MARTINIS & MANICURES

GORD HUME

ST. PETERSBURG PRESS

MARTINIS & MANICURES

A Samantha and the Sheriff Adventure

ST. PETERSBURG
PRESS

ST. PETERSBURG
—— PRESS

This is a work of fiction. Names, characters, businesses, places, events, locales, and incidents are either the products of the author's imagination or used in a fictitious manner. Any resemblance to actual persons, living or dead, or actual events is purely coincidental.

Composition by St. Petersburg Press and Isa Crosta
Cover and Interior design by W.D. Clements
The cover art is a compilation of works created by various artists who are generous to license for free usage. Images and characters used are found on vectorcharacters.com, freepik.com, all-free-download.com, www.vecteezy.com. and stock.adobe.com

Paperback ISBN: 978-1-940300-95-5

Chapter 1

THE CLOUDS HUNG painfully in the sky, skewered by a giant celestial pitchfork. They were the color of unfired charcoal briquettes. The air sweated.

Samantha Summers stood on her penthouse balcony looking west at the incoming Florida Gulf Coast storm. The waves were pounding the innocent shore, as they had done for millennia. Shell-pickers would find treasures on the beach in the morning.

Whitecaps were forming a mile out. One idiot kite-surfer darted over the water.

Rosie paced the balcony, sniffing anxiously. She was LeRoy Perkins' dog, but since Samantha and the Sheriff had become passionate lovers Rosie now had two homes. Perkins was at a law enforcement convention in Atlanta.

Rosie whined at the dimming sky. She pressed herself against Samantha's leg.

Samantha stared down. There was no one in the huge swimming pool at the Sapphire Blue condo complex. It looked as if there were whitecaps in the pool. Staff had tightly furled the umbrellas and secured them and the patio furniture.

The storm continued to brew. Winds were picking up. The palm trees swayed and bent.

Samantha stroked Rosie reassuringly. "It's just a summer storm. We'll be fine here."

Rosie looked at her. Doubt was in her eyes. She was too brave a dog to show fear, but certainly there was doubt.

The wind was beginning to whistle even louder. "I wonder if we should put down the hurricane shutters," Samantha asked Rosie.

A sudden loud BOOM shattered the evening.

"Just thunder," Samantha reassured the dog. Rosie went to the railing, looked out and yipped twice. Her nose was twitching.

Oddly, there was no repeat of the thunderclap; no lightning strikes followed.

The sky was dark now. No stars were visible. The temperature was still in the upper 80s but for some reason Samantha and Rosie both shivered.

"Let's go inside." Rosie practically leapt through the door into the condo. Samantha firmly shut the glass door and then hit the button to drop the shutters.

It was a dark and stormy night, she muttered to herself, mocking Snoopy's opening lines in his bad novel.

She fed Rosie a cookie, poured herself a reassuring glass of Pinot, turned on lights and soft rock, and hunkered down on the couch.

The storm grew in intensity.

Chapter 2

THE DOORBELL RANG at 6:59am. Samantha blearily buzzed Kim in.

"Good morning, Councillor Sharpe," Samantha said as Kim burst through the door. The title still gave her a kick. She poured each of them a large coffee. Rosie got some breakfast, which she inhaled in twelve seconds.

Kim had been elected to the Ward 3 seat in the municipal election last fall. Samantha had been her campaign manager. It had been a bruising battle.

Kim patted Rosie, grabbed her coffee and looked at Samantha. "We need to talk. Now."

"What?" Samantha didn't really get engaged in the day until her second cup of coffee. The world had found that out after she had administered a number of severe ass-kickings.

"Drink your coffee. Pay attention. Focus." Kim was unrelenting. Samantha quaffed a peevish cupful and looked at her.

Kim took a deep breath. "There was an incident last night. I get these notices from the Sheriff's department. Perk is fine," she continued quickly as Samantha paled. "Everybody is fine. But some idiot tried to blow up the new Delvecchio Bridge condo last night."

Samantha dropped her coffee mug. It splashed on the quartz countertop. Reflexively she grabbed a towel and mopped even as she asked, "What! What happened?"

The Delvecchio Bridge condo complex was a new project in an ungentrified part of the city. The initial proposed development had been the ugly scene of bribery and misappropriation of public funds in the previous City Council that had resulted in the mayor and two councillors being sent to prison for corruption and fraud.

New developers had been found and their exciting design concept approved. The Starwind Construction Company had just begun the foundation for a bold new two-tower complex. Samantha had befriended the neighborhood while designing a unique playground to be built as part of the $187 million development.

"Somebody set off some explosive...something...in the foundation about nine o'clock last night," Kim continued. She shook her head.

"My God! We heard that! I thought it was just thunder. Didn't we, sweetie?" She leaned down to pet Rosie. "It was a big boom. Rosie kept sniffing the air and whining." She stroked her again. "Yes, you are such a smart dog."

The phone rang. She reached over and picked up the receiver on the wall and stretched the cord out. "Oh, hi, Elliott. Yes, I just heard. Kim just told me. It's awful! How much damage? Oh, well, that's not too bad, I guess. Will it delay—wait, that's dumb. Of course, it will delay you. By how much? Really? Yes, of course we'll come down to the site. See you in an hour."

She hung up and turned to Kim. "I guess our power walk will be postponed. Elliott is at the site. He says there's damage to the excavation and the foundation they've just started pouring, but at this early stage of construction it won't be too much of a set-back. Let's go down there." She gulped more coffee.

"Sure. It's in my ward, so this is partly my problem." Kim swallowed the last of her coffee and then shook her head. "I can't believe you still have a land-line."

"Oh, I need it. I use it to find my cell phone."

CHAPTER 3

ELLIOTT WEBSTER HAD taken over his father's construction company several years before. The Delvecchio Bridge project would be the largest ever undertaken by the company. It had been enthusiastically supported by the new Port Manatee City Council, the neighborhood, and the local media.

"That's why I don't understand who might have done this," he said to the two detectives who were investigating. Crime scene specialists were poking around the ruins of the foundation.

There was a growing crowd of local residents, news media and lookey-loos gathering as word spread of the bombing.

"Was there security?"

"A padlocked fence around the site. No security guard. Well, there will be from tonight on," Webster replied grimly. He shrugged. "Nobody thought it was necessary. Who the hell would blow up a hole?"

Kim and Samantha walked over to him as soon as they arrived. Rosie was on a leash and was quite interested in this new vista and the unusual smells it offered.

They both hugged Elliott. Kim turned to the detectives. "Hi. I'm Kim Sharpe. I'm the Councillor for this ward. Any ideas yet?"

"Yes, ma'am. We know who you are. And no. But our investigators have just started looking through the site. They should have a preliminary report soon."

One of the deputies touched the brim of his hat to Samantha. The Sheriff's girlfriend was known throughout the department. Her reddish-blonde hair and her gorgeous slender body were the object of much envy.

A senior CSI approached the group. He looked at the senior detective with a raised eyebrow. The deputy simply nodded to go ahead.

"It was dynamite. Three, maybe four sticks. In the side of the foundation you've dug. We don't see dynamite used much anymore. No sign of bodies." Samantha and Kim both blanched. "We've found a couple of shreds of paper or something with a bit of printing. We can't make it out, but maybe our lab techs can."

He paused and then pawed the ground with the toe of his boot. "You probably can assess the damage better than we can," he said to the developer. "It certainly blew up a bunch of dirt and concrete and steel, but it doesn't seem that serious a set-back."

Webster nodded. "Yeah, we'll recover from this. At least it was early in the construction process. It will cost us a couple of weeks, but the—why would somebody do this now? The real damage would have been in six months or sometime after we've got the steel erected." He blew out his cheeks in frustration and anger.

Samantha patted his arm. "At least nobody was hurt. And you will continue."

He nodded.

"OK, good. I'm going to go over and reassure the neighbors." Part of Samantha's new consulting job with the project was to liaise with the local community.

"Yeah. Good. Go." Webster turned back to the deputies. "I don't suppose there were any surveillance cameras, any witnesses?"

"Nothing we've found so far. We'll keep looking, but this is such an isolated site."

Webster nodded. He looked hard at the now-misshapen hole in the ground. "It doesn't make any sense. Everybody loves the project." He shook his head again. Everybody looked at the hole. Nobody elucidated.

Samantha wandered over to chat with the watching mothers and community leaders. Several small, wide-eyed kids were restlessly trying to play on the hard ground. Rosie became an instant prima donna. She preened happily. The kids went crazy petting her.

Kim soon joined the group. "It will not be a big set-back," they both reassured those gathered. "Two or three weeks, that's all."

"We were worried it was going to be a big delay, or even scare off the developer," one of the neighborhood ladies admitted. Heads nodded. "You tell that nice Mr. Webster that we've got his back. We want this project. For our kids, for our community."

Samantha nodded. "He will be relieved to hear that. Thank you. And if anybody has any tips or information, please let the sheriff's department know immediately."

They chatted for a few more minutes and then the group broke up as kids headed for school and adults returned home or went to their jobs.

Samantha reported back to Elliott that the neighbors remained on-side.

"That's good to know. Thank you." He sighed in frustration. "I can't imagine who would want to disrupt this project." He shook his head. "I'm arranging for security at night from now on. The crews will start to clean up as soon as the CSI has cleared the scene."

He looked bleakly at the construction site. Nobody had anything to say. Nobody had any answers.

Especially not the Port Manatee Observer, but that didn't stop the daily newspaper from running three front-page pictures of the big hole in the ground.

Chapter 4

"THERE IS NOTHING more important than protecting the children of our city!" Councillor Mikayla Johnson was in full flight at the City Council meeting. She usually was. Shrill. Loud. Grating.

"That's why we need to shut down this Del-Vek-Ee-O project immediately! Close it! Save the lives of our children! Dynamite going off in a residential neighborhood! Lordy, Lordy! Shut it down! If the councillor for that area won't protect the kids and families in Ward 3, then we have to!"

She dropped heavily in her chair. There was stunned silence in the council chambers. It had only been a few months before that the council had unanimously endorsed the Delvecchio Bridge project.

Mayor Sonja Rodriguez was white-faced as she stared at the Councillor from Ward 5. City Manager Roy Crawford was pushing back his chair to rise and address the meeting when Kim Sharpe stood.

"Madam Mayor. I need to respond to the Councillor from Ward 5's rather dramatic comments." Kim breathed deeply to compose herself. The cable TV cameras swivelled to focus on her. "The very worst thing we could do would be to shut down this project. It is too important to the neighborhood, the city and our future economic prosperity. It will bring jobs, some affordable housing units and will rejuvenate a neighborhood that was ignored for far too long."

She sipped water. The other council members were riveted. "I was at the site the morning after the explosion. It was a terrible event, no question about it. But I spoke with community leaders and they were unanimous in wanting the project to continue. I spoke with Elliott Webster, the President of Starwind Construction. He remains committed. We should be grateful for that. He is also putting private security on the site at night, and our Sheriff's department will step up patrols."

Kim paused and collected her thoughts. "No one argues that protecting our children is a critical role for any elected body. But running away scared at the first sign of stress and hardship is not a good lesson we should be offering to those kids. We need to be stalwart and move forward. We need to— "

"Are you callin' me a coward!!? Is that what you sayin'?! I will come over there and slap you silly— "

"Councillors! Councillors! Come to order. Sit down! Both of you!" The Mayor was pounding her gavel. The audience was buzzing. This was high drama for the usually placid city council meetings.

"Sit! Now! Or I will rule you out of order!" Mayor Rodriguez again pounded her gavel. Kim sat down. Councillor Johnson continued to stand and shout at the mayor.

"Councillor Johnson! Sit down! Now!"

The Ward 5 representative threw out a few more choice words. The mayor pounded her gavel one last time. "Councillor Johnson! You are out of order! I am directing that you leave this council chamber for the remainder of this meeting! Sergeant-at-Arms!"

The security officer came forward reluctantly. Councillor Johnson looked around. She saw no support in the eyes of her colleagues. She glared once again at Kim. "I'm going to get you on this crooked deal! Just wait! I'm coming for you! You and your dirty friends!"

With that, she lifted up her printed agenda and papers and threw them up in the air. They floated to the carpet in the middle of the council horseshoe. A couple of the clerks and managers seated at the table in the middle ducked. City Clerk Kathy James was nearly hit by the edge of a binder.

The newspaper reporter was spluttering with excitement as he used his cell phone to shoot pictures of the scene.

With that, Councillor Johnson angrily shoved back her seat and stomped out of the council chambers. Her chair toppled and crashed to the floor.

There was dead silence in the room except for the mad clicking of the reporter's cell phone.

Wearily the Mayor tapped her gavel. "We will take a fifteen-minute recess."

CHAPTER 5

"WHAT WAS THAT all about?"

The question from Kim hung in the air. Nobody had an answer. The members of council and the senior staff had gathered in the mayor's office to recuperate from the public debacle that had just occurred.

They were all shocked. They were all confused. They were all upset. And most of them were getting angry.

"She can't say those things to any council member," declared Councillor March.

"She is an angry woman, but she can't bring that temper into our chambers," said Councillor Policy. He paused. "And what did she mean by 'I'm going to get you and your dirty friends'?"

Kim looked at him. "I have no idea. Nobody that I know of has any financial stake in this project. My friend Samantha did the playground design and is liaising with the community, but that's open knowledge. Heck, it was discussed in public when council approved the project. I have no conflict of interest." She shrugged. "No idea."

Mayor Rodriguez finally spoke up. "Listen. This is going to be a disaster. The media will ride it for days. I think we have to go back out there, finish the agenda quickly, and then get out with whatever dignity we can muster. I won't tell you what to say to the media after, but I would ask you to be discreet."

She paused. "I will have to confront Councillor Johnson tomorrow." She looked at Roy. "I would like you there to provide back-up and as an independent witness. Maybe with the City Clerk as well." They both nodded. "We can't tolerate that kind of behavior in the council chambers. This hurts the reputation of every one of us."

There were gloomy nods of agreement. The public tended to judge a council before they did a councillor. If the people of Port Manatee lost confidence in their new council, then all elected officials would suffer. The entire fate of their four-year term could be determined by one suddenly rogue council member.

It was not a comforting thought for anyone associated with the city.

CHAPTER 6

"WOULDN'T YOU LOVE to see him drop his phone into the pool?" murmured Samantha to Kim the next morning.

Kim offered a weary snort of laughter. She was emotionally drained after the explosive council meeting the night before. The media had not been kind to anyone on the council. The confrontation and accusations were the hot topic on local radio talk shows and across social media at #hissyfit.

Some imbecile wearing a faded orange hat, bathing trunks from the 1990s and a cloak of ego was standing in the shallow end of the pool talking on his cell phone. Loudly. Pretty much everyone in that part of the pool concourse could enjoy his conversation, whether they wanted to or not.

"We could jump in and splash him," suggested Samantha. She was trying very hard to get Kim's focus off the debacle of the previous evening. It wasn't working.

This was the first time that Kim had ever been publicly attacked by another elected official. It had obviously thrown her off balance. She was shaken by the sudden public turmoil and the media criticism.

The Port Manatee Observer had splashed pictures of the two feuding councillors on its front page, along with a picture of the papers flung in the air floating down to the floor. It was not an image to reassure local residents of the commitment to good, peaceful local government and a keen focus on community issues.

"I've got to get back to city hall after lunch," Kim said. "I don't know how I'm going to work with Mikayla again. It was as if she was enraged about me or something I did. And that threat about my friends! What's that all about?"

"I've always been very clear and open about my participation in this project," said Samantha firmly. "It is on the public record. It's been in the paper. No surprises there." She paused and sipped her ice water. "You have no financial interest in the project. It is privately funded by Elliott's company. Unless you're a secret partner in Starwind Construction, I don't see anything there." Kim snorted derisively.

The cell phone guy dialled another number. Please god, just let him drop it once, pleaded Samantha. Nothing. He hung on like it was Krazy-glued to his palm.

"Roy? Anything there?"

Kim and City Manager Roy Crawford were in a passionate affair. They had both openly declared their consensual relationship to the City Clerk. There had not been much of a ripple in the community about it. It was the 2020s.

"No. Heck, he negotiated the deal with Starwind on behalf of the city. Everybody had lawyers. Unless she's alleging some payoff to him. But Roy is the most honest man I've ever known. I won't believe for a second that there's anything there."

Samantha nodded agreement. Crawford was a straight shooter. She couldn't imagine his being on the take.

They went over a couple of other names. Nothing jumped out.

"Samira?"

Samantha paused as she thought that one through. The stunning Persian orthopedic surgeon who worked at the regional VA hospital was the third member of what Kim had nicknamed "The Sams Club." Samantha. Samira. And Kim, who claimed she was 'Sexy And Modest' so she also qualified.

Their club activities were mostly devoted to drinking nice wines, eating good food and discussing men.

Samira had been looking after Kim ever since she had been severely wounded in the Middle East. Kim had lost a foot in an IED attack when her squad was on patrol. She had been decorated for her heroism. She rarely talked about it. Samira had built three different prosthetic feet for her over the years, each one more advanced than the last.

Samira's family was very wealthy. Very. Samira and her brother and father invested in many projects, none of which Samantha or Kim knew anything about.

"Could she have some piece of this project?"

"I don't know. I don't think so. She's never said anything. And Starwind is privately owned by Elliott and his father."

"We'll have to ask her," Kim concluded, "but I don't see anything there." She blew out her cheeks in frustration. "Or anybody else that I can think of. Not to mention who would want to blow up the Delvecchio Bridge project. For what reason? What benefit?" She paused and thought about it more. "And why now? If you really wanted to hurt the project, wouldn't you do it when it was built up a lot more? Why just blow up a few walls in the foundation? It makes no sense."

Two kids jumped into the pool near the guy with the phone. He turned to them while still talking and gestured angrily. They ignored him. He waved with greater urgency. They kept playing. Finally, he finished his call, punched the button, and took a step toward the kids. His phone remained locked in his fist.

"Rats. I thought he'd blown it," Samantha remarked uncharitably. Kim smiled. "They should ban all cell phones from the pool area. That would shake up some people," Samantha grumbled. "And have you noticed how everybody speaks more loudly on their cells when they're outdoors? I really don't enjoy hearing about Aunt Agnes's gout."

They watched as the guy continued his pirouettes to dodge droplets and protect his precious phone. The kids were oblivious as they jumped and splashed. Desperate now, the guy turned away from the water geysers the kids were shooting up. He tried to hide the cell under his left arm to protect it.

Samantha groaned as he spun away from the kids. The phone was still intact. Ah well, maybe another—and that's when he stumbled. He waved his arms to regain his balance. It didn't happen. He and his phone sank below the waves.

Samantha burst out laughing.

Kim finally shook her head and began laughing as well. "Karma is a bitch," she grinned. Then she straightened up. "Maybe Councillor Johnson will find that out as well."

CHAPTER 7

"NO. I OWN nothing related to that project. I'm not invested in it at all. I do own some shares in a couple of regional banks that might be providing some financing for the development, but that would be just normal course of business," Samira declared firmly. "I'm not involved in any way. Neither is my family."

Kim and Samantha both nodded. They were all sipping a 2016 Italian Pinot Grigio. It was sliding down very smoothly. Some warm spiced almonds sat in the nut dish. A variety of olives rested on a china plate. A really nice triple-crème Brie, recently sliced open, was oozing gently.

"The whole thing doesn't make any sense," Kim repeated. She chewed a couple of the almonds.

"Perk's got his investigators working the case," Samantha reported. "So far I don't think they've got anything."

She selected two of the olives. One was stuffed with blue cheese, the other with preserved lemon peel.

Samira reached over with a surgeon's confidence to slice into the Brie. "What are you going to do about the bitch from the 5th?"

Kim sighed deeply. "She just seems to be an angry woman. Mikayla was on council a few years ago, got defeated, then came back in the last election and squeaked out a victory in Ward 5. She seems angry about everything. I've tried to get to know her, but I get nothing in return. The mayor is at her wits' end. She said her meeting with Councillor Johnson yesterday was a disaster. Just more threats, more shouting. It is exhausting. And it's hurting our Council's cohesion and effectiveness."

Silence.

Samantha finally broke the emptiness. "Well, then, on to other things. I want to start planning our "Martinis and Manicures" fund-raising party."

Kim perked up. "I think that's wonderful. Great idea. Great name. If we can raise some money for a future campaign, terrific. Even a couple of thousand would be welcome."

"Oh, I think we can do a lot better than that."

"Really?"

"What I'm thinking about is inviting twenty women. The top professional ladies from this city. Lawyers, business owners, bankers, doctors—Samira can help cull that list—the Provost from the university, the Publisher of the newspaper...and charging them $500 each."

Kim sucked in her breath. "Holy cow, can we get that?"

Samantha looked at Samira. "I think that's very doable," said the surgeon confidently. "The exclusivity will appeal. Many of them know each other, but some won't. Having it at Samantha's penthouse will be appealing, so they can judge her decorating and hostessing skills. And supporting a rising political star like Kim will intrigue some as well."

Samantha nodded her approval. "My plan is to serve a selection of martinis, from the regular dry gin to chocolate. Oh, maybe we can invent a special drink just for the evening. Let's see, let's see...well, we'll need to think about that. And then I'll get a couple of estheticians to set up in a corner of the lanai and guests can get their manicures done. I'll find a good caterer."

"Nobody has ever done a political fund-raiser like this," Kim exclaimed with enthusiasm. "It'll be a blast."

"Sign me up for the first ticket," Samira promised. "And I'll get you the names of three or four doctors who should go, and maybe the Vice President of the hospital. I am not a fan, but she's got money."

Samantha nodded as she made a couple of notes. She finished her wine and set the glass down on the side table. "Kim... Kim...martini...Kimmie...Kim uh, Kim...Wait! That's it! We'll invent a 'Kimtini.' That will be our own special martini concoction just for this party. That'll be fun!"

"Kimtini. That's a hoot. And really clever. I love it."

"So do I," agreed Samira. "Now we just need to invent the drink. That's going to be some fun experimenting."

"We'll need supplies, booze, uh, let's see...what else? Where do you go around here to buy party stuff?"

Kim turned to Samira. They grinned at one another as they told Samantha in unison, "Uncle Larry's!"

Chapter 8

THERE WAS NOTHING subtle about "Uncle Larry's Booze Barn."

It was a huge warehouse operation in an otherwise failing strip mall. The staff wore lime-green T-shirts, the decor was early slutty, and the prices were astoundingly low.

Samantha stood inside and gaped. "It's a department store of liquor," she exclaimed with reverential awe.

Racks of wine, liquor, beer, accessories and snacks in gigantic plastic tubs were strewn throughout the Booze Barn. Many of the snacks featured orange-colored fried balls of something. The shade of orange was not a color created by Mother Nature.

Kim and Samira chortled at Samantha's reaction. It was typical of first-timers. They each grabbed a cart and started pushing Samantha down the first aisle.

She was fondling bottles as she discovered whole sections devoted to French wines, Italian, Australian, South American, Californian—the racks just kept going. She became almost devout over the Côtes du Rhône section. Then she discovered the Sauvignon Blanc display.

"How did I not know about this?" she asked. She practically knelt at the Cabernet Sauvignon racks.

"We knew it wouldn't be good for you," Samira smirked. "Too much excitement."

"My gosh, if they had a cot in the back room, I would move in," Samantha whispered.

The staff in their fluorescent T-shirts hustled up and down the aisles. One of the twenty-something males took one look at the three women and promptly stumbled. He righted himself and began to whisper into his left wrist. Suddenly several other young men from throughout the store had urgent business in that particular aisle. It began to look like a wine convention for geeks.

Samantha remained oblivious. Kim and Samira got a kick out of the male attention. There were a lot of puffed up chests and soon-to-be deflated egos amongst the young men.

A middle-aged female manager finally pushed her way through. "Back to work, guys, the show's over." The young men slowly and reluctantly began to disperse.

"Sorry about that. Seeing you three here, well, that's about as much excitement as those idiots will get in a month. I'm Francine. Frankie for short. Now, how can I help you?"

Samantha was still too overcome by the racks and cases of wine that seemed to stretch to…well, not heaven, but really, really up there.

Kim explained about their party idea.

"Sure, that's a wonderful idea. We can help. You'll need a bunch of martini glasses. Shakers and cocktail stuff. Probably what, two bartenders? We can do all of that, plus deliver the liquor and wine you need."

"You deliver too," Samantha moaned. "How much better can this get?"

"Go look at the Burgundy section." Samira pushed her down another aisle.

"Ohhh, Burgundy…" Samantha left.

With Frankie's quick grasp of the party plan, it didn't take long to finalize the details for the fund-raiser. She got several gin and vodka samples to help them invent the Kimtini. Frankie loved the name.

"Heck, if it tastes good, maybe we'll feature it here at Uncle Larry's," she told them. She gave them advice on what might work in the Kimtini.

The two friends finally found Samantha wandering in the Provence Rosé section.

"C'mon, Samantha, time to go home."

"No, no. I am home. This is where I live now."

"Yes, we'll ask about that. But first we have to get you to your other home. Your boyfriend is coming back for you."

"Ohhh. But I don't want to leave."

They each grabbed an elbow and gently walked her to the exit. "You can come back and play another day," Kim promised her as they departed.

"Nooooooo…!"

CHAPTER 9

SHERIFF LEROY PERKINS strode into headquarters.

He was just over six feet tall, dark brown hair, lean and muscular with piercing blue eyes that turned icy on occasion. He was rugged rather than handsome. His face showed that he'd seen some of life's uglier sides. He had a scar on his shoulder from a failed assassination attempt. The bullet had left memories that sometimes pained as much as the stiff, angry scar.

He was well into his third year as Sheriff. It never got easier.

"Welcome back," said his assistant Mary as he walked into his office. "How was the conference?"

"Good. Good to be back. I spent an extra day with James Robertson who's now heading up the regional FBI operation in Atlanta. It's always useful to liaise with them."

"And drink some bourbon, no doubt," Mary commented tartly.

"Well, in that dry climate of Georgia, it is important to keep your throat moist."

"Hmphh. Well, I left the paperwork in your in-box. Shouldn't take more than a week or two to go through it." She knew how much he hated office paperwork.

He sighed. "Yeah. Any chance of a coffee?"

"Sure there is. Any chance of a raise?"

Defeated once again by the cruel realities of modern office life, Perkins grabbed the top file from the stack. It took a moment for the report to sink in.

"Hey," he shouted out his door. "What's this bombing thing at Delvecchio Bridge? Didn't anybody think it was important enough to let me know?"

Mary stuck her head in the door. "Not that big a deal from what I understand. Not much damage. Nobody hurt. Couple of sticks of dynamite that some idiot fired up." She shrugged. "No leads. Nobody's claimed responsibility. Detectives are stuck in neutral. It doesn't make sense to anybody."

"Huh." He finished scanning the report. He reminded himself to talk to the lead detective. It was Samantha's pet project, after all. He would have to ensure she remained safe.

He worked diligently through the pile, shaking his head at the detritus of life that any police force encountered:

* The thief who broke into a restaurant, fired up the grill, made a cheeseburger, and then fell asleep. It made for a rather easy arrest.

* The guy riding a Harley who had girlfriends in three different states—but made the really big mistake of hitting on the mother of one of the girlfriends. The carnage inside the rented house had been remarkable.

Well, that guy qualifies to teach a graduate course in stupid, Perkins thought to himself. He kept reading more files:

* A guy sitting in a beach bar drinking beer and eating peanuts had been attacked—by a squirrel. He had noticed the rodent on a tree branch. They made eye contact. The next thing he knows, the squirrel runs up his leg, sits in his lap and stares at him. The guy reaches for a peanut and the squirrel leaps up and bites his hand. He starts shouting and trying to shake it off. The other people at the bar are screaming. The staff is frozen. The squirrel finally lets go. The bar owner was gracious of course—he quickly produced a waiver for the guy to sign, and then comped his two beers. They trapped the squirrel the next day. There was an unconfirmed report that Brunswick Stew would be on the menu very soon.

* Deputies had responded to reports of a woman shrieking in a house. They burst in, guns drawn, to find the woman naked and tied spread-eagled to the bed. On the floor, bleeding profusely from a cut on his head, was a man in a Batman costume. It turned out they were married but planning some extra special fun in the sack. The guy had climbed up on a bureau wearing the superhero costume and leapt onto the bed—except that he forgot about the ceiling fan whirling away. The report indicated he

would recover from the scalp wounds. The woman was physically unharmed. The deputies might need therapy.

Perkins shook his head. This was Florida, where the crazies eventually returned to their natural home.

He read his department heads' weekly reports: A case of elder abuse; Perkins was disgusted at the very thought. A surprising rise in cocaine sales on the street. Also, more illegal prescription drugs seemed to be circulating. His detectives hadn't yet identified a source. Three shootings, thankfully none involving his officers. A pile of vehicle accidents—well, maybe he'd better rethink the word 'pile.'

He kept plowing through the paperwork. His thoughts occasionally wandered back to the faux-Batman incident. He would be re-uniting with Samantha that evening. Now, think hard, idiot: *does she have a ceiling fan in her bedroom?*

CHAPTER 10

FRIDAY NIGHT. THE Sams Club was meeting at Samantha's condo.

Perkins was the guest speaker at a high school awards dinner. Public speaking wasn't something he was really comfortable doing, but he recognized that it was part of his job description. He would be over later to join the ladies.

Rosie was dancing around the kitchen with the three women, making sure that snacks were shared appropriately. In her view, that meant one for her, one for any of the ladies, another for her…

She gulped down a nice piece of cheddar that Samira slipped her. She licked her hand gratefully. Samira patted her head. Kim offered a little slice of—would that be prosciutto? Rosie quite approved of that salty little piece of Italian heaven. She licked Kim's palm. It was a very nice party so far.

Conversation was wide-ranging as the ladies settled in. Kim mentioned the on-going difficulties with Councillor Johnson. Samira talked about how so many seniors were lonely, and how social isolation was becoming one of the greatest community, and medical, challenges facing our aging population.

Samantha brought out all of the glassware, pitchers, beakers, bottles and mixers that she owned. Tonight was to be the invention of the Kimtini. It promised to be a joyful journey—whether they succeeded or not.

The variety of gin and vodka samplers that Frankie from Uncle Larry's Booze Barn had given them were lined up. A couple of different kinds of vermouth. A wide variety of citrus fruits. Olives. Pearl onions. Gherkins. Ice in a large bucket. Both of her cocktail shakers. One tall silver spoon. Napkins. Two sharp paring knives. A reamer for the citrus.

Any army had to be properly equipped before going into battle.

They started with the basic gin martini. They tried adding unique condiments—a dash of chilli oil; a large splash of vermouth and pimento-dill olives. Well, not every experiment in a science lab was going to be successful.

The failures were poured down the sink. The dregs would no doubt remove any plaque build-up in the sewer lines.

The hunt continued amidst much laughter and licking of fingers by all three of them. Vodka and pickle juice. Good lord, NO! Gin, pineapple juice and lime, no tonic. Vodka and orange peel, with a splash of Cointreau. Vodka and vermouth and lemon and whatever was in that little bottle on the counter. That was an oops moment.

The evening drifted along. Voices were raised and music turned up, Rosie was running around, laughter echoed around the kitchen and the recipes got more and more...interesting? Unique? Bizarre?

"We definitely need something to sharpen the taste," Kim reported. "I still like a citrus addition."

"Vodka or gin?"

"Gin seems to have a little sharperer taste. Oops. Shar-per," Kim corrected herself. The multiple tastings had loosened tongues and taste buds. Samira and Samantha giggled.

"We need some color in them," Samira observed. "They are too...clear." She looked around the kitchen. "Ah hah!" She reached over to grab a pomegranate. She sliced into it with her deft surgical skills. The halves fell apart neatly.

Kim looked at the inside of one half with suspicion. "So this is what a poma, pomi, pomgrnt-thing really looks like. Huh. How do you get the little seeds out?"

"You have to spank it," Samira told her. Laughter erupted. Rosie pranced around the kitchen looking at the three ladies as they choked out their giggles. The parade of snacks had stopped. The party, in Rosie's considered opinion, was going downhill pretty fast.

Samira grabbed a bowl, took a large spoon, flipped over the pomegranate half, and proceeded to whack the skin side with the back of the spoon. The glistening ruby seeds began to fall as Kim kept laughing at the spanking.

"It reminds me of a boyfriend a few years ago," she began, before breaking out in laughter.

Samantha covered her ears. "TMI! TMI!"

They finally got a bunch of seeds. Suddenly inspired, Samantha grabbed a grapefruit and pared it open. "Let's try this." She poured gin into the cocktail mixer, squeezed in some fresh grapefruit juice, a dash of vermouth, added lots of ice and shook vigorously. She poured it into three glasses and added a few pomegranate seeds. They all stared and then sipped.

"Wow." Samira's eyes opened wider. "That's pretty good."

Kim took a cautious mouthful. Then another. "You know, I think we're really close."

Samantha took her own mouthful. Swallowed. She nodded. "I like it. I do." She paused for a minute. "Now how the heck did I mix it?"

More howls of laughter.

It took several minutes of serious work, false starts, much laughter, sloppy note-taking and dedicated sipping to finalize the official recipe for their MARTINIS & MANICURES party drink:

THE KIMTINI

Pour 3 parts gin and 1 part vermouth into a large martini glass. Add a splash of fresh-squeezed grapefruit juice.

Pour into a martini shaker with lots of ice. Shake to mix and chill.

Pour back into the large martini glass.

Add 5 pomegranate seeds.

Garnish with either: grapefruit twist (like a lemon peel twist) OR grapefruit and mandarin orange segments on a martini stick.

Sip. Enjoy.

"They look like little ruby jewels in the bottom of the glass," Samira said with affection as they stared at their finished product.

"Women and jewels. And martinis. What a wonderful combination," Samantha sighed happily. "The party's going to be a smash."

"Well, they are certainly going to get smashed," Kim chortled. They all broke up.

Rosie sniffed around the kitchen floor. Nothing. Gosh, Samantha's party-making skills had certainly deteriorated.

Perkins arrived to find a big mess in the kitchen, three giggling and very happy women, and his dog grumbling quietly.

He was soon honored to be the first man to ever try the Kimtini. "Not bad," he admitted. "Not bad at all." He looked at the three. "Was it hard to invent?"

That elicited gales of laughter which he didn't understand. He had a final sip and then took Rosie out for her evening walk.

He came back to a kitchen that was still the 'after' picture of a hurricane disaster zone. Samantha was in bed, Samira was asleep in the guest room, and Kim had tottered back to her own condo in the White Building of the Sapphire Blue complex.

Perkins bent down and looked at Rosie. "I left you in charge of these three tonight. What happened?"

Rosie looked at him adoringly. She yawned, licked his face, and went to her doggie bed. She turned around three times, curled up, and promptly went to sleep.

Perkins looked around the condo. Well damn.

He cleaned up the kitchen, ran the dishwasher, scrubbed the countertop, set the coffee-maker timer and took two bottles of water into the bedroom. He put both bottles on Samantha's bed-side table. He loosened the cap on one. He brushed his teeth, hung up his clothes and finally slipped into bed with Samantha. She didn't stir. He grimaced. Geez, he cleans up the kitchen and doesn't even get a kiss goodnight. The abuse a good man takes. Awful.

He rolled onto his left side and went to sleep.

CHAPTER 11

CITY IN SECRET LAND DEAL screamed the headline on the front page of The Observer the next morning.

The story disclosed that a confidential source had revealed that the city was in private negotiations to acquire a large piece of land for future development. There was speculation by the reporter that it would be used for a new community recreation center.

City Manager Roy Crawford stared in disgust at the newspaper. He had confidentially briefed the members of City Council on the proposed new project just two nights ago. He had emphasized the need for secrecy as negotiations with the owner of the property continued.

It was a very short list of people who had been in the council chambers. Who knew about the property acquisition 48 hours later was undoubtedly a much broader list. Including, now, the entire city. And, even worse, the landowner.

Crawford had arranged for a lawyer to negotiate as a third party with the seller's real estate people so the city as the prospective buyer would not be revealed. Experience had taught him that as soon as a government wanted to buy property, the price skyrocketed.

Mayor Rodriguez called him at 7:12am.

"Look, Madam Mayor, there are only four reasons for somebody to leak this story. One, they are angry with the city or somebody connected with the city. Retribution. Stealth attack. Whatever. Two, they are trying to curry favor with the paper or the TV station. It is an ego trip for him or her—they are more knowledgeable, more powerful than anybody else. They think they will get better future coverage by being a leaker. Three, they are trying to scuttle the project or the negotiations or the person proposing the project. Political infighting. Mean-spirited. Trying to push their own agenda. Or four, their ego is so big that they think they are above any constraints or norms or protocols that we follow at city council."

He was very angry. "What I can tell you is that the price just went up a couple of million dollars and some members of the public will now oppose the project just because of how it is being perceived."

"You're right, Roy. This is a disaster for us. Who would...?"

The key question hung in the air.

"The problem now," said the mayor cautiously, "is that it taints everybody on council. Everybody in the chambers that night. And it was a pretty small list."

"I can talk to my staff, but I am 99% certain that it wasn't any of them."

"Yes. I agree with that." She sighed loudly. "That leaves my esteemed council colleagues." The sarcasm dripped viciously. "Not Kim. Not me. Not Councillors Policy or March, at least I doubt it. They are both veterans. They understand the game. That leaves the other three. Damn."

Crawford said nothing. For him to take a role in investigating a council member would be exceedingly awkward, since ultimately, they had the power to hire or fire him.

Finally he spoke. "I will leave that to you. I am here to help as you request. But we also need to think about the on-going implications. Is this going to trigger a break-down of trust on the council floor for the rest of this term?"

The mayor said nothing for a long moment. "I hadn't even thought of that, but you're right. This could irrevocably split the council and pretty much kill our plans to move the city forward." She took a deep breath. "I am really upset, Roy. Why would somebody do this to us?"

Crawford cawed an ugly laugh. "Somebody angry. Somebody who wants to hurt the city."

He didn't mention any names.

CHAPTER 12

"I AM CALLING THIS special meeting of the Port Manatee City Council to order," declared the mayor. "Clerk?"

Kathy James stood. "Madam Mayor, there is a confidential report dealing with property and legal matters for the municipality."

"Motion to go in camera?"

"So moved."

"Thank you, Councillor Policy. Second?"

"Second."

"Thank you, Councillor Sharpe. All in favor? Opposed? Then…"

"Wait! Hold on! I'm objecting to this whole thing! I believe in doing the people's business in public, not hiding behind closed doors."

"Councillor Johnson. This is a routine motion to allow the council members to receive important legal information and a report on a property matter. These are allowed by State law to be dealt with in closed session."

"No! This council has been shutting out the public for too long!"

The mayor banged her gavel. "That is an inappropriate and inaccurate comment! Please sit down. I'm going to proceed with the vote."

It was 6-1 to go in camera. The audience left and the doors were locked.

Mikayla Johnson continued to fume as the city solicitor outlined the legal options the council had to try to discover the leak. There weren't many.

Roy Crawford took over. "The land we have been negotiating for would be used for a new multi-purpose facility. A recreation center. A new library. A swimming pool. Exercise and gym facilities for kids and seniors. Two outdoor basketball courts. A skateboard park. A community meeting room, which is badly needed in that area. It would be a very ambitious project for this city, but one that would serve the needs of our families in that part of the city for decades. But it is costly if we're going to do it right—probably in the $35-40 million dollar range. So if the cost of the land just went up a million or two because of this leak, then that impacts the entire project's viability. It hurts the city badly. And it also hurts our reputation as a corporation, because businesspeople and landowners will just laugh at us when we ask for confidentiality on tenders or other contracts with the city. They just won't trust us. That will increase the price of our doing business not just now but also for future projects."

Silence around the horseshoe.

The implications were withering.

Crawford waited. No one spoke. He cleared his throat. "I have spoken to the outside lawyer we retained to negotiate on the city's behalf. He indicated to me that the owner of the property now wants to renegotiate. I doubt if the price will go down," he concluded dryly.

"Well, this is what happens when you run around behind closed doors! Hiding from the public!" said Mikayla Johnson. "This is all your fault!" She pointed at Crawford. "All your secrecy! Screwin' around with a councillor! Shame on you!"

Crawford swallowed hard to restrain himself. He gripped the edge of the table tightly. "The Councillor is certainly entitled to her opinion," he grated. "I would respectfully disagree in the strongest possible terms. My personal relationship is a matter of public record. Councillor Sharpe and I are consenting adults." Kim looked on, red-faced and angry. "I would strongly suggest that that subject is not a matter for Councillor Johnson to question."

He took a deep breath to try to calm himself. "I have conducted this entire land acquisition process in the best way possible. I have kept the mayor informed. We briefed the entire city council." He paused. "And then this leak occurred."

The implication was unspoken but clear. One of the elected officials had leaked this, and it was now coming back to bite the city on its ass.

"I think we have to accept our city manager's very blunt assessment," offered Councillor Policy. "It makes me sick that somebody is leaking this kind of confidential information. It makes everybody on this council a suspect. It makes the entire council look sloppy, badly run and incompetent."

"I don't know who did this," began Kim as she tried to regain her calm, "but it is hurtful. I despise leaks like this. I think Roy is right: it will cost us money and time and credibility. To be blunt, I completely reject Councillor Johnson's allegations about our city manager. I can tell her that our consensual relationship is one of the best things I've ever had in my life. And as to her insinuations and allegations, I would suggest that the Councillor needs to stop indulging in her hit-and-run relationship with the truth."

Laughs from around the horseshoe at Kim's put-down. That set off Councillor Johnson one more time.

"Don't you be talkin' to me like that, you skinny white bitch!" The mayor started pounding her gavel as the spittle and vitriol spewed out of the Councillor's mouth. There were audible gasps from the staff and the other elected officials in the room.

"ENOUGH! STOP!" shouted the mayor. "You are out of order! Sit down! NOW!"

Mikayla did not sit down. Instead, she gave Kim the finger, turned, and stomped out of the council chambers.

She left behind a limp and breathless group.

Ward 6 Councillor Alex Miller finally spoke. "I've been on council for eleven years. I've never seen anything like this. I hope I never do again. The idea of a member of this council attacking another member on race or personal relationships makes me ill." He drew a deep breath. "We can't let this fester. I'm going to talk to our lawyer and city clerk about a motion of censure against Councillor Johnson." He paused. "Maybe she needs anger management classes."

He slumped back in his chair.

Ward 4 Councillor John Kelly roused himself. He was an older man. He had been on and off the council for years and tended now to focus on keeping out of trouble and avoiding controversy. He was not noted for bold leadership.

"Well I didn't leak the damn thing," he began. "I'm with Alex. We need to put a lid on this thing before it blows sky-high in public." He creakily turned his head to look at Kim. "By the way, that was one of the greatest put-downs I've ever heard, that hit-'n-run thing." He grinned at her.

Tensions eased just a bit. The Mayor finally looked around the horseshoe at her council members, then at the City Manager's desk. He stood.

"Madam Mayor, perhaps the council would like to instruct me to now pursue direct negotiations with the landowner for the multi-purpose complex. It is such a needed and important project for this city. I don't want to see the opportunity lost." He shrugged. "I don't think I can do any more harm."

Mayor Rodriguez looked around the chambers. There were nods from the councillors. "Good idea, Roy. And good luck." She sighed. "I fear we're all going to need that."

CHAPTER 13

THE WIVES WERE busy making dinner. That meant phoning their restaurant of choice for reservations.

There were about a dozen Wives who composed the social leadership of Sapphire Blue. There was absolutely no doubt that they ruled the condo complex. Even General Manager Virginia McIntyre kowtowed to their rigid reign.

Samantha and Kim would never be part of the inner circle around the pool. They wouldn't even make the outer circle of the inner circle. Over time, they might make the inner circle of the second outer circle. It was a very confusing social structure.

The husbands of The Wives were still their husbands—so far today. But the day was still young. Among their group, marital contracts were always in doubt.

The boys were clustered around the perimeter of the tables, lounge chairs and umbrellas that made up the center court where their ladies reigned.

Two of the lesser Wives were absent today. A couple of the husbands speculated—in hushed tones—that they were probably stirring the bones of some poor wretch who had royally pissed off The Wives in the bottom of their coven's caldron that was no doubt bubbling and boiling, troubling and toiling, as ravens and vultures flew overhead.

It was a sobering vision, enough to keep the husbands mostly obedient. That didn't include visits to the Bonga Bonga room to watch certain young ladies perform their, ah, artistic dances. Or visits to Krazy Kenny's for the noon burger-and-beer belch fests.

The husbands had also learned that if you wanted people in the big condo complex to know something, by far the fastest and easiest solution was to tell Mary Lou—in strictest confidence.

Instagram should work as efficiently.

This underground information railroad was important as it often deflected the attention of The Wives from certain sins and misdemeanors of their beloveds.

Eight women from Indiana, as white as the snow they had just left, poured themselves onto lounge chairs clustered around the pool. They were amply supplied with pitchers of a strange mixture of cranberry-pomegranate juice with a lot of cheap vodka in it, accented with a splash of OJ and one lonely lime. It was not their first drink of the day. Their drunken screeches turned the pool concourse into a shrieking cacophony, much to the disgust of the regulars. These were obviously interlopers, down for the birthday party of one of the eight. They didn't understand that re-hydrating meant water, not more vodka.

Kim and Samantha huddled in a distant corner under a cluster of shady palm trees blowing softly in the breeze.

"Roy is really angry about the leak over the property acquisition," Kim confided. "Mikayla made some ugly charges at the meeting. He batted her down. I creamed her. She stormed out, angry at me and everybody else. It is toxic at City Council right now."

They applied suntan lotion. Sadly, the octet from the Hoosier State was not as careful. There would be massive regrets later. Sunburn plus hangover equals a gruesome vacation combination.

Kim continued, "Sonja is upset. All of a sudden, her leadership is in doubt. The question now is if we can hold this council together for the remainder of the term, or if we just become completely dysfunctional." She blew out her lips and shook her head angrily.

"Did Mikayla admit to being the leaker?"

"Heavens no. That's part of the problem. We are all under suspicion."

Samantha stared at the pool. She had no answers to this difficult problem.

More of the lethal vodka concoction got poured. The decibel level went up another notch. Two of the women rolled into the pool. The remaining six screamed with laughter. A cell phone shot the carnage. Tik Tok would be busy tonight.

"Remember what Samira was saying the other night about seniors and how so many of them are lonely?" Kim said, changing the subject.

Samantha nodded.

"I was thinking. She's correct. Maybe we should volunteer at that big senior's complex. The Whispering Palms Retirement Village, I think it's called. A couple of hours a week? Just talking with the residents, doing whatever we can to help. It is in my ward. It's always good to have a strong connection with seniors, and I think we might do some good."

"That's a nice idea. Sure, I'll go with you."

"OK. Good. You sort something out and let me know." Kim was quickly learning the art of delegation.

The afternoon warmth was lovely. They both sipped ice water from their thermos bottles. They waved at The Wives. They waved back. They had become a lot friendlier since Samantha and the Sheriff had returned the half million dollars that a couple of con artists had swindled from them. One of the culprits had been a woman. Samantha had chased her to Singapore and tackled her into submission in Amsterdam. It had been quite the adventure.

To this day, the husbands had no idea what had gone on with the fake Asian crypto-currency scam.

"Oh, before I forget," Samantha said, "book the 26th of next month for the "Martinis & Manicures" party. I've got a list of 29 leading women in the area—business, legal, the university, retail, advertising, media. I'm sending out the invitations tomorrow. We'll probably be lucky to get half of them to attend."

"Do you think this will really work? Will anybody show? Will anybody contribute?"

Kim's rookie year in politics was a steep learning curve. Truthfully, however, Samantha was equally uncertain about the success of the event. Especially after she had priced the exclusive invitation at $1,000.

"Hey, go big or go home! It's fun to try. And we did invent the Kimtini! If nothing else lasts from the party, if nobody comes, we've always got that."

Kim laughed at the memory of the cocktail invention night.

They got up for a swim. Samantha looked carefully around the pool and the lounge chairs as they stepped into the huge swimming pool.

"Have you noticed that women's bathing suits seem to be getting smaller and tighter, while men's are getting bigger and baggier?"

Kim surveyed the evidence arrayed around the pool. "Probably a good thing," she said as she slipped under water.

Chapter 14

THE WHISPERING PALMS Retirement Village was a four-story stucco building on a couple of acres of land in the southwest of Port Manatee. Two additions over the years made the building an oddly-shaped 'E' design. It was pleasantly landscaped with tropical shrubs, walking paths that curved through the property, brightly colored flower beds, and lots of the ubiquitous palm trees.

"We have 187 residents, most of them in their own room," said Connie Brighthouse, the GM of the home. "We provide assisted living, but we don't have a secure area for people suffering from Alzheimer's or other long-term dementia issues. We refer those people to our sister facility in Sarasota."

Samantha and Kim sat quietly in the office as Brighthouse and Head Nurse Nicholas Nurse interviewed them. "I'm a bit embarrassed about having to ask you these questions," she continued, "but our protocol demands that we clear all of our volunteers—just to protect our residents. The background checks are purely routine."

They both nodded understanding. Brighthouse was a pleasant woman in her early 50s. Her hair was turning silver at the tips. Nurse was dressed in casual male nurse attire. He was about 45, Samantha guessed. He had a sallow complexion and a weary demeanor. His brown hair was thinning. His nails were neatly trimmed.

The interview proceeded quickly as Mrs. Brighthouse explored their personal and professional histories. "We are so grateful to have volunteers who want to assist at Whispering Palms," Brighthouse assured them. "Loneliness—social isolation—is one of the biggest challenges that our residents face. Here or at any seniors' home. Often their family is no longer in this area, or they are simply busy with their own lives and can't visit as much as our ladies and gentlemen would like. We care much more about a volunteer's character than experience with seniors."

"I can't be tied down to a specific schedule," Kim reminded the administrator. "My work at City Council is erratic in scheduling and meetings that I have to attend often come up at the last minute."

"I understand completely. Both of you are busy. We get that. That's why we don't demand a regular schedule of visitations. We do ask for some continuity in visiting, perhaps once or twice a week so that the residents become familiar and get comfortable with you."

The two women nodded.

"Wonderful then. Thank you. Nick, any other questions?"

"No. Thank you for coming." His voice was gentle. His face was expressive behind thick glasses.

Mrs. Brighthouse pushed her chair back and stood up. "We'll confirm your background checks immediately. Perhaps now you'd like to see the facility? Nick, could you do that?"

He nodded as he stood and waited for Kim and Samantha to shake hands with his boss and turn to the door. He led them onto the first floor corridor.

"We do most of the social activities on this floor. The movie theater is down there. The card room is here," he said as he opened a door to reveal half a dozen square card tables. There were four sturdy chairs with arm rests at each table. "Our library is down the hall in the corner. And the dining area is in here," he said as he walked into a comfortable, spacious room. Windows opened onto the attractive garden outside.

"We've started to grow some of our own herbs and vegetables," he told them proudly. "A few of the residents help with the gardening. The meals are really important to our residents. The food is very good here."

They continued the tour of the main floor. "This is one of our sitting rooms. The other one is a little smaller, in the corner down there. Pretty view though. It looks over the flower garden."

The threesome walked down the hall as residents passed slowly. A number of walkers were in use, as were canes of varying designs. Staff hurried along the corridor. Two staff pushed wheelchairs.

"Ah, this is one of our nursing support staff, Elmer Krackle." Krackle was a small man in his early fifties. He had thinning brown hair, close-set eyes and the evidence of a bad case of childhood acne. He avoided looking directly at either woman as he nodded and scurried down the corridor.

Kim and Samantha continued to peer into the rooms. They looked clean, tidy and comfortable. A few residents were reading in quiet corners or chatting with friends. Several sat alone in a chair or stared out the window. Others began to drift into the card room.

"This is Mrs. Harris," Nurse announced as a bright-eyed African-American woman in a wheelchair rolled up to them. "Mrs. Harris has been with us for six years now. She was a teacher in high school for what, 40 years?"

"42. Loved it. Loved the kids. Loved educating them. Hated the school system. Hated being underpaid. Hated the dumbing-down of our educational system in the last years of my career. Bunch of dumb politicians screwing up the schools and a couple of generations of kids. Hmmph."

Her aura of teacherly authority was still shining brightly. Kim seemed more than a little intimidated by the woman with such high standards and a bright mind. Samantha stepped forward, hand out-stretched.

"I am very happy to meet you, Mrs. Harris. My name is Samantha Summers. This is Kim Sharpe. We're hoping to become new volunteers here at The Palms."

Mrs. Harris eyed them carefully as they shook hands. "You're my city councillor," she said, her eyes fixed on Kim. "And you're the lady who designed the playground for the Delvecchio Bridge project," she announced to Samantha. "Are you still dating that handsome Sheriff?"

Stunned, the two women looked at each other in shock.

"Oh for heaven's sake. I'm old, not stupid," Mrs. Harris said tartly. "I pay attention to what's going on around here. I read the local paper. This is my city. I always taught my students to really focus on their local government. That's where the action is, that's where you can have the greatest influence. Not in Washington. Or, Lord help us, Tallahassee." She shuddered as she considered the latest crop of Florida state legislators.

Nick Nurse stood by. A smile broke out as he watched the older woman dismantle the two new volunteers. She was a smart woman, was Mrs. Harris.

"I'm in a wheelchair because of the arthritis and my two hip replacements and because I'm tired and hurting. Well, that just helps to focus my mind on other things. You two come and see me next time. I'll get you straightened out."

With that, she rolled down the hall. She left two limp women behind.

"She reminds me of the nuns in my Catholic school," said Kim finally. "They scared the hell—sorry, Sister, heck—out of me."

Samantha laughed. So did Nurse. "I love her," announced Samantha. "I want to see more of her. May I?"

Nurse Nurse grinned. "If you can handle her, go right ahead. She is a terror around here. Scares the...heck...out of everybody. She's smart. Really smart."

They finished the tour. Just as they were about to say their good-byes, Mrs. Brighthouse came bustling out of her office.

"Hang on. I just wanted to let you know that, well, I expedited your background clearances with the Sheriff's department. A Deputy Chad was very helpful." She smiled. "He seemed to know of both of you." Her smile got bigger. "It probably won't surprise you to learn that you both cleared the security check. Welcome to The Whispering Palms Retirement Village."

Samantha promised to return the next day to pick up their Volunteer badges and complete the rest of the paperwork. Kim was scheduled for a Planning Committee meeting at city hall.

Handshakes and smiles all around as they left the retirement home.

Kim was quiet on the drive home. Finally she turned to Samantha. "I'll make you a deal. You get Mrs. Harris; I'll take the rest of the place."

Samantha laughed. "Deal. But I'll bet you that in a few months you'll be really good friends with her."

Another silence in the car. Finally Kim spoke. "Geez, can you imagine if we'd flunked the security check by our own Sheriff's Department?"

Chapter 15

"SO WE'VE GOT nothing?"

Silence around the table. Perkins' senior staff was meeting for their daily 8am briefing.

The Sheriff tried again. "Two weeks after somebody uses dynamite to blow up a building project in our city, and we've got nothing?"

An Inspector finally spoke up. "We know where the dynamite came from. It was stolen either from a construction site in Jacksonville or from FSU. The police there have no leads. They don't think it was internal. Nothing else was taken in the robbery."

"There were a couple of scraps of paper CSI found. They're working on them."

"A local resident we interviewed said he thought he heard banjo music just before the explosion. Probably a radio or something." He shrugged.

"CIs have offered nothing," reported a senior Detective. Confidential Informants were usually a fairly reliable source of what was going on in the underbelly of the city. "Nothing. Not a hint."

"We've heard no street talk," confirmed another detective. "Nobody is boasting. We've got no big bang theory."

Snickers. Perkins' temperature rose another degree. "We're looking like incompetent idiots!" The mood around the table straightened up quickly. "The Mayor's on me. Local TV won't let it go. The developer keeps asking me what's going on. This guy is dropping $187 million into this city and we can't even keep some nutcase from blowing up a bunch of dirt on his property? Get on it, people!"

The group fled the meeting room. Perkins didn't blow up very often. He was usually cool and reserved. When he erupted, it was for real.

Perkins sat alone at the head of the conference table. He was fuming. Why wasn't someone out there bragging about what they'd done? And why on earth would anybody blow a hole in the ground where they were already digging a hole in the ground?

It made no sense. None at all.

Regardless, it was making the Sheriff's Department look bad. That Perkins couldn't tolerate.

CHAPTER 16

SAMANTHA PICKED UP the volunteer badges for herself and Kim the next morning. She strolled the halls and stopped in one of the reading rooms. She introduced herself to several residents. She helped a couple of ladies get their morning tea and cookies. She sat and chatted with a man sitting by himself. He seemed to be brightened by the attention.

It was later in the morning when she found Mrs. Harris again.

"So you came back? I wasn't sure you would after yesterday. Your friend looked a little wary."

"Kim? No. I think she just had a flash-back to her high school days. Catholic girl's school. Strict nuns."

"Ah, yes. I always approved of a little discipline in the classroom. Not like the mess we've got today in so many schools. Teachers dress worse than the kids. There's no respect any more for teachers. You need some separation in the classroom. There has to be an authority figure. Kids need boundaries. They respect that, even if they say they don't like it."

Samantha got coffee for both of them. She tucked a chocolate cookie on each saucer. She returned to sit beside the wheelchair.

Mrs. Harris eyed her. "So what's your story, honey? How did you end up in this steamy little city of ours? You're not from here. Wait. Let me guess. You don't have that disgusting New Joisey accent. Not New England either, you don't roll your Rs. Has to be Connecticut, Delaware or New York. You're way too pretty to hide in the sticks. Has to be NYC."

"You are correct," Samantha laughed. "I moved here a year and a half ago after I divorced my idiot former husband. He was a stockbroker on Wall Street. He made a lot of money and lost a lot of friends." She paused. "He cared more about the money than friends. Or me." She sipped her coffee. "I caught him having an affair with one of my best...well, used-to-be friends. Old story, I guess. I never suspected."

She shook herself. "Anyway, I decided to get out of town. I fought for a really good settlement, jumped in my car and ended up here in the middle of February. It was warm! I bought a condo and moved in. I'm pretty much severing all my ties with New York and that life." She paused again. "I don't miss it."

"And of course you've got that cute Sheriff down here," Mrs. Harris noted tartly.

Samantha flushed a bit. "Yes, we are very happy. He's a special man. He has been very good for me." She smiled a coy smile. "Of course, I like to think that I've been good for him too."

Mrs. Harris hooted. "I just bet you have, honey, I just bet you have. You might have to bring him over here sometime to put the fear of God in some of the men. They'll all fall for you. A few of them might get rather handsy, if you understand what I mean."

"I do. Thanks for the warning. I'm sure I'll be alright, though. I've dealt with grabby guys before," Samantha smiled.

"I just bet you have, the way you look. I love your hair. What is that shade? Uh, let me guess. Copper? No, too reddish. Dark blonde with...no. Wait! I have it! Burnished gold. That's it, that's your hair color."

Samantha reflexively patted her hair. "That's lovely. I've never heard that description before. Burnished gold. I like it. Thank you."

She looked at Mrs. Harris. Her face had suddenly slumped; her eyes were tired. "I am going to go for a rest now, but I enjoyed our chat, dear. Maybe you would push me to my room? I get...suddenly tired now. Getting old is not for the faint of heart." Her head drooped a bit. "I hate it," she muttered almost under her breath as Samantha unlocked the brake and wheeled the chair to the elevator.

She escorted Mrs. Harris to her room and got her tucked in. She quietly turned out the lights and shut the door.

CHAPTER 17

"THE PROPERTY OWNER has now hiked his asking price for the land for the new community center to $2,950,000," Roy Crawford reported to the in-camera meeting of city council.

There were a few angry glances at Councillor Johnson. She ignored them all.

"What about another site? Why are we focused on that particular parcel of land? Don't we have other options?"

"That's a good question, Councillor Miller. The answer, as it usually is with real estate, is simple—the location. The site has easy access to two main arterial roads. That part of the city is sadly lacking in municipal facilities, and there will be a lot of growth in that quadrant, so the neighborhood fit is great. The location is by far our first choice for the new sports and community complex."

'What will this do to the final budget for the project?"

Crawford paused. "Obviously it is going up. Our staff is currently reassessing costs and what we might be able to trim to bring the budget more in line with our original estimate. However, we also believe that if we're going to do this project, we need to do it right. If we start skimping and cutting too severely it will never be as good a facility as it should be." He shook his head. "Council is between the proverbial rock and a hard place on this. We will try to come up with some alternatives and I will meet again with the landowner on the price."

He turned to the mayor. "I know it is difficult to get everyone together for these special council meetings. If it would be easier, I would undertake to talk with each council member for a private update as things evolve."

Councillor Johnson erupted. "You are still determined to hide everything from everybody, ain't you? The webs of lies and secrecy that you—"

"That is out of order, Councillor! Stop it! I will not have you attacking our city manager when he is simply trying to salvage a situation that y—uh, that someone, has caused." The Mayor looked around the horseshoe. "Councillor Sharpe?"

"I think getting on-going briefings from the City Manager is a very good idea. It will keep us informed and up to date without having to have a series of special meetings. I know it takes a lot of staff time and effort to put together a full council meeting. This situation is still evolving. I want to stay informed."

"Yeah, you can get briefed while you two're foolin' around in the sack," Councillor Johnson muttered in a low voice. Kim whirled to face her. Apparently, no one else had heard the venomous comment. Kim stared at her nemesis. The other councillor dropped her eyes with a smirk.

"Councillor Sharpe?" It was a puzzled question from the mayor when Kim didn't sit down after her speech.

Kim continued to glare at the other councillor before looking up. "Sorry, Mayor." She sat down.

"I agree with Councillor Sharpe," said Councillor Kelly. "It makes all kinds of sense in a fluid situation like this. And it lets Roy get on with trying to salvage this mess."

The Council quickly agreed to allow their city manager to continue to negotiate the land deal and to review plans for the project itself. He would report back to the council members on an individual basis from time to time, as events warranted. The mayor would call a special meeting of the council if and when formal votes were required to authorize action or spending.

The vote was 6-1 to proceed. Nobody was surprised at the dissenter.

Nor were many surprised when The Observer had a headline story the next day about allegations of more secret dealings at Port Manatee City Council involving a land purchase and civic project.

Roy Crawford was livid. He saw the price for the land jumping again. The leak at city council was getting more and more expensive.

Chapter 18

"SHE HAD AN unlimited budget for her wedding…and she exceeded it!"

Samira was laughing as she told the story of one of her friends who had recently been married.

"Her family is Indian. The wedding went on for three or four days. Feasts every night. Gold everywhere. Live elephants. Receptions with fountains of iced Dom Perignon. Seafood flown in from all over the world. Celebrity chefs hired for the night to prepare delicacies that were…well, incredible. Her wedding dress cost almost $250,000. It had spun gold thread in the fabric. It was…astounding. And her jewellery! My God, the jewellery!"

Kim and Samantha sat, entranced, on Samantha's lanai.

"There were maybe four hundred guests. The cost of the women's outfits would have bankrupted a small country. The wedding gifts were…unbelievable. Custom designed jewellery. Several cars. There were rumors of a jet plane. Just a small one, but still…" Samira shook her head at the memories.

"And yet here I am, stuck drinking cheap wine with you two bozos! Not an elephant in sight! Not one lousy Rolls Royce!"

Samantha looked at Kim. "As the hostess, I want you to know that I am highly offended. Lousy wine, my ass. I'll have you know that I paid almost $12 a bottle at Uncle Larry's Booze Barn for this fruity and well-balanced French Côtes du Rhône."

"And I notice she hasn't declined any refills," Kim added with a malicious grin.

"Twelve dollars a bottle?" Samira retorted. "At the wedding, they would have used that cheap swill to wash the dishrags in the kitchen." She sniffed. "I need a refill."

Laughter greeted her request. Samira gave out one last shot. "Twelve bucks, huh? At Uncle Larry's? What, did they give you part ownership of the joint?"

After the laughter faded, the three friends sat in companionable silence for several minutes, enjoying the sultry weather.

"Oh! Golly. I almost forgot," announced Samantha. "The invitations for the MARTINIS & MANICURES party went out." She swallowed the mellow red wine. Kim looked at her nervously.

"The RSVPs started coming back immediately. I had hoped we might get ten or twelve people coming out of the 29 invitations we sent out. We didn't get that. Not even close." She paused and sipped. Kim slumped back in her chair. She was disappointed. This was her first fund-raising foray. It was, well, dreadful.

Samira looked on, concerned and frowning. She had supplied several of the names of the prominent women who had been invited.

"No," Samantha continued slowly, "we didn't get the ten or twelve that I'd expected." She paused again, drawing out the suspense. "But we did get 23!"

Kim whooped in glee. And relief. Samira said with a slow grin, "Way to go, you bum. You almost gave her a heart attack." She gestured towards Kim who was slumped on a chair.

"For whatever reason, the party seemed to resonate with the women leaders in town. They liked how unique it was, and how it was such an exclusive event. We only had three people say no. Two of them are out of town on business, and one is committed to hosting a big corporate conference. We never heard from the final three. Rude, but whatever," she concluded.

"That...that is fabulous!" Kim was ecstatic. "That's going to raise, what, over twenty grand?"

"No." Kim quivered at the response. Samantha again waited. "Several of the women wanted to make an additional donation. We're going to end up with more than $40,000 in the bank!"

Kim sagged back, clutching her chest with one hand and her wine glass with the other. "Don't tease me, Samantha! I can't take any more! Seriously?"

Samantha took pity of her friend. She nodded. "Yes, absolutely true. This is going to give us a fabulous bank roll for your future political ambitions. And we'll make some great contacts with professional women throughout the community. That is a base we'll be able to tap in the future."

Kim's smile lit up the night.

"Great job, Samantha." Samira was sincere. "Of course," she continued after a pause, "I still think it would have been easier just to marry her off to some rich Indian prince who could pay for all her future campaigns." She thought some more. "Gosh, her wedding reception would still be going on!"

Chapter 19

THE HEAVY-SET MAN walking down the street was wearing a faded tie-dyed shirt right out of the 60s. Psychedelic didn't even begin to describe the pattern. The brightly colored swirls on the shirt would make a peacock vomit.

Perkins shook his head as he patrolled the city. He insisted on getting out once or twice a week to do on-street police work. That kept him in touch with the city and what was going on. Smart cops always want a feel for the street.

Still, that didn't mean he had to approve of everything he saw. Like the woman with scraggly gray hair and a royal purple sweat suit walking her pet pig on the sidewalk. The pig rumbled along like an NFL blocking back. Pedestrians parted like waves before it. The pig was on a leather leash that looked insubstantial for animal control purposes.

Perkins looked at the pig one more time. Maybe a BLT for lunch?

"All units! All units! 10-31. 10-31 on Abigail Avenue at River Road. Store robbery."

Perkins checked traffic around him as he accelerated towards the scene. "Sheriff enroute. Two minutes out."

"Sheriff two minutes. Car 39 one minute. Car 27 arriving now. Officer on scene reports a 10-32. Repeat, 10-32. Proceed with caution."

Damn. Somebody at the scene with a gun. That always ratcheted up the risk level to high. Usually very high.

Perkins hit the light and siren bar as he manoeuvred around the traffic. Adrenaline kicked in. He drove with controlled speed but was moving swiftly through the vehicles clogging the street.

Abigail Avenue was a main street through a neighborhood that had seen its best days half a century ago. The two-story retail shops had once been warm red bricks and bright, newly painted doors and shutters. Today it was a shabby hang-over from those days. No paint brush had been used on any store-front in a decade.

Passers-by were pressed fearfully against building walls and in doorway recesses when Perkins pulled up. His officers had sealed the street at both ends and were hustling the by-standers to safety. Two officers were crouched behind their SUV. Both had guns drawn.

Across the street in a pawn shop, a man peered through the front window. He was waving a gun. Perkins couldn't see any other people inside the store.

He opened his car door after parking near the other police vehicles. He crouched down as he swiftly moved toward his officers. The air crackled with tension.

"Hey, Sheriff. Nice of you to join us," said Deputy Sosa. A ten-year veteran of the department, Sosa was a street-smart cop. Perkins looked at his partner who was crouched behind the left rear tire. "Officer Tranh," introduced Sosa. "Sheriff Perkins."

They nodded at one another. "Officer Tranh started yester-day," Sosa continued. It was said without inflection, but it was a warning to Perkins about the experience level of his partner. New recruits were always paired with knowledgeable veteran cops for their real training after their graduation from Police College.

"We got an alarm signal from inside the pawn shop," Sosa continued. "We pulled up and were getting out when this guy inside takes a shot through the window. We got behind the car and radioed in for assistance. We don't know how many are inside the store. Gotta be at least the store owner. Maybe others."

"Do you need the Tactical Unit?"

"Yeah. I radioed in. We just don't know what we're dealing with here." Perkins nodded agreement. "What else don't we know?" Sosa asked his newbie partner.

Tranh thought for a moment. "We don't know what mental state the gunman is in. Whether he is on drugs or not. We also don't know if he has partners inside." He paused, thinking more. "Or a partner outside."

Perkins grunted as he looked at Sosa. "Good call, Tranh," said the veteran cop. "Not many think of the possibility of an accomplice on the outside. They might be keeping watch. Maybe in a get-away car. There could be a possible shooter from the back or side."

Perkins still didn't speak. It was important for the two new partners to build a rapport. It was also a teaching moment for the young officer.

"So," Sosa continued, "what does that mean to us?"

Tranh again thought for a moment. "Clear the perimeter?"

"Good. Get the people out of here, make sure our backs are clean. That's happening now. Then we can completely focus on the perp inside the pawn shop."

Sosa used his radio to confirm with the other units that had arrived to finish clearing the street. To help distract the man inside the store, he used his police car radio system to 'talk' to the gunman.

"Why don't you lay down your gun and come out?" Sosa started on the microphone. "You will be safe. We don't want anyone harmed. That includes you."

No answer from inside.

"We have police all around the store. There is no escape for you. Let's put the gun down and end this right now."

Perkins could see the gunman's head moving inside the store window. No other heads were showing. The TAC unit truck rolled up. The black-armor-clad officers scrambled out. The situation was escalating.

Sosa looked at Perkins for a brief moment and shook his head. Perkins immediately got on his radio. "TAC, TAC. Officer on scene asks you to stay back. Negotiations are under way. Repeat, stay back."

The TAC team retreated to their truck.

"What is your name?" continued Sosa. "I'm Manuel Sosa. Who are you?"

"Jimmy," came a faint response from the store.

"Jimmy. Good. Call me Manny. What's goin' on, Jimmy?"

"Stuff...not so good. Lost my job. Family needs to eat. Just... shitty."

"Yeah. I hear you. Look, Jimmy. Your family doesn't want you to get hurt or do anything silly. How about this? You put the gun down and come out of the store with your hands up, and we'll get somebody who can help you? Get some food for your family. Maybe help you find a new job?"

"That...that would be...nice." A long pause. "Nobody's offered to help me for a while." Another pause. "OK, I'm coming out."

"Good, Jimmy, good. Just toss your gun out first. Then you walk out, hands in the air. That's all it will take."

The door to the pawnshop swung open. An automatic pistol hit the pavement. A moment later a whip-thin man in dirty blue jeans and a faded T-shirt came out. It had been several days since he'd shaved or shampooed. His hands were up. The TAC squad rushed over, put him on the ground and cuffed him. The gun was collected, unloaded and bagged.

Sosa and the other officers stood up. Two TAC officers went into the store. They came back a moment later. "Store's clear," they announced. "Just the pawn broker inside. He's fine. Well, shaken-up, but physically OK."

A sheriff's car drove off with Jimmy in the back seat. The street slowly came back to life. Sosa went up to check with the TAC squad.

"You got really lucky today," Perkins turned to Tranh.

"Nobody got shot?"

"Well, that too. But today you learned some huge lessons from your partner."

Tranh paused as he recalled the incident. Perkins could see awareness building in his eyes. Finally he blinked and refocused on Perkins. "Yes, sir. I see that now. Thank you."

"Thank your partner. You are learning from one of the best we've got. Listen to him. I think you're going to make a very fine officer. Welcome to the department."

Perkins offered his hand. Tranh shook it gratefully.

Perkins nodded and walked over to the TAC truck. "Good job everybody." He looked at Sosa. "Outstanding, Manny. And a good lesson for the kid."

Sosa nodded.

"You'll follow up with social services to get the family some help?"

"I will. I promised that to Jimmy. I think he's a good man but another one who got trapped in this economy and the pandemic. We'll get his family fed."

Perkins nodded.

Just another day of policing on the streets of Port Manatee.

Chapter 20

"I'VE GOT HIM down to $2.55M," reported Roy Crawford to Mayor Rodriguez, "after some really hard bargaining. We're kind of stuck there. Now that he knows it's the city that wants the land, he is holding us up. I practically had to promise him your first-born to get him down another half-million."

Rodriguez smiled. "Javier's about to turn 13. The dreaded teenage years. I'd probably take that trade."

Crawford laughed. "I think I can drive him down a bit more. Would you consider awarding him a nice certificate of appreciation or something? You know, for civic contributions?"

"You get the price down another half-million and I'll award him the nicest Commendation Plaque that we've ever created." She thought. "And we will honor him at the opening ceremonies. No! Wait! We'll put up the plaque in the foyer of the new building so his kids and grandkids can see it. That should help."

"Great idea. I'll have another run at him." Crawford paused before looking straight at the mayor. "I have come up with an idea that might help us identify the leaker. We know it is someone senior at city hall, either staff or elected. I suspect we both have suspicions." He cracked his neck. The tension was very real over this whole leak issue. It was starting to affect him physically on top of the mental stress.

"I am reluctant to share the details with you because you need, well, let's just say I don't want to make you vulnerable to any internal attacks. You need complete deniability of what I'm going to do. If it works, we would know for sure who the leaker is. If you don't want me to proceed then tell me now and I'll shut it down, because if we identify the person there will be repercussions."

The mayor sat looking at him for a long time. Finally she blinked and looked out her office window. She sighed and looked back at her city manager.

"Look, Roy. I think you're a heck of a good city manager. You've done great things for this city at a time when things could have crumbled, and you could have just walked away and found another job in about two seconds. I appreciate that you've always supported me and the council."

Her face twisted with frustration as she continued. "But this situation is starting to tear the Council apart. It's becoming a joke in the community amongst a number of business leaders. We are looking bad. The negative feelings and personal animosities around the horseshoe are getting worse. We're losing the trust and respect of each other. If it continues, if we can't get rid of this poison inside our chambers, then our entire term will be unproductive and that will hurt the city."

She shook her head in growing anger and despair as she thought about the implications. Her own legacy as mayor would be tarnished forever. To say nothing about the negative impact on the city's growth and development.

Crawford watched carefully but said nothing. There were times when an elected official really must step up and elevate over his or her own political objectives. They had to assume some personal political risk and not fear retribution. It was a test that many failed as their own self-interest about getting re-elected too often took priority.

He could see Mayor Rodriguez struggling through the issue and the implications. This was the painful Olympic moment for her.

Finally Rodriguez re-focused. "I simply won't have this mess continue. I tell you to your face that I am not the leaker. That said, and without knowing what you are planning—" she held up her hand in a stop signal to Crawford "—and I don't want to know anything about it. Period. Nothing. But the condition that I put on this idea of yours is that you have to treat me exactly the same as any other elected member. The same test or whatever you're thinking about doing. If I fail it somehow, then your duty is to report that to the other council members."

Crawford was about to speak when she again held up her hand. "And if your test or whatever finds incontrovertible proof of the culprit, then I will take appropriate action. Or at least urge the Council, if it is an elected member, to do so. If it turns out to be administrative, then I will back whatever decision you make to discipline that person. Including termination."

Crawford sat there. He raised an eyebrow. She nodded and finally he spoke. "I cannot tell you how much I respect what you have just stated. Thank you. You should be immensely proud of what you have said this morning. I am honored to be working for this city and its mayor."

A quick hug seemed appropriate to both of them. It turned to be a bit longer. They both suddenly understood that they were crossing a dangerous bridge in their working lives. It could easily collapse or blow up, and leave one if not both of their careers plummeting to disaster.

Chapter 21

THE MOOD SEEMED sombre when Kim and Samantha walked into the front lobby of Whispering Palms. The reason became clear at the front desk. A black frame surrounded by a black velvet ribbon held a stark notice: "We are saddened to announce the passing of a beloved resident of Whispering Palms, Mrs. Lillian Goldschmidt. A memorial service will be held Thursday at 11am in the chapel."

"She was a nice lady," Nick Nurse told them. "She lived here nearly five years. She had a couple of daughters who were regular visitors. She'll be missed."

They walked into the main sitting room. A number of residents were there, talking quietly. Kim drifted over to a group of women and sat down. Samantha quickly gravitated to Mrs. Harris.

"I liked her," began Mrs. Harris. "I am black, Baptist; she was white, Jewish, from Michigan as I recall, but we quickly became friends here. We talked a lot. We solved several world problems together," she chuckled. "We both liked a little sip of bourbon at night. Don't tell anybody."

Samantha smiled. "Is it, uh, difficult here when someone passes?"

"Listen, it's an old folk's home. Most of us are pretty realistic. We're all on that trajectory. Most of us just hope for a good death. We want to keep our faculties, so we don't get moved into some facility for the physically infirm or the mentally—well, I won't even go there. It is pleasant here. We make friends. We socialize with nice people like you." She sipped her tea. "But something happened in the last few months. Lillian started to withdraw. She said a couple of times her wrists were sore. She had some bruises on them. It was odd." Mrs. Harris stared out the window.

"Still," she said after a moment, "there have been several deaths here in the past year or two." She frowned. "Maybe more than the statistics would project. I used to teach math and English," she said as she smiled at Samantha. "I know about mathematical projections like bell curves and stuff. It seems to me that we're having a bit of a bump on the far side of that curve." She shrugged and paused. "Listen, people die in a senior's residence. It happens." She shrugged again.

Samantha didn't quite know what to say. Mrs. Harris patted her knee. "Don't you be listening to an old broad like me. You keep enjoying your life. I want to meet that handsome Sheriff of yours someday soon. Now, do me a favor and go over and talk to Mrs. Williams. She's sitting by herself in that corner. She needs a friend. She's become increasingly...withdrawn. I worry about her."

Samantha hugged her new friend in her wheelchair and walked over to stand by Mrs. Williams.

"Hi. I'm Samantha. May I join you?"

The woman peered up through thick glasses. She was clutching a well-worn handkerchief. She wore a beige dress with a shawl around her shoulders. A half-drunk cup of tea was on the side-table. The peanut butter cookie was untouched.

"Oh." A cautious response.

Samantha sat down on an adjacent chair. "That's a very pretty shawl," she said.

Mrs. Williams raised her left hand to stroke the shawl. "Cashmere," she announced. "My son gave it to me."

"It is lovely. And I bet it's warm."

She raised her other hand to touch the shawl. Samantha blanched. "Yes, it is very warm and soft," Mrs. Williams said.

"Would you like some more tea?"

"No, thank you. I'm not very...hungry today."

"Did you know Mrs. Goldschmidt?"

"Oh yes. We used to play cards together. Then her arm and wrist started to hurt her. She sort of withdrew from socializing here. Well, from everything. It was sad." She dabbed a tear. "And now she's dead."

They chatted for a few more minutes before Samantha left to find Kim. She had a luncheon meeting at city hall, and Samantha had to finish planning the fast approaching MARTINIS & MANICURES party. And she wanted to talk to Connie Brighthouse, the General Manager, about an idea she had for a special visitor to Whispering Palms.

Chapter 22

IT TOOK ROSIE about 12 seconds to become the star of the show. The. Star.

When Samantha walked her into Whispering Palms the following Monday, it was with mild trepidation. Rosie could be rather exuberant in her affection. Samantha had had a long, serious talk with her in the car while they were driving over.

"No slobbering kisses. No jumping up on laps. You're too big a dog for that. And these are older, delicate people. Many of them have trouble walking. They have canes or walkers or wheelchairs. Those are called mobility issues. You have to make sure you don't push them down or anything."

Rosie looked at her with panting affection. She squirmed with excitement about the car ride and seeing new places.

"I'm serious. Don't give me that happy stare. Pay attention. This is a trial. If you blow it, I'll probably get thrown out on my ear. Or my rear. I'll probably be the first volunteer at Whispering Palms to get excommunicated."

Rosie grinned happily. She let her pink tongue loll. She stuck her head out the car window. She tried to climb into the driver's seat.

"Now stop it. That's the sort of thing you can't do there. If you do that, they won't give you any treats."

That certainly got her attention. Rosie was very big on treats. She was both a knowledgeable and a motivated consumer.

She licked Samantha's right ear. "No. Your daddy can do that. In fact, he does that very well," Samantha smirked to herself. "Not you. Not at the retirement home. No licking of ears. Just be gentle. Be a perfect little lady."

Rosie barked at a squirrel in the park. Rosie didn't approve of squirrels. They were nasty little rodents. Fast, though. Hard to chase—they kept hiding in trees. It wasn't a nice way to play the game.

"Oh, and no barking. Absolutely no barking. You hear me?"

Rosie turned her big beautiful eyes onto the pretty lady who smelled of sunshine and lemons. What was she babbling about? There were squirrels to chase.

What she discovered a few minutes later wasn't squirrels, but a whole bunch of nice old people in a big building. That's when she became the star of the show. Everybody loved her. She soon broke away from that silly leash that she used to make sure her human friends didn't get lost on their walks. Now she could wander freely to meet these interesting new smells and sounds and people.

Everybody wanted to pat her, pet her, stroke her, kiss her, and tell her sweet things.

Rosie was very mature in her role. After all, she was the Queen. She stood patiently as shaky, veined hands caressed her. She laid her head onto the lap of a woman in one of those chair-things with wheels. She gave a little kiss to an old man in a brown checked shirt who seemed to need some special atten-tion. She sensed the most vulnerable and spent long minutes bestowing her attention.

Samantha finally gave up even trying to follow Rosie. The cluster of people around her was constant. Mrs. Brighthouse and Nick Nurse stood at the back of the room with Samantha, watching.

"I am absolutely amazed," the GM finally said.

"She is a wonderful dog," agreed Nurse. "And you said she didn't have any special training for this?"

"No. But we did have a long talk about her decorum during the drive over."

The nurse and the GM stared at each other before side-eyeing Samantha.

Samantha looked at her watch. "I should get her out of here. She probably needs to have a little run outside. I've got bags to pick up after her, not to worry. Is that alright?"

"Alright? Heck, right now she could be elected President of our Resident's Council. Nick, see if the kitchen has something special for her, will you?"

The nurse disappeared down the corridor.

The GM watched for another minute. "This is...terrific. What a great dog. Thank you for the idea. You bring her in anytime you want." She thought for a moment. "Maybe we'll have a special volunteer badge made up for her, or something."

Samantha smiled happily. Whew. It had been a nerve-wracking experiment. She went over to find Rosie. On the way back, she stopped at Mrs. Harris's wheelchair. "This is my special friend, Mrs. Harris," she said to Rosie. "This is Rosie."

The dog immediately dropped her head into Mrs. Harris's lap. She seemed to understand the physical limitations of the elderly woman. She got petted. Mrs. Harris soon found that spot between her ears at the back of her head. Rosie scrunched her eyes in pleasure.

"What a gorgeous animal. And she has almost the same color of hair that you do," Mrs. Harris exclaimed to Samantha. "You are just so special, yes you are."

Samantha smiled back. Then she realized the last remark was directed at Rosie. Ah well.

On their way out, Nick Nurse appeared from the kitchen with a plate of—Rosie sniffed appreciatively—sliced steak. He put it down and Rosie scarfed it up in an instant. Well, she'd been working hard all morning. A queen needs nourishment too.

She gave the nurse a little tongue in appreciation. He laughed and patted her as Samantha led her down to the front doors.

Once outside, Rosie enjoyed a nice little run on the lawn. She kept a wary eye out for those interloping squirrels. Her vigilance paid off. Not a squirrel in sight. The home and the nice older people she'd met today would be safe tonight.

CHAPTER 23

"HONEY?"

"Yuh?" Perkins was almost asleep after a vigorous round of lovemaking. Samantha was nestled on his shoulder. Her hand gently caressed his chest. It had been a glorious time. He was still catching his breath. And stretching out a little cramp in his left thigh.

"You know I've been volunteering at the Whispering Palms Retirement Home?"

"Yuh."

"Well...I don't really know what I'm talking about—don't even go there!" she swatted him as he took a breath to comment. "But...at the home. Nice people. I'm becoming friends with some of them. And Rosie was a spectacular success." He could hear the smile in her voice. "She is such a diva." He shifted just a bit as her hand drifted lower.

"Here's the thing. I've seen on oh, two, maybe three, of the residents what look to me like bruises on their wrists or lower arms. You know the skin gets kind of what, more translucent? as people age. Maybe it just bruises more easily. I'm not an expert. But—"

Perkins shifted again. "Just what are you saying? And don't stop what you're doing."

She giggled. But didn't stop. "I really care for these people. Some of them are all alone. Most are lonely. I don't know what they could do if something...nasty...was happening to them."

He pushed up on the bed to look at her. Her hand dropped away. His face was serious in the moonlight. "Are you suggesting elder-abuse? That there is something wrong going on in that home? Because that's really serious, Samantha."

"Yes. No. I don't know. I'm no expert in this. I'm not accusing anyone of anything. But I have seen bruises on the wrists of two ladies, and one man flinched when I patted his arm. He was wearing a sweater so I couldn't see, but I just felt that he was bruised."

"Well, you shouldn't be feeling-up the male residents." The joke fell flat. "Sorry. Look, honey, sadly there is a lot of abuse that goes on in seniors' residences. Sometimes homes use restraints, I guess to protect the person from self-harm or something. Sometimes staff members are just mean. Job interviews can't always root out the cruel or incompetent ones. There is such a high demand for workers in retirement homes."

He dropped his head back to the pillow. "We actually had a seminar about elder abuse a few weeks ago. The fear is that as more of us age, society won't have the facilities or the resources to look after our senior citizens properly. Hiring support workers, nurses, therapists, well, it's all falling behind badly. Residences are struggling with staffing and nobody talks about that. It is a big problem now and soon it is going to be a huge problem. Homes are so vulnerable to influenza or any virus. So many people in long-term care homes die." He paused. "The risk is that retirement homes become so desperate to hire anybody that they end up with unqualified or uncaring staff." He paused again then gasped as her hand resumed its downward path. "Apparently in Japan and other places, they are now using robots for a lot of routine care and even companionship in nursing homes and retirement residences."

Samantha was thoughtful as she listened. She continued her gentle touches. He responded well. In fact, he soon responded with considerable vigor. The next half hour left both of them exhausted, satiated and asleep.

Chapter 24

"WE'VE REPAIRED ALL of the foundation that got blown up," Elliott Webster told Samantha as he pointed at the big hole in the ground from which the twin-tower complex would arise. The Sheriff's department had finally released the site back to Starwind Construction after the criminal investigation.

"It took us a bit longer than planned because we had to let some dirt settle and then really pack it tight. The new foundations are now re-poured. It set us back about 15 days altogether. We'll try to make up a couple of those during construction, but it will still cost us over two hundred grand."

"Wow. That's awful. No further problems?"

"Not so far. We've added security at night. More fencing. The neighborhood has been fantastic, watching for strangers. I'd like to thank them somehow."

"Lovely idea. They will appreciate that. Leave it with me. I'll come up with something."

Webster nodded. He strode off to check with the foreman in the construction office trailer. Samantha stared at the big hole one more time. It was hard to imagine that such a beautiful structure would rise from this dirt and bare concrete.

She carefully walked to the back of the foundation. She was wearing her pink hard-hat with *SAMANTHA* on the front, and her safety boots. She stopped to look over the land at the back of the building site that would become her playground and community garden.

Her vision had excited the neighborhood. It would be winding paths through the new vegetation, shrubs and flowers that would create a wonderful new community gathering place. There would be benches, bird baths, and a placid secret glen in the center. A community herb garden would be a feature.

The kid's playground would swoop toward the beach adjacent to the garden. It would be securely fenced to keep the kids safe. There would be playground equipment but also toys and materials so the kids could make up their own games and be creative within the safe space.

Finally, there would be a small beach area with open public access that would provide swimming and sunning and beach games and activities. The City had agreed to equip and maintain the beach.

Everyone agreed that Samantha's vision had been the driving force in separating Elliott Webster's bid on the project from any other. That was when he had hired her part-time to liaise with the neighborhood and to supervise the playground and garden installation.

"Samantha! Samantha!" The shouts from some kids racing towards her shook her out of her dream.

"Hi, guys! How are you?" She bent down to hug the little girls and bumped fists with the boys. A few mothers followed behind, laughing at their kids as they clustered around Samantha.

They hugged Samantha and then stood there looking at the site. "So, this is going to be our garden and playground," one finally exclaimed. "My kids can't wait. It is hard to imagine, though, just seeing this mound of dirt."

The kids were running around in the dirt, making up some game that involved lots of shrieking and dodging.

"It will be wonderful when it's done," Samantha reassured them. "They won't start to lay it out until the towers start to rise, but that will happen in a few months. Until then, make sure the kids stay away from the construction site. And if you ever see anyone suspicious, call the Sheriff's Department. And please let me know as well."

Wise nods from the mothers. A couple of the littlest girls returned to grab Samantha's leg and catch their breath.

"Oh. Listen. My boss here, the guy building the project, wanted me to tell you how grateful we are for all of you keeping an eye on the site for us. It is really valuable."

"We've formed a sort of Neighborhood Watch thing," Marvel d'Agostino told her. "We take turns patrolling around here. We've made friends with the security people. They check with us if somebody they don't know is snooping around. Our families are all together on this."

"That is so fantastic! Thank you! In fact, Elliott would like to put on some party or something to thank you. What do you think?"

Samantha had really prided herself on the close relation-ships that she'd developed with the families in the Ward 3 neighborhood. Kim had begun visiting on a regular basis as well. It was a great foundation for her political career.

That's why Samantha was stunned when the ladies all looked at one another and shook their heads. "No, honey. Thank you, but no."

Shaken, Samantha stared back. Had her work all been in vain? Had she done something to offend the community? My God, this was a disaster! What would Elliott think? She'd have to resign, of course. She would miss—

"Oh, honeychile!" Mrs. Barkley came over to hug her. Mrs. Barkley was the alpha mother in the neighborhood, which meant she ran the entire district. She weighed probably 210 pounds, wore bright floral dresses, ruled her kids with an iron hand, and had gone through two or three husbands—she laughed when she tried to recall. Maybe it was four.

"No, no! We love you! It's jus' that, well, we was talkin'. We wanna throw a big pic-inic for you an' the crew an' that nice Mr. Webster. A big thank you from us to you. What you think, Marvel, a pic-inic?"

Samantha sagged in relief and wonderment. The Community wanted to thank them? Wow. She wondered if that had ever been done before.

"That…would be fabulous! How nice of you all! But you have to let us contribute something…"

Mrs. Barkley was shaking her head. Her jowls quivered, along with some other parts of her big strong body.

"Nope. This is from us to you. We wanna cook for you. Have fun. Have a party."

Samantha hugged her. Then the other ladies who had gath-ered. The kids weren't quite sure what was going on, but they ran around hugging everybody as well.

It took a while for Samantha to extricate herself from the impromptu celebration. She finally found Elliott just as he was finishing a meeting with some suppliers. Something about rebar, whatever that was.

When he had a minute, she grabbed him and told him that she'd raised the idea of Starwind Construction hosting a com-munity party.

He looked on; a bit impatient. There were some big decisions to be made on the project and he was anxious to push it along.

"They turned us down," Samantha told him with a straight face.

Elliott turned back to her. His face was shocked. "They turned us down? For a party? What the hell, Samantha..."

She couldn't hold the grin back any longer. "The reason," she explained to him slowly, "is because they want to host a party for us!"

Elliott looked at her in disbelief. "What?"

"The mothers in the neighborhood cooked up this idea to have a picnic or something to say 'thank you' to you and Starwind for building this. I had nothing to do with it," she hastened to add. "This is completely their idea. I think it is marvelous."

Webster shook his head. "I've never heard of anything like this in any construction project I've ever..." His voice trailed off. "That is beautiful." He stopped and looked at her. "What can we do? Pay for it? What?"

Samantha shook her head. "I don't know. It all just happened. I think they would be insulted if you wrote a check. This is really a neighborhood outreach. But let me think about it. Maybe I can come up with a little way to help out without, you know, helping out."

"They want to do a party for us." Webster was still shaking his head in disbelief. "Huh." He wandered off to his next meeting. Then he turned back and shouted at her, "I guess this means you're hired for another week." He laughed and went into construction office trailer.

The door banged behind him.

CHAPTER 25

THE DISTINCTIVE OPENING notes of *Duelling Banjos* from "Deliverance" rang out in the darkness. The security guard cocked his head and then got out of his truck. He walked to the far end of the construction project. His big flashlight reflected off the locked fenced site.

He looked around but saw nothing. He peered into the darkness. Still nothing. The music had stopped. He heard no movement. He unsnapped his gun holster. He had never fired it except at the range. He was 21 years old. He swallowed hard. This was supposed to be an easy job.

The plucking of the banjo started again, farther away from the big site. A radio? He shone his flashlight towards the noise. He saw nothing. He slowly edged his way in the direction of the noise. He paused, listened and then fumbled for his cell phone and hit speed-dial to connect him with headquarters.

"Whatta ya got, Freddie?"

"I...I dunno. Some banjo music at the Delvecchio Bridge construction site. But there ain't nobody there. Here. I'm out lookin'. Nuthin."

"I'm calling the Sheriff's department. You stay there. Keep looking. Use your flashlight to make big arcs. I'll get back to you."

The phone clicked off. Freddie thought about his orders to keep looking. He thought about his girlfriend waiting for him. He glanced at his watch. 1:34am. No way was—

The explosion lit up the night. The concussion knocked Freddie down. He banged his head on the hard ground. The flashlight flew from his hand. The gun dropped into the dirt.

His ears had been deafened by the explosion. He dimly heard a vehicle accelerating away from the site when the dust and debris stopped flying and he recovered some of his hearing. He shook his head, trying to regain his equilibrium. That's how the second unit from the Sheriff's department found him.

The first unit had secured the site and checked quickly for causalities. They called in Fire, EMS, more police units, the Crime Scene Investigators and the Canine unit.

Scared neighbors were beginning to drift closer to the site. The next two police units set up a wide perimeter around the explosion site to keep back the crowds and protect evidence.

This time the hole in the ground was a lot bigger. The foundations had exploded and were now broken bits of concrete. Several of the initial steel beams to be erected that had been sitting adjacent to the construction site were now a twisted tangle of metal. The explosion had caused major damage to the project.

A dusty haze hung over the block. The putrid odor of explosives lingered. From a thriving construction site to a crime scene of wreckage: a dismal reality for civic officials.

"The future of this neighborhood-saving project is in jeopardy now," guessed Marvel d'Agostino as she huddled with some of the other mothers. "Poor Mr. Webster. What will he be thinking of our neighborhood now?"

(HAPTER 26

"WHO COULD BE doing this to us? Why? Why now?"
Elliott Webster asked the key questions. They hung in the cool morning air as the sun fought to break through the morning cloud bank.

Sheriff Perkins and several senior investigators were in a loose circle just outside the taped crime scene. Coffee was being drunk.

"Anything from the security guard?"

"Nothing much, Sheriff. The kid is pretty shook up. Slight concussion. He says he never heard anybody approach the site. No sign of lights or anybody sneaking in. He said something about deliverance or delivering or something, but we don't know what that means until we interview him again today. Maybe some supplies or equipment?"

"I wouldn't think so," replied Webster. "Who would deliver material late at night?"

Silence. The hushed slurping of rapidly cooling coffee. Everybody looked at the big hole in the ground. Chunks of metal and concrete littered the site.

Webster kicked the dusty ground with a well-worn construction boot. "Shit. This makes no sense. A locked fence. A guard on site. Why would anybody be against this project?"

He looked bleakly at the mess. "This is going to set us back three, maybe four weeks. It's going to cost us over a million dollars. We're a mid-sized company and we can't afford to drop another million."

He shook his head and kicked at the ground once more. "The entire investment is in jeopardy." The mayor had just arrived and heard the last statement.

"The Sheriff will find out who did this," she proclaimed. Perkins and his senior staff blanched. Law enforcement officials hate it when politicians make promises about investigations

69

and pledges of swift justice. The system usually just doesn't work that way.

"In the meantime, what about insurance? Won't that help?"

Webster shrugged. "I don't know. They weren't very happy about the first explosion. This one will really piss 'em off."

He sighed and threw the dregs of his coffee on the ground. "My crews will clean up once you release the site back to us. Unless some of the guys start thinking it is too dangerous." He paused, thinking. "I've never failed to complete a project, Mayor. But I have to tell you, this thing is either jinxed or somebody's out to get me or you or something else. Either way, it is getting harder to proceed. Our expenses are going up. There'll be another delay in revenue coming in which will stretch our bridge financing. The numbers have got to work for us to continue. I can't risk the future of my company and the jobs of all my employees on one project." He spit on the ground. "I need to talk to my people."

It was said pragmatically. It also sent a wave of terror through the Mayor. She had a huge political stake in seeing the project completed. So did the Council. So did the entire city.

The law enforcement people looked on. Perkins finally broke the silence.

"Whoever is doing this is making us look like bumpkins. I won't have that. Not on my watch. Mr. Webster, we're going to double-down on this investigation. I will commit whatever resources it takes."

Webster nodded. "Thanks. I hope it is..." He trailed off. He looked at the devastated site once again. "I've got to go." He nodded to Sonja Rodriguez and then the members of the Sheriff's investigation team and headed back to his truck. He walked slowly. His shoulders were slumped.

As Webster slid into the driver's seat and drove off, he didn't notice the three big black SUVs that pulled in behind him. Doors opened and a phalanx of black-clad officials poured out. A big man, 6-2, 225 pounds, led the way. He sported short brown hair. The edge of a snake tattoo peeked over his collar. He had a small scar on his left cheek. He headed directly towards the Sheriff.

"Perkins? You the head honcho here?"

Perkins nodded. The guy reached into his pocket and drew out a small black case. He flipped it open briefly. "Michael Crunciman. Homeland Security. This looks like a probable terrorist incident. We're taking over."

"The hell you are." Perkins voice was soft but there was steel in the phrase. "My city. My investigation. My people." The two men stared at each other. "Look, Mike..."

"Michael."

"...Michael. We appreciate the offer. If we need your, uh, expertise, we'll be happy to work together. We want this solved. Quickly. But this happened in my territory. I've got very smart people already working on this. We need to continue."

"Two bombings on the same site? Bullshit. You've got nothing so far." Perkins flushed one deeper shade of red. "There was another bombing at a construction site in Clearwater a couple weeks ago. Some terrorist organization is obviously trying to send a message of fear and hate. This is a conspiracy of terror that is threatening the United States. We need to stop it. Now. What's this town called?" he demanded of an aide.

"Port Manatee."

"Really? Crappy name. Big fat sea cows. Whatever. We'll..."

"You'll do nothing." The voice of Sonja Rodriguez cut through the morning air.

"Pull back your PR girl or whoever the fuck this is, Perkins."

The Sheriff offered a tight grin. There was no warmth in it. "Let me introduce the Mayor of Port Manatee, Her Honor, Sonja Rodriguez."

An awkward pause. "Ah. Well. Sorry about that. We'll be happy to let you know how our investigation turns out, Mayor."

"Sheriff Perkins will keep me well informed, Mr. Whoeveryouare. From Whateveragencyitis. Our Sheriff has my complete confidence. Now, thank you for visiting. Have a safe trip back to...well, wherever."

Crunciman stared at her for a long moment. Then his gaze shifted to Perkins. "Federal authority. I say we're taking over, we're taking over. Your people can't handle something like this."

There was stirring from the local authorities at this insult. Perkins flushed and stepped forward. Crunciman took a step towards him. The air bristled with animosity. Aides from both sides stepped between the two men and prevented what would have become an ugly battle.

Perkins took a deep breath. "Look," he ground out as he stared daggers at Crunciman. "I have full confidence in my department. We have been offered the assistance of the FBI by the Regional Director, James Robertson in Atlanta. I met with him recently. We will be fine. We keep authority."

Crunciman snorted. "Bunch of fuckin' amateurs," he muttered to an aide.

"I stand with my Sheriff and his team," repeated Mayor Rodriguez as she locked eyes with the brutish federal agent.

Finally Crunciman shrugged. "You're both making a big mistake. Huge. You're not equipped to handle the international aspects of terrorism and how complex their cells are. How big this might be. But." He shrugged elaborately. "Your funeral. I've got bigger cases than this little pissant explosion. Washington's orders are to work with local authorities where possible." He sniffed. "I don't think that's possible here." He spit. "We don't need this. Just tryin' to help. The hell with you and Port Seacowshit."

He turned to his aide again. "Make a note of their refusal of federal assistance, Agent Winslow. Date and time. Quote 'em. That way when the shite hits the proverbial fan, the media will have a full explanation from Homeland Security as to the competence of local law enforcement." He stared evilly at the mayor. "And the political leadership here in Hicksville."

His stare swept across the assembled officers, at least two of whom looked ready to pull their service weapons.

"Huh." With that dismissal, Crunciman turned and strutted back to the SUV parking lot. His aides followed. A moment later the cavalcade was gone.

The vacuum left behind took a long moment to fill. It was the Sheriff who recovered first.

"Geez I hate the feds. Especially Homeland Security. Arrogant bastards. Ah, sorry, Mayor."

"No need to apologize, Sheriff, when the description is correct." She shook her head as if to clear it. "Unbelievable. Thank God you stood up to them." She looked at the officers assembled. "Understand me. I have absolute confidence in your collective ability to solve this. But we need it done quickly. Our city needs this development. We have to earn Mr. Webster's confidence again. And the neighborhood will need reassuring. The best way to accomplish all of that is to find the perpetrator. Soon."

With that she nodded to all and returned to her car to head to city hall.

Perkins looked after her. "OK, that's a vote of confidence. Now let's earn it. I want a senior staff meeting at 11 this morning to plan our new investigation. Keep the crime scene people working here. We can coordinate with them later. Think creatively, people. Our credibility is now at stake. The Mayor has us on notice."

He kicked the ground. "And the feds have us on notice," he said under his breath. Not just political eyes but law enforcement eyes would be watching every step in this investigation, because the showdown with Homeland Security would get flashed across the infamous Blue network of police officers. Perkins had a strong feeling that Crunciman had not gone very far away. He'd be watching like a vulture, waiting to swoop down on the dead bodies in the desert.

The pressure was just starting to build for his investigating officers. And for his own reputation and professional standing. He kicked the ground again and strode to his car.

CHAPTER 27

"LOOK. STARWIND IS not some huge multi-national corporation. This is a family business that has been very successful, but it can't keep taking hits like these explosions. Elliott Webster made that very clear to me this morning," said Sonja Rodriguez forcefully.

Roy Crawford nodded agreement. He, the mayor, the Ward 3 Councillor and the head of finance for the city were meeting. The ward Councillor was his lover, Kim Sharpe. Neither of them even looked at one another. That was their solemn vow—city business inside city hall remained focused, private and secure.

"The project is a huge benefit for Port Manatee," Crawford confirmed. "It is the largest single construction project ever in our city. It has immense importance to the neighborhood around Delvecchio Bridge, which has been under-serviced for a very long time. If it is delayed or its completion is jeopardized, then we have a lot of problems. We'll lose over three million dollars a year in new taxes. We'll lose the job creation throughout the construction period and the on-going jobs at the new complex. We'll lose the new affordable housing units that we need so desperately. We'll lose a new public park and children's playground. Most of all, we'll lose the confidence of the business community in our ability to protect and grow this city. It would be tragic if this development collapsed."

Left unsaid was the political price that the Mayor would pay. As would Kim. It was her ward and she had been a leading proponent. In fact, the entire city council would be seen by an angry public to be incompetent. And with the already fractious relationship between Mikayla Johnson and the rest of the council, the media and the public were beginning to circle in the shark tank. There was the acrid smell of blood in the water.

The city's finance director was a very sharp Latina who was working on her MBA as she handled the city's finances.

"We could offer a reduction in development charges," Carmen Molinara suggested. "That would save the company some money up front, but it would anger other developers. We could offer a property tax deferral of a couple of years to let them get established and stabilize their cash flow before we send their first tax bill."

There were risks with either strategy.

Finally Kim spoke. "What if we developed some kind of new policy, so this is not seen as favoritism, to allow developers to seek a tax credit for any community amenities they build? I know that is considered during assessment, but we might be able to implement it for development charges as well."

"Possible," acknowledged Molinara. "And it could be good public policy to encourage development of parks and provide public art and other amenities."

"I know we can do bonusing where we allow greater density in return for more public space and landscaping and so on," Kim continued. "What if we allowed a couple more stories to be built as part of this project?"

"I like that," replied the mayor. "More housing. Bigger development. It would improve his financial projections. Do you think Elliott would be interested?"

"I could get Samantha to sound him out," Kim responded. "She's helping with the neighborhood liaison and the park design."

"Good. Let's quietly try that. We need to salvage this project, people. And we need to get the bomber behind bars."

CHAPTER 28

THE LOCAL MEDIA went nuts over the story. TV clips of the big hole in the ground and the scattered debris on the site led all the local newscasts that evening. The producers at Channel 7 developed a brightly-colored title for the explosive situation: *"THE BANJO BOMBER."* It featured an exploding banjo and a lot of fireworks in a night sky.

Somebody had leaked the playing of banjo music before the explosion. The TV people had grabbed onto the connection like piranha on a pig.

Perkins was livid that a possible clue had been compromised. His investigators quickly traced the leak to the kid security guard, who had traded his integrity for 12 seconds on camera.

The sheriff met with the investigative team late into the evening. There wasn't much progress to report.

Chapter 29

Two men in their mid-twenties marched into Whispering Palms without acknowledging the receptionist or any other staff member. They hustled up a stairway to the second floor.

Samantha looked at them. She then turned to look at Mrs. Harris.

"Deveron Snively and a cousin, I think. He's the grandson of Mrs. Snively. She's in 209. She's a bit of a loner. Doesn't socialize much." She paused. "They visit her almost every day." She paused again. "You'd think that would make them poster-children for looking after granny." She sighed loudly. "I'm not so sure. My teacher instincts have alarm bells going off every time I see them in here. I don't know why."

She picked up her cup of tea and sipped. Samantha did the same.

"How are you feeling?"

"About the same, thank you, dear. My joints hurt. My body aches. I've lost a lot of my mobility. I don't like this darn chair. But I endure."

"Do you worry about diseases in here?"

"Oh, Lordy, yes. Let's face it. Old folks' homes and cruise ships are petri dishes for nasty bugs. Once they invade either place it is almost inevitable that a lot of people are going to get infected. Some are going to die. It's terrifying, so we don't think about it too much. I wash my hands a lot. I wear a mask sometimes. I get vaccinated."

She sipped more tea and then leaned closer to Samantha. "I've been secretly stock-piling my own supply of medical masks and gloves to protect myself when the next pandemic hits. And it will. Don't tell anybody."

Samantha gave her a sad smile. "That's smart of you. I'm sorry you have to be in this position. How is the staff in a situation like that?"

"Mixed. Very mixed. Some are really caring and dedicated. Some are indifferent. A couple are cruel. Some go home and never come back. A few just don't care." She paused. "Don't tell on me. I don't want to get in trouble."

"I would never do that. You know that. But I worry about you and the other residents. I never realized how vulnerable residents of a long-term care facility truly are."

It was quiet in their corner of the parlor. Other residents moved slowly from their chairs and wandered into the hall or towards the card room. The clacking of walkers could be heard down the hallway.

Nurse Elmer Krackle stuck his head into the reading room. He gave Mrs. Harris a long look and then a quick glance at Samantha before retreating down the corridor. Samantha turned to her new friend and was startled at the look on her face. She had always known Mrs. Harris as a strong person. Now, there was a look of…was it fear?

"Are you OK?"

Mrs. Harris shook her head and her face recovered. "Yes. Sure. But let's go. I think there's a movie in the theater that I'd like to see. And you have other things to do."

Samantha wheeled her down to the theater and made sure her chair was secure before saying her good-byes. She waved at a couple of other residents she had met, and one of the nursing assistants, a subdued woman named Ethel who helped with personal care and doling out medications to the residents.

The movie was beginning, and the lights dimmed. Samantha left the theater and headed back to her condo. She was confused. And worried. In the rear-view mirror of her car she saw Deveron Snively and his cousin exit through a side stairwell door. They were each carrying a backpack. They jumped into a shiny new black pick-up truck and roared out of the parking lot.

CHAPTER 30

"THE NEW REVISED price for the land is $2.25 million," Roy Crawford reported to Councillor Policy. "The revised price for the entire recreation complex is now $39.7 million."

"That's pretty much the high end of the budget, isn't it Roy?"

"Yessir. But we can just handle it with our reserve fund for recreational projects and a modest borrowing cost because interest rates are so low right now."

"OK, thanks for the update. This is an efficient way of briefing council members, isn't it?"

"It is. And we can get together at a formal and public council meeting when we're ready to ratify the final land sale and issue the tender call for the project."

"OK, I'm on board. How does everybody else feel?"

"You're the first one I've called. I did talk to the Mayor earlier this morning and briefed her on the numbers. I'm calling the rest of the councillors now."

"Fine. Thanks, Roy. Good job in salvaging this for us."

"My pleasure, Councillor. I hope it all works out."

"Yeah. Anything else I need to know?"

"That's it. Thank you."

"Bye."

Crawford looked at his list of city councillors and dialled the next one. Councillor Mikayla Johnson. He groaned just a bit as he bravely punched the phone buttons.

CHAPTER 31

"THIS GUY WAS running for City Council. I forget which city. It doesn't matter. It was his first campaign. He was desperate for publicity, anything to get his name out there. The city had a big annual RibFest each fall. You know, a bunch of ribbers come in, lots of smoke and barbecue sauce all over. Big deal, right? Anyway, he knew somebody who knew somebody who was a cousin of one of the organizers. He finagled an invitation to be a guest judge for the rib contest. Thousands of people attending. Great exposure, right?"

Samantha and Kim smiled as they listed to P.J. Hozworm recount the story. They were at La Casa Adrianna, the small, exclusive Cuban hacienda that had been converted into a luxury boutique hotel. The quiet bar was dimly lit and offered a peaceful respite from the noise and confusion of the outside world. They were all sipping unsweetened iced tea.

"So there he is on stage, ready to judge the highlight of the festival: baby back ribs with barbecue sauce. Everybody's looking at the stage. They bring out the platters of ribs. They start serving them to the judges. And somebody in the audience hollers out to him, 'Hey! Ain't you a vegetarian?'"

The three of them laughed. Hozworm wore his customary gray suit, white shirt, black tie and highly polished black shoes. Kim was in a copper pantsuit. Samantha wore a demure turquoise dress.

They all sipped from their glasses. Hozworm was the political fixer for Central Florida and had been for many years. He operated strictly in the shadows of the political system. He was very good at what he did.

"A new mayor got elected in that little city north of here. After she'd been sworn in and had taken office, somebody asked her how many people worked at city hall. 'I'm not sure,' she replied, 'maybe two-thirds of them.'"

Appreciative chuckles. Hozworm was on a roll.

"I had a rookie running for the state legislature once. The guy was so new. We sent him out to do door-to-door for a while. You know, get to know the constituents, listen to their concerns. It looks good to the voters. Of course, most of them lie to you at the door about who they're going to vote for, but whatever. Anyway, he comes back to campaign headquarters one night, eyes as big as saucers. I asked him what happened. He said he rang a doorbell and a 300-pound Italian man answered—wearing nothing but hair. A lot of hair. I asked him what he finally did. He said, 'I have never made more intense eye contact with somebody in my entire life.'"

La Casa Adrianna's veteran hostess, Rosita, peered at the table in the corner. That much laughter was unusual in this lovely quiet bar, especially with Mr. Hozworm. He and the two beautiful women were obviously enjoying the conversation.

"I can't tell you how much this means to me," Kim finally said when she regained her breath. "Samantha has told me how insightful your comments have been. And your idea to do fund-raising now was inspired."

"We are sold out," reported Samantha. "We have more than twenty of the most influential women in the county coming on the 26th. I think we'll net over $40,000. And Kim will get some important new supporters."

"Very impressive. And I love the name. "Martinis & Manicures." How on earth did you come up with that as a theme?"

Samantha and Kim giggled at one another. "It was a brain-storming session. Sort of," Kim confessed, remembering the liquids that had fuelled the evening.

Hozworm nodded. "I understand. It is brilliant. I'd trademark it if I were you. Once the results of your fund-raiser get out, every quack wanna-be politician in the state will run something similar."

"I am sorry I wasn't invited, but I understand. Women only. Very smart." He looked at his watch. "I know you have to get back to city hall for a committee meeting," he said to Kim. "This has been lovely. I enjoyed spending the time with you; thank you for joining me. I hope we might do it again sometime."

"I would like that a lot. Thank you." With that Kim rose and shook hands with Hozworm, kissed Samantha on the cheek and headed for the door.

"She is just what I'd hoped," Hozworm confided to Samantha when they sat back down. "Smart. Personable. Caring. She's going to go far if she wants it enough."

"Yes, she's really settling in at city hall. She does her homework, reads the material carefully, comes prepared for the meetings and doesn't try to dominate the debate. And she's enjoying it. Except for this Delvecchio Bridge construction disaster. Who on earth would blow up the foundations of such a project? It's making the city look bad."

"Are there any leads, any clues?"

"From what I understand there aren't many pieces of hard evidence because, well, they got blown up. Perk told me something about banjo music before the explosion, but nobody knows what that's all about. Nobody can figure out who would be against this development. It will do nothing but help to rejuvenate that neighborhood."

Samantha blew out her cheeks in frustration. She gulped the last of her tea and shook her head.

Hozworm sat, head tilted, eyes staring into the dark corner of the bar. "There is...well, let me try to remember. The banjo thing...odd." He shook his head and kept staring into the distance.

He finished his own glass. Finally he grunted in satisfaction and refocused on Samantha.

"I would never suggest to your Sheriff how to conduct his investigation. However, I may have a small piece of information that may be useful for him to pursue. I know that law enforcement looks on these situations through the law-and-order prism. I look at it perhaps a bit differently. If no one is profiting from the destruction, then perhaps that is the aim. Who gets hurt if this doesn't go forward? The current Mayor. The current Council. Kim as the Ward Councillor. Who would want that? I think it might be personal. Perhaps the perpetrators see this as a statement about the current politicians' inability to move the city forward, to successfully complete this biggest project in Port Manatee's history. Perhaps the incidents are a longing for a past administration?"

Samantha was hanging on his every word now, trying to follow his circuitous way of thinking. It was fascinating to watch his mind work.

"It is often useful to me to figure out not just who might win something, but who might lose. In politics, as you know, there are many motivations for actions. Often, they are competing. It can create very convoluted scenarios."

He absently sipped ice water. "I bring a different perspective. In this case, who would be angry at the accomplishment of this new development?" He paused and waited. Samantha said nothing. "The former Mayor," Hozworm concluded.

Samantha sat back, stunned. The previous mayor had been thrown in jail for corruption, misuse of public funds and a couple of other charges relating to the fraud that had reeked through the previous city council's effort to build at that site.

"I thought about the former developer who wanted that project, Castillo, but he is too stupid to think in this fashion," Hozworm continued. "Besides, he's up to his ears in the FBI investigation. Other developers? No, the contract has been signed. They'll have moved on to other projects. Who else would care? It can only be politically motivated."

"That is ingenious. It makes a lot of sense. But who is behind this? The former mayor, Smithfield? He's still in jail."

Hozworm nodded slowly. "Yes, yes he is." He waited a moment. "But his sister and brother-in-law aren't. I've met them once or twice at political events. A while back. That's what took me time to remember. The man seemed solid. But maybe Smithfield's controlling this from behind bars, and maybe his sister is trying to rewrite the family history." He shrugged. "God help us, maybe she thinks Smithfield can make a political comeback. The entire family was certainly invested in Smithfield when he was mayor."

Samantha sat back. "I'm going to talk to Perk. Right away."

"Of course you are. Just keep me out of it."

"But what if—"

"No. I don't get involved in investigations or anything with official paperwork. I'm happy to speculate with you, but nothing official. Promise me."

"Alright...but I don't think Perk will be very happy about this..."

"Perhaps not. But if my—well, it won't matter, will it, if your Sheriff solves the case?"

Samantha mentally squirmed. It was going to be an exceedingly awkward conversation with Perkins. He was a stickler for knowing about informants or where clues originated.

"If that is your condition, then I will honor it and do everything I can to keep you out of this." She paused. "What made you think of the former mayor's sister and brother-in-law?"

"One of their cousins was obsessed with the movie "Deliverance." He looked a bit like one of the characters, the pudgy guy, whatever his name was. Anyway, he kept humming those very distinctive notes from the song. You know, the banjo plinkin' 'n pluckin'. I just kind of put it all together. There's no way your Sheriff and his investigators would have that kind of insider background knowledge. And of course, I may be totally incorrect."

Samantha smiled at him. "Maybe. Who knows? That's what the investigation will find out. Oh, do you know where this family lives?"

"My recollection is St. Augustine on the Atlantic Ocean side of Florida. Near Jacksonville. I forget the family name, but that should be easy to check for your Sheriff. I hope it works out."

"I can't thank you enough. I'll get this to Perk immediately. I hope it helps. He's really frustrated over the lack of progress of the investigation."

Hozworm bowed his head slightly as they both pushed back their chairs.

"I hope this anonymous tip that you received will be useful," he smiled as they departed.

Chapter 32

ROSIE WAS A very confused puppy. Mommy and Daddy were not cuddled together on the couch as they usually were. They were not enjoying the yummy little tid-bits of food on the side table. Even more importantly, they were not sharing any snacks with Rosie. But most of all, they seemed to be almost barking at each other. Rosie didn't like that at all.

"You are telling me that some anonymous little angel just flitted down onto your shoulder and whispered in your ear that I should investigate the former mayor's sister and brother-in-law about the bombings at Delvecchio Bridge?"

"Of course not," Samantha snapped back. "It was more someone breathing fire and brimstone. Like you right now." She slammed her wineglass down on the table.

"I don't need the sarcasm, thank you very much. I need names. I need facts. I need to know who and why. That's what we call an investigation."

"And that's what I call idiotic. Here I am giving you this great tip when you and your investigators have got bupkis on these bombings and you're looking really bad out there. I'm trying to help you! Don't you get that?"

"Yeah, yeah. I still need to know who the informant is so we can open a new leg in our investigation. There has to be a reasonable belief that we will discover important evidence before we can ask the FBI for assistance such as background checks. There must be a certain continuity of the investigation if we are ever going to get a judge to issue search warrants. We need a clear chain of evidence for the prosecutors if we ever get to trial. We need to be credible in our assumptions, and frankly some wild story about the former mayor's brother-in-law's family who likes banjo music is not a very solid foundation!"

He steamed for a moment. "The courts would laugh us out on our butts." He finished his IPA and set the mug down. Hard.

"I can't go to court because some fairy swooped down from the heavens to sprinkle..." He sputtered to a conclusion.

"Oh, the sarcasm is really helpful. Yes, that's very good." Samantha ran her fingers through her long reddish-blonde hair in frustration and mounting anger. "Look. You have, what are they called? CIs? Confidential Informants? Right? Well, just think of this as one of those. Why can't you say thank you and get your ass in gear?"

"Because the CIs are known to law enforcement! It may be to only one detective or cop, but that gives it legitimacy. Don't you get it? How can I go to my detectives based on some wild conjecture when I can't offer any background? I'd look like an idiot to them! And rightly so!"

"Oh for heaven's sake! Just put away this phony macho act of yours for once and accept that sometimes you don't know everything! Step up! Be the bigger man! Stop this whiny crap! Get over your ego! Just go and do your job! Be a leader! And you might even say 'thank you' to me!"

As soon as the words tumbled out, Samantha regretted them. She could see his face flush with anger. Two red spots appeared on his cheeks as he clenched his teeth. His jaw muscle popped.

He slowly and consciously breathed deeply as he stared at her. A very long moment passed. Apologies whirled through Samantha's head as she stared back. Then abruptly he rose, grabbed Rosie and her leash and headed for the door.

"Thank you for the advice. Good evening."

His tone was cold. The words clunked down like gravel off a dump truck.

Stunned by his rapid departure, Samantha wasn't even near the front door as he pulled it open and walked out. He didn't even slam it, which somehow might have been more comforting.

"Wait! Perk! Stop!"

There was no response as he stomped down the corridor to the elevators. Rosie followed. She looked back at Samantha in a bewildered way. She had a doleful expression on her doggie face. Samantha started down the hallway after them, but the elevator door opened quickly and they disappeared into Otis hell.

Samantha stopped halfway down the hall. She slumped against the wall, her words ricocheting in her mind.

She was stunned at his reaction. What had she said? Something about his macho—oh god. Would he take that to demean his personality? Impugn his manhood? Reduce his sense of—she suddenly realized how cutting and hurtful her remarks could have been to him.

She sagged down the wall and crouched on the shiny burnt orange tiles of the hallway. Her shoulders began to shake as her emotions overflowed—anger, frustration, shock. She held her head in her hands.

The elevator dinged suddenly. She looked up, hoping he had returned. The door slid open. The elderly couple in 603 tottered out. They walked slowly down to her. Both stared openly at the woman in agony on the hallway floor.

"Everything all right, dear?" Mrs. Weatherby finally asked.

Samantha burst into tears.

CHAPTER 33

"SO, NOTHING?"

Samantha shook her head. "Nothing. It's been two days."

The emergency meeting of the Sams Club was in full swing. Kim and Samira were flanking Samantha as they sat on her big living room sofa.

"And you've emailed him?"

"Of course. And I get a form email back: 'Sheriff Perkins is on assignment. He will respond when available. If this is an emergency, call 911 or 1-800-555-6509.'"

"And you've called his home?"

"Yes. And left two messages. Nothing."

"What about calling Mary? His assistant? She likes you."

"I tried yesterday. She was pretty...cool. Wouldn't promise anything." Samantha pursed her lips. "I think the word is out: I'm Number One on the Shit List."

There was a pause and Kim and Samira thought that one through. More wine was sipped. Michael Bublé trilled softly in the background.

Samira was the first to bravely step forward.

"Uh, sweetie. Do you think you were, uh, maybe a bit, ahh, wrong in this thing?"

"I don't know! That's what is so frustrating. Here I thought he'd be grateful and thank me for giving him this great lead. Why should he care who the source was? Just investigate and solve the darn thing. That's all he had to do. I was just trying to help."

"But, uh, when you said about that, er, macho thing...how do you think he reacted to that?"

"Not good. Not good at all. I didn't phrase that very well; I will concede that. Didn't pick my words as well as I...oh heck. I don't know. We were just talking and all of a sudden, he goes ice cold and is out the door. Poor Rosie didn't know what was going on." She grimaced. "Neither did I, obviously." A sigh. "But I still think he is over-reacting!"

Silence.

A touch more of the nicely-chilled Petit Chablis was poured.

A couple of jumbo shrimp that weren't an oxymoron were dipped into the spicy cocktail sauce and munched.

Kim leaned over to pat Samantha's left hand. She too summoned her courage and moved onto the firing line. "Do you think that really matters right now?"

"But he did! Over-react. He still is!" Samantha's voice was firm although her hand shook just a bit as she reached to pick up her wine glass.

Kim continued after a short pause. "Samantha. Look at me." She waited until Samantha's pained and drawn face looked at her. "You know I was a captain in the army, right?" Samantha nodded. "Well, this is what you need to understand. A police department is a quasi-military organization. Even though women are advancing today, the system and the command structure in law enforcement has been quite traditional. It was very male-dominated and rigid for a long time. Perk isn't tied to that and he's transforming the department, but the history is still in place. When you attacked him and said that macho thing, you were also attacking his professional standing and his leadership abilities. But when you hollered about his being a man it became really personal to him, and a grave professional insult. It would have cut him deeply. I think he felt your words were disparaging his command of the Sheriff's department as well as his personal male status. Those wounds are lingering. And I suspect will fester for a while."

She looked at her friend with compassion. "You really hurt him, Samantha."

Samantha sat back to absorb Kim's words. A minute passed. Then another one.

"I...I...I do remember the pain and the anger etched into his face," she finally admitted softly. "And then...he was just...gone."

Samira shook her head as she observed the mixed emotions play across her friend's face.

"Do you think either one of you is a winner in this fight? And does that matter anymore?"

Samantha swivelled to stare at the Persian beauty. She switched her gaze to the darkening sky as the sunset concluded. It had been a glorious display of pinks, oranges, purples and reds suffusing the fluffy clouds, but had been ignored by the three women during their intense conversation.

"I know that I can be a bit stubborn," Samantha began. She ignored Kim's snicker. "But I can also be right," she continued. "But I would like to go back and undo a few things I said," she concluded with a sigh.

"Yeah. That's not going to happen. I don't think you're ready yet to admit how deeply you've scarred him. I think he is really insulted by the manhood thing. And I think you're going to have to apologize to him before you can start to reconnect."

Samantha stiffened as she listened. "I still don't understand! Here I practically solve this whole bombing case for him and I don't even get a 'good job, thanks.'"

"What if your tip doesn't solve it? What if the lead is useless? What if Perk puts his own reputation on the line with his staff and then he ends up looking like an amateur?"

Well. That was a nasty right hook to the jaw. After a count of 8 Samantha got up from the canvas, waved off the referee, and vowed to continue fighting.

"That would be tough. I'd be sorry. But let's face it, cops follow false leads all the time. They eliminate suspects. They look for new clues. They are constantly testing crime scene evidence and the people involved. An investigation's outcome is always a moving target. These are veteran detectives. Leads come and go. They would understand that. Why would any of that be my fault?"

"I'm not sure if you're ready for the reconciliation if—well, let me ask first. Do you *want* to stay in the relationship with him?"

Ah. The key question that had been hanging over the entire discussion. The question that Samantha had been scared to confront as she had thought repeatedly about their fight in the days since it had exploded. And worse, in the nights. Sleep had become an elusive companion.

She pushed the waves of hair off her face in exasperation. She kneaded one cheek. "I have such great respect for Perk. He is a very strong man. I love being with him. I treasure our time together. It's fun. It is exciting. The sex is great. I trust him. I thought we were building a wonderful relationship that had a future." She stopped. There was breathless silence from her two friends. "That's why I was so shocked at his reaction, at his walking out on me. We should be able to handle something like this. Maybe there is some hidden flaw that I haven't seen, something in his psyche that is dangerous." She paused again and then wailed, "I just don't know and it is making me crazy!"

The words hung in the dimness of the advancing twilight. It was almost as if the three of them were scared to move in case it shattered the revelations that were being suddenly and nakedly exposed.

"That's what I can't get past right now," continued Samantha, sniffling. "Does he have these triggers? Do I somehow set them off? Are there secret places that I can't go near with him? I don't get it. And he won't even talk to me."

"You are angry, you are confused, you are unsure. All perfectly understandable. But I think you also need to take some responsibility for this situation, Samantha. I think you've got to understand that before you can resolve it," Samira said.

"Maybe. Maybe. I am hurting so much though," Samantha moaned. Her two closest friends reached over to hug her. The awkward triangle on the sofa lasted for a couple of minutes before they all shook themselves and separated slightly.

The energy had left the room. All of them felt it. Kim and Samira soon departed. Samantha cleaned up desultorily and packed the dishwasher. It hadn't gotten much use lately. She had no appetite.

She wandered out to the lanai and dropped onto a patio chair. She looked at the black vastness of the sky. The red and green flashing lights of a few airplanes passed overhead. A satellite in geosynchronous orbit stared down at who knew what—or whom. The moon was a gloomy three-quarter. Stars could be seen through the wispy clouds in the night sky.

Alone. That's how she felt. All alone in this great big universe.

Alone.

Chapter 34

"HIS NAME IS Grigori Kowalski. He goes by Greg. His grandparents emigrated from Russia in the 50s. They landed in Brighton Beach in Brooklyn. His parents later ran the food store that his grandparents started. He moved to Florida in the 80s, met the former mayor's sister, they got married in 1997. Two kids, boy and girl. Both in their twenties. He is a foreman for a construction company. Lives in St. Augustine, works construction projects up and down the Atlantic coast. His reputation in the construction business seems pretty solid. Works hard. Trusted."

Perkins reacted to that. "Foreman? Construction? So he'd have access to dynamite?"

"Yeah. Not sure it is used that much anymore, but I guess he'd have knowledge about explosives for construction." Detective Ortega stopped and thought about that some more. "I presume he'd know where to get the stuff, at least."

Perkins grunted agreement. He pushed back from his desk and grabbed his coffee mug. The residue was cold. He grimaced and set the mug back on its coaster. He looked at the counter. The donut fairy had yet to magically appear. So far it was a lousy morning. Not to mention the whole mess with Samantha that he couldn't even bring himself to think about.

Shit.

"...and where they get it."

"Sorry, Carmela, once more?"

Detective Carmela Ortega looked at her partner and then across the desk at the Sheriff. Rumors had been flying for a couple of days that Perkins and his stunning girlfriend were split, or splitting, or splitting heads, or something. As a result, everybody in HQ was walking on eggshells around him.

"I said, we could ask the sheriff in St. Johns County to find out where construction companies over there would be allowed to purchase the stuff and where they get it. Our checks of local suppliers around here haven't showed any problems."

Perkins thought about it for a brief moment. "OK, good idea. Let me know." The two detectives nodded and got up. "Oh, and let's keep this quiet. We don't know if this is a good lead or not."

Ortega looked back from the doorway. "Got it."

Perkins rolled back in his chair. He thought about the suspect. It didn't feel right to him somehow, but the circumstantial evidence was interesting and certainly worth pursuing. Maybe Samantha had—stop! Don't even go there.

He was still steamed about what she had said. He was hurt. He was angry. He was—. His desk phone interrupted.

"Sheriff Perkins. Oh, morning, James. How is the FBI making my life better today?"

James Robertson laughed. "By not telling the rest of the law enforcement community what a complete idiot you are. Dumping Samantha? Are you crazy?"

"Not real sure that's any of your damn business," Perkins flared, his voice cold.

"Everything is my business. I am the regional supervisor for the South-East United States of America. Coordinating with local law enforcement is paramount in my busy, busy life. And when the sheriff of an important central Florida jurisdiction goes nuts, then obviously I have to be informed." There was amusement in his voice.

There was no amusement in Perkins' response. "Well, then, here's a suggestion. Why don't you take your service revolver, cock it and then stick it up your—"

"Now, now. No need to get vulgar." Robertson's voice changed. "I really was sorry to hear of this, Perk. You know that I like you both. What happened?"

Perkins regained his composure. "Yeah. Sorry. It's all pretty raw. And I don't want to talk about it."

Quiet on the phone circuit. "OK. I get it. Well, I don't really, but maybe you'll both come to your senses. You were head over heels about her. And everything I heard about Samantha is that she's a pretty special woman."

Perkins grunted into the receiver. Then he rasped, "I don't even know what happened, James. She said something, I got angry, she said—I don't know, it is all a jumble of…well, let's just say it is a big, putrid mess."

"Yeah. Well, I hope it works out. I think she is really good for you."

Perkins grunted again.

"Anyway, the real reason I'm calling is to ask why you're interested in buying dynamite in St. Augustine?"

"My detectives are following a lead in the Delvecchio Bridge explosions. Hey, wait, how would you know about buying dynamite in St. Augustine?"

"Oh. Well. The NSA in Washington monitors on-line and phone transmissions. Anyway, the Artificial Intelligence nerds alerted me. It took them, let's see, fourteen seconds after somebody in your office Googled 'where to buy dynamite in St. Augustine.' You can see where that topic might get our attention. A.I. is pretty quick to alert us in such a situation. So I just thought I'd make a friendly call to my favorite sheriff and see what was going on."

Perkins was still feeling pretty wounded. "You got me. I'm guilty. I'm secretly planning to buy two sticks of dynamite and light them and shove them up your—"

"My, my. You are certainly fixated on that particular orifice of my body. And so violent." Robertson couldn't keep the amusement out of his voice.

"Sorry. I'm just really upset over this whole bloody thing with Samantha."

"Why don't you go over and apologize? That's what you've always done in the past whenever you've screwed up." He paused. "All of the times." He paused again. There was a touch of smirk in his voice. "The many, many times."

"I don't think this one is my fault. I really don't. But I'm frozen about what to do. About the only pleasure left in my life is the idea of blowing your sorry butt to Timbuktu."

"Ah. I've never visited Mali. Sounds lovely. But perhaps not today. I have a massage planned later. And then dinner with my wife."

"I am so happy for you," Perkins ground out slowly. His teeth were clenched.

Robertson's voice continued his amusement. "Well, since I'm in Atlanta and you're not, I guess my very cute and very taut butt is safe for another day. Have fun chasing your bomber. Let me know if I can help." His voice turned serious. "And Perk... fix this thing with Samantha. You two need to be together."

He hung up. Perkins slowly replaced his own receiver in its cradle.

The secretive NSA geeks were going to have a field day parsing that phone conversation.

CHAPTER 35

"MR. KOWALSKI SEEMS CLEAN," reported Detective Ortega two days later. "So does the wife."

"He's had a couple of traffic tickets, the usual stuff. He's never been charged with anything serious. Never been in court. Good worker. His crew respects him. Good reputation in the local construction industry. He's been married for thirty-four years. Wife's a part-time accountant. His son just graduated from UF in Gainesville as a dentist and has joined a local dental office. His daughter is taking political science at FSU. They've lived in the same house for nearly twenty years. I don't think he is particularly close to his brother-in-law." She stopped and flipped through her notes. "We are still checking his location the night of the second bombing." She looked at her notebook once more. "That's our report."

The detective shut her notebook and looked at Perkins. Her partner sat quietly in the adjacent chair.

"So. Nothing."

Ortega shrugged. "He obviously knows about dynamite, how to use it and how to store it because of his job. We couldn't trace his every move, but we talked to the main supplier of explosives for his company and everything they've sold to the construction company has been used and recorded in the construction log. The construction office people keep track of all the dynamite that is purchased and is then exploded. It all matches up, according to the local detectives who looked into this for us."

"What about his wife? After all, she is the former mayor's sister?"

"From what we heard, she was more embarrassed than angry about his fraud charges. They grew up together but she claims they haven't been close as adults. She moved away to go to college. Living across the state from one another, they just drifted apart. Normal. The families got together for holidays and so on." She paused. "I'm not sure we see an accountant as a primary bombing suspect."

Perkins nodded slowly. This was going nowhere fast. He thought back to what Samantha had told him. Oops, that was a bad idea. Still...

"Didn't we get that tip, what was it? Banjo music? What the TV stations are blowing up." He winced at his choice of words.

"Yeah. The security guard said he heard banjo music, that Deliverance song, duh duh duh duh duh dut dut dut duh; you know it."

"Anybody in the Kowalski family fluent in banjo?"

"Ah, never came up. But if they did play a banjo, wouldn't that be more of a misdemeanor than a felony?"

For the first time in several days, Perkins laughed.

Chapter 36

THE EXPLOSION LIT up the night sky in Orlando.

The construction site for a small office tower was in early-stage development, but enough progress had occurred so that it rained down chunks of concrete, steel and dirt.

No one was killed in the explosion. The Orange County Sheriff's department announced that was a miracle. Kids had been playing near the site only hours before. Two cars parked near the site were wrecked by the explosion. A power pole was shattered and 356 homes were blacked out.

No group claimed credit for the bombing.

Perkins certainly wasn't laughing the next morning as he studied the Intel summary of major Florida incidents. The Orlando bombing seemed to have eerie similarities to the two Delvecchio Bridge explosions in his own territory and the first one in Clearwater.

He quickly phoned Sheriff Ramos and explained what his jurisdiction had gone through.

"It seems pretty similar to me," Perkins told his counterpart.

"It does. I'm waiting for the ballistics report, but my people think it was dynamite. Same as yours, as I recall."

Perkins grunted agreement.

"We can't figure out why somebody would blow up an early-stage project like this," Ramos continued. "It's an office tower, fer gawd's sake. What's that all about? Who would hate that?" He paused. "Nobody's stepped forward to claim the bombing. Funny, that. Usually the assholes want the publicity."

Perkins grunted agreement. He paused, then asked, "This sounds odd, but was there, did anybody, uh, hear any, uh, banjo music?"

A long silence. Then finally, "Geez, Perk, you've gotta stop topping up your morning coffee with that little jar of bourbon in the bottom left hand drawer of your desk."

"I'm serious," responded Perkins indignantly. "Besides, I have no bourbon in my bottom left desk drawer. Maybe a bit of amber liquid in my bottom right drawer for purely medicinal purposes in case of a snake-bite or something, but that's it. Anyway, a couple of witnesses claimed they heard some banjo music before the explosion. The "Deliverance" theme; you know it."

"Uh, the answer would be NO. At least not as far as any of my investigators have shared."

"OK. Just asking. Oh, I've been liaising with James Robertson in Atlanta. The FBI has offered any help we need. I tell you that because of one final caution. Some Homeland Security asshole named Michael Crunciman. He swept in here like an avenging demon, wanted to take over the entire investigation. Tried to claim federal jurisdiction. I said no. He then insulted my mayor who kicked him out of town. He was not happy. I didn't like him. He didn't like me. But I would be careful."

Perkins could hear Ramos breathing hard through the phone. "I hate those damn feds trying to bust in and—wait, hang on. Who? From where? Oh good. Somebody named Crunciman is on my front doorstep. Won't this be fun. Thanks for the heads-up, Perk. Keep in touch."

Chapter 37

"What's wrong with you?"

Samantha looked down at her hands. They were clenched. She made a conscious effort to relax them.

It was her first time returning to Whispering Pines in a week. Mrs. Harris had immediately noticed her pale complexion and subdued manner.

"It is, well, I..."

"I can see that you are troubled. Do you want to talk about it?"

"I am...it is...he was..." She stopped. Then it suddenly all gushed out. Mrs. Harris listened intently. Forty years of teaching had exposed her to most of life's goods and bads. The world and the people in it held few surprises for her.

Samantha's story finally ended. She sagged back in her chair, exhausted.

No one else in the residence was close to their corner of the north reading room. The big window beside them looked out over a nicely landscaped flower bed. Two squirrels ran across the lawn. Rosie would have been outraged.

Mrs. Harris took her time responding.

"Were you trying to insult his manhood? His manliness? His male ego?"

"Of course not!"

"But you do understand that he probably took it that way? That he would have felt attacked, personally and professionally?"

"I guess I understand that now. At the time, I didn't think that."

"Or maybe you just didn't think," Mrs. Harris noted tartly. Samantha flinched. "Listen, dear, I've lived a long time. I've mentored good kids, I've helped dumb kids, I've fought with bad kids and tried to save some of them. I've intervened in family crises. I've comforted people when a relative got killed.

I held one of my students after he'd been shot on the street in a gang war and he died in my arms. I've buried two husbands and I've got three grandchildren who think the sun rises and shines on their granny. And one of the things I've learned through all of those good things and bad, all those ups and downs we have in our lives, is that finding the right person to share your life with is a blessing beyond most others. It doesn't always happen, even to good people. When you get the chance, when you find that man, or that woman, then you'd better not screw it up."

Samantha stared at the woman in the wheelchair dispensing wisdom and experience with a conviction that only a lifetime on the front lines of human interaction can deliver. Her gaze shifted to the outside view. Her mind was whirling.

Finally she turned back to stare into the gentle, caring face of her new friend. Mrs. Harris sipped the last of her coffee and watched her closely.

"All I was trying to do was help his case. I thought he'd be really grateful. Somehow, I'm still not entirely sure how, it all blew up. He got really icy. It was almost scary how he shut down. Then he was gone."

"Do you think that was to avoid saying something to you that he would have really regretted? You were both pretty intense at that moment from what you've told me. One of the things that police officers are taught is to de-escalate a situation before it gets out of hand. Maybe that training kicked in and he decided to get out before the fight erupted further."

"I never thought of it quite that way. You may be right. I know that I hurt him and I'm sorry for that. But now he won't even communicate with me! How do I tell him that?"

"You're in his doghouse, that's for sure. But you're a smart girl. If you're ready to get past this and apologize and move forward with him, then I think you're going to have to take a big step. Show some real initiative. There are too many walls around each of you right now. You've got to knock down some of those so you can have a real conversation. That's how to start the healing."

Samantha gazed out the window for a long time. Finally she turned to the woman in the wheelchair who was watching her intently. "You're right. Thank you. It *is* up to me to take that first big step. I know he's hurting too, but I think he probably blames me the most. I've got to sit down with him and talk this through.

But how do I do that when he won't even return my calls or texts?"

"Oh, Samantha. You're very clever. You'll figure it out," Mrs. Harris smiled. She waited a moment. "But don't forget the two secrets of how smart women get what they want from their men, and have for centuries." She broke into a grin. "Food and sex."

CHAPTER 38

"HI, ROSIE."

At the sound of her name, Rosie woke instantly from her nap on the grass in the shade of a large palm tree in Perkins' back yard. She leapt to her feet, barked twice, and then charged pell-mell toward the gate. Mommy was back!

Samantha laughed as she slipped into the yard, secured the gate and then braced herself. Rosie indulged in a brief orgy of kisses and tongue-lapping before dancing away and spinning around as her tail flared. She then head-butted Samantha's leg only to run around some more. She was a very happy puppy.

It took them a minute or two to settle down. Samantha looked around the yard with interest. She'd been in the house several times, but she and Perkins rarely seemed to visit more than the kitchen, the living room and the master bedroom. The yard was fenced, with a few flower beds that could use a little TLC, some mature palm trees, a couple of flowering bushes and one big bougainvillea that needed a trim.

There was a water dish for Rosie in the shade of the back porch. Rosie kept by her as Samantha walked to the porch. She had already tried the front door, but like a good homeowner, Perkins had it locked. There was no security alarm company sign posted on the property; on the other hand, what criminal would be stupid enough to break into the Sheriff's house?

Samantha and the Sheriff had talked about exchanging keys. It hadn't happened, for reasons Samantha couldn't recall. It hadn't seemed like a big deal to either one of them at the time.

Now that she was trying to illegally enter his home, the key thing became a little more important. She hoped the back door would be unlocked. If it wasn't, she would ask Rosie for permission to enter. Surely a judge would accept that as good faith.

Rosie hopped onto the porch and looked over her shoulder. Samantha slowly climbed the two steps and then hesitated before trying the doorknob. Locked. Naturally. Well, he was setting a good example for other homeowners.

She looked around and then watched as Rosie suddenly disappeared. Her doggie door led into the kitchen. Of course. Rosie reappeared in the door, curious that Samantha hadn't followed her inside.

"I don't suppose you could unlock the door for me?" Samantha asked Rosie. The dog wagged her tail affectionately but made no move toward the deadbolt.

Samantha looked around once more. All the windows seemed secure and shut as the AC cooled the house. Nothing there. Neither door was unlocked. Well, as Mrs. Harris had noted, she was in the doghouse. This would be the next step in her humiliation and penance.

Samantha dropped down on all fours. At a casual glance the doggie door had looked to be a good size. Now that she was actually trying to squeeze through it, it didn't seem all that large. She sighed, shoved her purse through the door and crawled the first couple of feet. Rosie immediately took to this new game and enthusiastically licked her face to greet her. Samantha laughed as she squeezed her shoulders through and gently pushed Rosie aside.

She shimmied her waist through. Rosie thought this was all great fun, although she didn't quite understand why Samantha just didn't use the big door. Then Samantha felt her hips nudge the sides of the doggie door. Hmmm. That couldn't be right. Heck, she'd lost four pounds worrying and fretting in the last week or two. Besides, Perkins had always claimed she had the cutest little butt in all of Florida, maybe the entire SE USA.

She briefly contemplated the sight she must be making if any of the neighbors were spying. Or, she thought with sudden panic, if they phoned Perkins to let him know his house was being broken into by some crazed redhead in white linen shorts. That would be a very difficult conversation.

Her slender waist was through the door. Her 400-pound hips, not so much. At least she had worn shorts, not a miniskirt, so some modesty was still in play. It wasn't much, however.

She would not get stuck in a doggie-door. She simply would not. She would never, ever, live that down. What if somebody had to call the Fire Department to rescue her? The humiliation would run her out of town, the hoots and cat-calls following her.

Everybody would simply know then that Perkins had been correct to dump her for being a complete and brainless idiot.

She wriggled a little more. Stuck. She retreated a couple of inches to give herself more breathing room. Rosie remained an enthusiastic participant in this strange new game.

Think. The doggie door was higher that it was wide. Hmmmm. So if she twisted her torso, wouldn't that provide a little more room for her 600-pound hips and butt to squeeze through?

She gradually scooted over onto her left elbow. She breathed deeply a couple of times and then held her breath. That made no sense, of course, as her waist was fitting through quite nicely, but it seemed to her to be the right approach at that moment.

She shimmied like a stripper at the Bonga-Bonga Room on a Friday night. Rosie was prancing around watching, no doubt trying to figure out how to play this fun new game. Samantha was stuck again. Her 800-pound derriere would not go through the damn door.

She paused for a moment, cursing every bite of Mint Chocolate Chip ice cream that she'd ever indulged in. She could not stay stuck here. Rosie wasn't that good about dialling 911. In or out, make up your mind.

Samantha sucked in another breath, squeezed her butt muscles tighter than a miser's check book, swivelled her hips once again and pushed hard. With a couple of desperate pelvic jerks and a final squeeze of her left butt cheek, Samantha's 1,000-pound bum suddenly popped through the doggie door.

Rosie immediately kissed her in congratulations and then went looking for treats. Surely after the main show was over the audience deserved refreshments.

Samantha sat up slowly. She collected herself and her purse. She clambered to her feet, patted her hair, straightened her blouse and shorts and took a deep, cleansing breath. The first stage of OPERATION DOGHOUSE was complete.

CHAPTER 39

SAMANTHA GOT A couple of cookies for Rosie. She went through the cupboards in the kitchen and pulled out some pots and pans, including a heavy Dutch oven.

She went to her car and brought in a bag of groceries. Rosie sniffed with admiration as a package of lamb shanks was unwrapped. Samantha opened a very good bottle of Napa Valley Cab Sauv that Frankie at Uncle Larry's Booze Barn had highly recommended. She needed a little splash to revive her after the doggie door debacle. She put the second bottle in the fridge to chill slightly.

She seasoned each lamb shank and browned them in hot oil in the Dutch oven. She chopped onions, carrots and garlic and tossed them into the pan after removing the shanks. She let the aromatics become soft and golden, and then added half the bottle of wine—a top-up for her glass was necessary first—as well as a can of diced tomatoes, tomato paste, some beef broth and a splash of chicken stock. She added several sprigs of fresh rosemary and thyme, submerged the shanks in the flavorful liquid and brought it all to a boil. She then covered the pot and put it in a medium low oven. It would simmer happily for a couple of hours.

She sank onto a corner of the couch in his living room. She swallowed another mouthful of the very good red wine. She'd have to remember to give Frankie a little something extra. Rosie wandered over to sit with her.

Now, Samantha thought, let's just hope this crazy plan of hers worked. So many things could go wrong. He might have to work that night. There could be a police emergency he would have to supervise. He might be out of town. Maybe he was playing poker with some buddies. Or, she gulped as she went down the list of potential disasters, he could be out with somebody. A female somebody. Hhmmpppfff. The hussy. Samantha could already picture the bitch. What was he doing with her? She wasn't right for him!

She swallowed more wine and tried to calm down.

Finally she rose, shook herself and finished the dinner prep. She set the table, arranged the flowers she'd brought, and tidied up the house just a bit because men will be men when they live alone. She went into the master bathroom to change into her dress. It was new, it was black, it was short, it was sexy and it was expensive.

She slipped on her heels, checked her hair and make-up. Rosie admired her. So did the mirror. Samantha smiled at both and returned to the kitchen.

She took out the nicely cooled bottle of wine from the fridge, opened it, poured and left it to breathe in the decanter. She trimmed the asparagus and threw together a salad ready to be dressed. The mini chocolate cakes were still in the fridge.

She checked her hair once more and then sat down, her legs crossed elegantly. Now it was pretty much in the hands of the gods.

Chapter 40

WHAT THE HECK? was Perkins' reaction when he pulled into his driveway. Why were there lights on in his house? Really, Rosie was a smart dog but come on!

He parked in the driveway and cautiously got out. What burglar would leave the lights on? Still. He unsnapped his holster and held his service weapon along the side of his right leg. He walked beside the garage rather than on the front walk. He could hear Rosie with her welcoming bark. That was a good sign.

He quietly edged open the front door. Rosie came bounding out and barked a couple of times before she rushed back into the house. Strange. She usually stayed with him until he entered the house.

Some very enticing aromas came from inside his house. Meat and wine and herbs and—and his former girlfriend.

Samantha was standing in the main hallway, watching him with nervous eyes. She looked incredible in a little black dress. She smelled pretty good too—maybe not as good as the lamb shanks, he thought, but pretty close.

"Hi," she said softly. She looked at him with a bit of fear and a lot of uncertainty.

Perkins returned his gun to his holster and snapped shut the cover. He closed the front door slowly and walked towards her.

"Hello." He looked around the house.

"I, uh, sort of broke in. Sorry about that."

"Uh huh."

Rosie circled around the two of them. There was a very odd atmosphere in the room, she thought. And wasn't it about time for that really interesting meat dish to get served? The smells were quite intoxicating to the poor starving dog. She hadn't eaten for hours. Treats didn't count.

An uncomfortable pause as they looked at one another.

"Would you care for a glass of wine?"

"Uh huh."

"Great. I'll get it for you." Samantha turned and walked toward the kitchen. Perkins enjoyed the view. Then he shook his head. He went into his bedroom, took off his service belt, locked up his gun, changed clothes and freshened up.

When he returned a few minutes later, Samantha had poured him a glass of the smoky red. She had put it on the side table by his favorite recliner. Rosie was on the floor between the two of them where she could watch them both. Her head was on her front paws. She was alert.

Perkins sagged into the recliner. The battered leather chair had a Perkins' butt-shaped depression in the cushion. It had been there for a few years. He took the glass of wine, tilted it briefly at Samantha and sipped.

"That's very nice," he told her. "Thank you."

For frickin' $84 a bottle it had better be, she thought as she returned his small salute.

They sat there for a couple of minutes. The silence was growing a bit uncomfortable. Finally Perkins broke it.

"Uh, how did you..."

"Oh. Rosie showed me the way in," Samantha replied with a smile.

"Hmmph." Perkins looked at Rosie. "Great guard dog, aren't you?"

Rosie thumped her tail in agreement.

More silence. This time it was Samantha.

"Perk. Listen. Please."

She stopped and looked at him. He was stony-faced, but attentive.

"I want to apologize," she continued hesitantly. "For what I said. I didn't mean to say...what I said. What came out. I...I was wrong. I'm sorry." She paused and looked down at her hands. "And I've missed you," she blurted out. She peered up at him as a tear trickled down her left cheek.

Rosie got up and went over to her and pressed herself against her leg. Samantha absently patted her.

After a moment Perkins also got up and went over to Samantha. She absently patted him.

"I have missed you too. A lot." He paused and considered his next words. "I was really hurt and angry with you. What you said. It wounded me."

Samantha gulped in a big breath. She dried her eyes and kept listening. Rosie remained frozen against her thigh.

"I left that night before things really exploded. I didn't think you understood what I have to do in investigations and how precise we have to be these days. Defense lawyers are swarming all over every police procedure, checking for misconduct so they can get evidence thrown out of court."

He swallowed hard. Samantha could hardly breathe as she listened.

"It felt as if you were attacking me. My profession. My leadership. I was really hurt." She could hear his voice stiffening. "I have to follow the protocols. If I don't lead properly, the entire Sheriff's department is weakened. That is a burden that I have taken on gladly, but it is a heavy cloak to wear."

He swallowed audibly. "I felt betrayed by you. That you didn't understand what I do and what I have to do. It was cruel, Samantha, and that shocked me."

Her tears were starting again as she listened to his heart pour out. How dumb had she been?

Very.

"I didn't understand where you were coming from. Why you were attacking me like that. It was hurtful, Samantha."

She fought the tears as she listened to him open up. It hurt her too, but maybe she deserved it. "I...I guess I got caught up in the investigation. I thought it would be a really important new lead for you. But the situation between us just suddenly kept getting uglier. I should have stopped. Sometimes my temper gets to my mouth before my brain does. I really am sorry, Perk."

She bowed her head and sniffled as more tears leaked out. "You didn't deserve what I said. You're a great guy. You deserve better of me." She grabbed some tissues and blotted her eyes. A distant thought crossed her mind about what she must look like right now—a raccoon with red-blonde hair and a tear-stained blotchy face with mascara running down it. Nice. That's a look that will attract the men.

Perkins put his hand back on her shoulder. "Thank you for saying that. I think—I hope—that we have something stronger building in our relationship. Look, I am so far from getting my life together that most days I'm not even in the ballpark. I screw up all the time, but I try to work through the mistakes. Like with our...misunderstanding. I...I just didn't know what to do about our...well, it."

Perkins wiped his sweaty palms on his pants. "You are the best thing that's happened in my life for a very long time. That's why I was so surprised and so hurt by our fight."

He took a nervous swallow of wine and drew a deep breath. "I think we can survive this. I want to." He stopped again and swallowed hard. "Maybe we both learned a little something. Maybe we both emerge from this in a better, a stronger relationship." He paused to look at her. "Now I think we should close the door on the whole episode." He paused again. "What do you think?"

With that Samantha tilted her head up, grabbed him by the collar and pulled him down to her tear-stained face for a long kiss. That sealed the agreement. They kissed again just to make sure it was notarized. And then once more for the judge to stamp it and file it away.

When they came up for air, Rosie stood staring at them. It's dinnertime. All this lovey-dovey stuff can wait. Dinnertime. Now!

They got the hint. They rose from the couch and headed into the kitchen, hand in hand. Rosie led the way to make sure they didn't get lost. Samantha swung into the bathroom for some badly-needed touch-ups. She returned a few minutes later and turned off the oven, removed the lamb shanks, covered them in foil to let them rest and stay warm. She paused to kiss Perkins rather firmly. He affectionately patted her butt. She smiled and then strained the sauce and reduced it on the stove to a syrupy goodness. Perkins tossed the salad, grilled the asparagus and most importantly, fed Rosie.

The sat at the table devouring the feast. The lamb shanks were gorgeous, the sauce rich and piquant, the salad crisp, the wine fabulous—and neither one of them tasted any of it. They both knew there would be a very special dessert right after the dinner, and it wasn't going to be the chocolate cakes.

CHAPTER 41

"SORRY TO SAY, your lead about the brother-in-law didn't pan out. Greg Kowalski is his name. We had the local police check him. He was bowling with a bunch of guys the night of the second explosion. He's in the clear."

Samantha listened, surprised and disappointed. She was snuggled into the Sheriff's arms as they lay in his bed. The make-up sex had been fantastic. Her LBD was thrown over a chair. Her bra was hanging from a lamp. Her panties were lord knows where. One shiny black shoe was under the bed. She had no idea where the second shoe was.

They were both still panting from their exertions.

Rosie was banned from the bedroom. She had lobbied for a lamb shank bone, but Perkins knew that it would be dangerous for her to chew a cooked lamb bone. She was stuck with a rawhide bone. After enjoying the smells of the lamb cooking, Rosie thought the rawhide was a rather poor alternative. Still, she thought contemplatively, a dog had to accept what she got offered in the chewable department.

"We've still got no solid leads in the bombing," he said with frustration. "Kowalski's wife is the former mayor's sister. She's pretty quiet. Part time accountant. Son is a new dentist; daughter is at FSU in poli sci. There was another explosion in Orlando the other day, a big one. Seems to be escalating, assuming they are connected. I think they are. The FBI is leaning to some kind of big conspiracy. This whole thing is really freaky. Nobody's got any ideas. Terrorism is becoming a theory but no organization has claimed credit. Odd."

He exhaled loudly and scratched an itchy spot on his stomach.

"We found a couple of Nike shoe prints, size 7 ½, plus lots of other shoe prints at the Delvecchio site. Could be from the kids who play around there. Or from somebody just walking through the site. No way to trace it. Pretty small for a man's foot. More likely a woman's. Nothing there to follow-up. The explosion didn't leave many traces. We've got nothing."

Samantha was silent. She had been so certain that the sister and brother-in-law lead from Hozworm would crack open the case. Her promotion to Detective First Class was obviously in serious jeopardy.

"I feel like an idiot having to tell Elliott Webster about our lack of progress," Perkins muttered. "Poor guy is spending millions trying to build this great new project and we can't even protect his site." He frowned. "I've got a patrol out there every night. They haven't seen anything suspicious."

Samantha sighed. "I'll ask around the neighborhood. Maybe somebody saw something and they'll tell me." She snuggled down. She let her hand wander around under the sheet. Perkins responded quickly. So did she. They had their own simultaneous explosion a few minutes later.

It was as they were drifting off to sleep that Perkins closed the final issue in their fight.

"I'm going to get you a key for the house," he said. "It looks bad if my girlfriend has to crawl through the doggie door to get in."

CHAPTER 42

"THE FINAL PRICE for the land for the community recreation center that we negotiated is $1.83 million," Roy Crawford reported to Councillor Kelly.

"OK. Thanks," the Ward 4 Councillor said on the phone.

"We'll bring the contract to next week's City Council meeting," Crawford continued. "We'll discuss the contract in camera, and then approve the deal in public session if the Council is supportive."

"Everybody good so far?"

"I've informed the mayor and the councillors from wards 1, 2, and 3. Now you. So far everybody's OK, although a couple flinched at the final price. Ward 5 is next."

There was sympathetic silence from the long-time council member. They both knew that Mikayla Johnson would be her usual nasty and venomous self.

"Better you than me," joked Kelly. "Good luck."

"Yeah. Thanks. I'll let you know when my funeral will be held."

Kelly laughed and hung up.

City Clerk Kathy James ticked off another name on her list and noted the conversation's details.

Crawford looked across his desk at her. He was still holding the phone receiver. He hesitated, groaned and then depressed the button on his office phone to regain a dial tone. He started to punch in the phone number of the combative Ward 5 council member.

Chapter 43

"A YOUNG WOMAN AND a guy. They was walkin' around the property, 'ccording to some of the kids. They said the guy had one of those garnet and gold jackets. You know, the Seminoles."

Samantha was about two steps behind in the report from Mrs. Barkley.

"Funny to see that jacket here. Mostly USF or UCF supporters in this part of Florida."

"Sorry. I'm still new. Seminoles?"

"Oh, sorry, honey. The Florida State University team. From up there in Tall'hassee. On the Panhandle. Good school. We hate 'em. Their football team keeps beatin' the crap outta our boys."

She paused to shoo her kids away while she talked to Samantha.

"A coupla teenage boys rode their bikes through the lot the other night. A coupla cars cruised by slow, lookin' at the bomb site. Nobody got out. That was it."

Samantha thanked her for the report. She kept on looking for some lead for Perkins—something that might actually pan out this time, after her previous failure at playing Sherlock Holmes.

She looked over at the foundation of the first tower. Webster's crews had again patched the hole, were re-digging the foundations, and would soon be ready to start pouring concrete and erecting the steel structure. They were running nearly a month late because of the two bombings. Webster had told her it would be a $1.1 million hit. The insurance company was being the typical friendly insurance company: really good at cashing checks, really bad at writing checks.

"We thought maybe we'd have the barbecue next Friday night," continued Mrs. Barkley. "Suppose' to be a nice night. We want you and Mr. Webster and all his crew. You good?"

"That will be lovely," Samantha responded instantly. "But I'd really like to do something to help."

"Preciate that, really do. We talked about it. This is something we want to do for that nice Mr. Webster. He the one takin' all the risk to build us this bee-you-tee-ful new development. You just come and enjoy."

That was that. You didn't argue very much with Mrs. Barkley. Her kids had figured that out real early in life.

Samantha hugged her, hugged her kids, hugged the rest of the kids hovering around, hugged two other mothers who had appeared, and wandered over to the construction office trailer.

Webster happened to be there, studying the architect's drawings. He had enthusiastically agreed to add two floors to each building. It would help the long-term financial outlook for the project.

"We are all invited for dinner next Friday," Samantha dutifully reported. "All the guys and the three girls on the construction crews. A community thank-you barbecue."

Webster shook his head. "Astonishing. I still wish they'd let us pay for it or something."

"No. Definitely not. This is their event, their way. You don't want to get on Mrs. Barkley's naughty list. She'll whack you into next week."

Webster laughed. "OK. You're in charge. We'll all be there."

Samantha left the trailer. She looked over the site once more. She wanted to add some special surprise to the evening. What?

CHAPTER 44

"CITY TO PAY $2.14M FOR REC CENTER LAND" screamed the headline in the Port Manatee Observer.

The story quoted anonymous sources 'who were not authorized to speak on behalf of the city.'

Several council members were outraged.

The article sparked a lot of comment and commentary on the Boomer Bronsky talk radio program on AM 1410. Very few of the callers thought the city had made a great deal. There was a lot of grumbling about the lack of leadership in city hall. Old fights about old issues were re-aired, since most of the callers were men in their 60, 70s, 80s, and a couple in their 90s.

This was the highlight of their day. If they actually got on the air they bragged for weeks. The callers' opinions on most issues never changed. Ever. Their opinions would not change because of the airing of points of view contrary to theirs. Ever.

It was a dull life most of them led. The radio-fuelled outrage was about the only bump in their heart rates.

Roy Crawford stayed above the fray and refused to comment. Mayor Rodriguez defended the deal although she said the price wasn't right. Correct, she quickly corrected herself to local media.

She questioned Crawford privately about the details, but he would only tell her that it would all become clear at the council meeting.

CHAPTER 45

"I CALL THIS SPECIAL meeting of the Port Manatee City Council to order." Mayor Rodriguez banged her gavel until the hum in the room quieted. "Clerk?"

"Yes, Madam Mayor. The City Manager has requested this special meeting to discuss a land acquisition. Under state law the council is allowed to go into an in camera meeting to hear the details."

"Motion to go in camera? Councillor March? Second? Councillor Miller. All those in..."

"Wait! Just hold it!" Councillor Mikayla Johnson rose ponderously from her seat. She bristled with animosity and indignation. "This is just another example of this council and the senior administration trying to hide critical information from the public! I object to his manipulation of elected officials! The people's business should be done in public! But apparently I am the only one on this Council who believes that!" She sat down heavily as she glared at Crawford, who promptly rose.

"With respect, Your Honor, I suggest to the Councillor that it would be in her interest to have the information I will be revealing to the Council be presented during the in camera session." Crawford sat down.

Councillor Johnson pushed herself up. "Yeah," she sneered across the council floor at the city manager, "I just bet you do." She snorted in derision and fell back to her seat.

Crawford rose again. "If it is the Councillor's wish to do this in public session, Your Honor, despite that I have recommended that Council go in camera, then I am fine with presenting the complete and total information on this matter in public session."

A look of surprise crossed the Ward 5 Councillor's face. Crawford had never acquiesced to one of her demands before. The council had always honored his recommendations, so she had been safe in voting against going into private session knowing that the rest of the council would vote to do so. That protected her self-anointed title as 'Queen of the little guy' in public matters.

Her eyes narrowed as she studied the city manager. She couldn't stand what she took to be his smug professionalism. He was a skilled city manager, she had to concede that, but she just didn't like him. And she certainly didn't like the fact that he and that skinny bitch from Ward 3 were shacking up.

Ward 6 Councillor Alex Miller rose. "I don't see what the objection to going into private session to receive the information could possibly be. And of course we always report any key information back to the public, and we vote in public on any resolutions. But frankly, Mayor, I'm tired of the Ward 5 Councillor's constant effort to establish herself as the only council member who wants to protect the public interest. She is wrong. We all do." He cast a disdainful look at the woman sitting beside him. "I don't know what our City Manager will be reporting, but if he says it can be done in public, then let's do that. Maybe this will stop the posturing we've been getting from some council members."

He sat down, a bit red-faced. He refused to look at the Ward 5 Councillor, who was now steaming. The audience began to buzz at this early clash. The cable TV camera peered into the horseshoe where the elected officials sat on a dais. The newspaper reporter discreetly unsnapped his camera bag. There might be an interesting photo op coming if this thing exploded.

Councillor March rose. "I'll withdraw my motion if the seconder agrees. Let's get on with this. We've been accused too often of hiding in private session on issues. I'm tired of it. And I'm sick of the pious screeching and preaching from the newspaper." The reporter grinned. "Let's get on with it."

Ward 2 Councillor Fred March nodded agreement. Mayor Rodriguez looked around the horseshoe. Councillor Johnson was fidgeting. She couldn't quite believe what was happening but she didn't know how to pull a U-turn at this stage.

"Seeing no objection, we will proceed. Mr. Crawford?"

"Thank you, Madam Mayor." The elegant City Manager rose and began his presentation. "As the Council knows, I was tasked with negotiating a price for the acquisition of the property the city requires to build a new multi-purpose library, community and recreation center. The price has been, uh, speculated about in the local media despite our requests to keep negotiations confidential. That leak hurt our ability to negotiate a better price."

The councillors were riveted. This was a highly sensitive matter. It had exposed internal problems and worse, made them all look bad. Except, Councillor Johnson thought with a smirk, her.

"Because of that reality, and the way my negotiations with the landowner proceeded, I decided to try to solve both problems. I want to emphasize that this was my decision and my decision alone. I did not talk to anyone on the council, and only to one other senior administrator, City Clerk Kathy James. She assisted me throughout and was an independent witness to my actions. But I am responsible for the plan and for the outcome, no one else."

The buzz in the audience got a little more excited. This was rare fodder indeed. It was better than the ditziest afternoon soap on TV, the old farts assured one another.

"The Council also gave me permission to keep each council member up to date through a phone call or private meeting. I have done that at each stage of this process. Tonight we have a potential deal for the land." He paused, shuffled a couple of papers and then looked up at the council members. "We may also have new information on the leak of confidential information."

Most of the council members simply looked puzzled. Councillor Johnson furtively wiped her brow as she stared at the city manager. She didn't know what was coming, but suddenly she felt her stomach fluttering uncomfortably.

"When I phoned each of the council members in the past few days, I had the City Clerk with me as an independent witness. She made her own notes. She will be happy to corroborate any details that council wishes."

Crawford took a deep breath. He was about to dive off the cliff. There were a lot of sharp rocks below.

"I wonder, Madam Mayor, if you would indulge me by allowing me to ask each council member one question?"

Puzzled, the mayor looked at him and then shrugged. "Certainly."

"Thank you. Perhaps I could begin with you, Your Honor. When we talked, what price did I tell you the land acquisition price would be?"

"$1.92 million."

"Thank you. Clerk, is that correct, is that what your notes indicate?"

"Yes."

A look of dawning horror crossed Councillor Johnson's face. She pushed herself to her feet. "Mayor! Mayor! This is a ridiculous thing, some effort to embarrass council members or something. Maybe to deflect from the city manager's own incompetence. To save him, I move we go in camera for the rest of his report."

Her fellow council members looked on in amazement.

"We have a motion. Is there a seconder?" The mayor looked around the horseshoe. "I see no seconder. The motion is lost. Proceed, Mr. Crawford."

"Thank you. Ward 1. Councillor March?"

"You told me the price would be $1.79 million."

"Clerk?"

"According to my notes, that is correct."

The reporter scratched his head. A different price? Then it hit him. He focused his cell phone on the councillors and started snapping pictures.

"Ward 2. Councillor Policy?"

"2.42 million."

"Clerk?"

"Correct."

"Ward 3. Councillor Sharpe?"

"I was told $2.81 million."

"Clerk?"

"That is what my notes show."

"Councillor Kelly, Ward 4?"

"2.59."

"Clerk?"

"Correct."

A pause now. Everyone knew what was coming next. There was a collective intake of breath. Crawford sorted his papers. He looked up directly at Councillor Johnson.

"Ward 5? Councillor Johnson?"

"I object to this nonsense. This charade. What a foolish and dangerous game the city manager is playing. It is time to end our city's contract with him and hire a new city manager who will better respect the members of this council! We are the elected representatives of the people of this city! We don't have to stand for this kind of phony grandstanding stunt!"

Silence in the chambers. Everyone was staring at the Ward 5 Councillor.

The mayor finally broke the silence. "I think it is rather late for that, Councillor. All other members of this council have responded. The city manager asked you a question, Councillor Johnson. Please respond."

"No. I refuse to be part of this nonsense." Councillor Johnson crossed her arms and looked defiant.

The mayor shrugged. "As you wish. I believe the City Clerk would have that answer from her notes of the conversations. Ms. James?"

"Yes, Your Honor. When the City Manager and I talked on the phone with Councillor Johnson, the price Mr. Crawford told her was...$2.14 million."

There was a collective gasp as everyone let out their breath. There it was. The same price that the newspaper had headlined. Anonymously. The leak. And now the leaker.

Crawford let a moment pass before continuing. In the same flat voice he asked Ward 6 Councillor Alex Miller.

"2.37 million."

"Ms. James?"

"That is correct."

Crawford looked around the dais. "I am truly sorry that I had to resort to such a strategy. I emphasize that I did this on my own. Again, neither the mayor nor anyone else inside city hall or on the council had any prior knowledge. Only the city clerk was made aware, and I did that only for independent confirmation purposes. If the council wishes to blame anyone for this action, it is solely and completely on my shoulders."

He started to sit down, and then straightened up. "Oh. As to the land deal itself. After much discussion, the owner of the land has now agreed to make a very significant contribution to assist the community. He will be recognized appropriately at the opening ceremonies and also with a permanent plaque that will be erected in the lobby of the new building. The actual price we agreed upon for the land acquisition is $1.66 million."

With that he sat down. Six council members sat stony-faced. The seventh was slumped back in her chair, her face pressed into her hands.

No one spoke.

The newspaper reporter snapped some more close-ups of the faces of the council members. The TV camera split time between the mayor, the Ward 5 Councillor and a wide shot of the council chambers. The social media blogger didn't quite understand what was happening so she just sent out a frownie-face emoji.

The reporter from The Observer knew that his confidential informant on council had just been burned. There was no longer any benefit to protecting Councillor Johnson. His twitter posts from now on, and his full-length morning story in the newspaper, would express shock and outrage at this betrayal of the public trust by an elected official. The editorial page would be blistering.

Hypocrisy was neither uncommon nor unknown fare for newspapers.

The audience hummed with excitement. You didn't get to see many public executions anymore. This was great fun.

Kim Sharpe was the first to rise. "Mayor?"

Sonja Rodriguez focused slowly on the rookie councillor. "Yes. Councillor Sharpe."

"Thank you. I suggest that we have witnessed a rather extraordinary situation tonight. I want to state publicly that I had no prior knowledge of any of this. I say that because you are all aware of my personal relationship with the City Manager. You deserve to hear me state that."

She cleared her throat. "Second, let's not lose sight of the fact that this whole mess was because the city was trying to acquire a site for a really important new development for our city. The price that the City Manager has negotiated, to buy the land for $1.66 million, well, that seems to me to be a terrific deal. So let's proceed with that. I move approval of the land acquisition at the price and terms recommended in his report."

"Second. Here, second it. Yeah, let's go."

The comments from around the horseshoe were swift.

"Moved. Seconded. Any discussion? Those in favor? Six in favor. Opposed? No one. One abstention, then, the Councillor from Ward 5." She banged her gavel.

Kim rose again. "As to the other matter that the City Manager has exposed. I suggest, Mayor, that we all need some time to absorb that situation and the implications of these, ah, circumstances. I would suggest that we ask the City Solicitor for a report on our options as a council and we consider that report at our next meeting."

"I will second that," intoned Councillor March.

"We have a motion. Discussion? Those in favor? Six. Opposed? One. The motion is carried. Is there any other business, Madam Clerk?"

"No, Your Honor."

"In that case, a motion to adjourn? Councillor Kelly. Second. Councillor Policy. In favor? Six. Opposed. Whatever. We are adjourned."

Her gavel came down with ferocity.

CHAPTER 46

THERE WAS NO sense of elation amongst those sprawled in the mayor's office after the council meeting. They were drained. All of the councillors, except for Councillor Johnson, had instinctively gathered together for a private post-mortem.

Councillor Johnson had fled city hall, hotly pursued by the local media, cameras flashing and microphones waving.

Exhaustion mixed with relief, with just a soupcon of malice, created a frothy brew of emotions in the room. Once again, the Port Manatee City Council's internal operations had been exposed to the citizenry, and once again it had failed the test. The mayor and the five councillors knew that they would all be tarred a little by this latest brush of scandal.

When any legislative body explodes, all of the members suffer collateral damage. Some of the shrapnel would get sprinkled on them. Voters would remember only the broadest aspects of the scandal; none of the sitting members of council would look great over this issue in the rear-view mirror of public opinion.

"It had to be done," Fred March said finally. "The poison was seeping into our entire council."

Nods from around the room. Most of them were enjoying a little snort from the Mayor's private stock of aged bourbon. The outside doors to her office anteroom were shut firmly and guarded by the Sergeant-at-Arms. No reporters would be allowed to get close.

Sonja Rodriguez kicked off her heels and sat slumped behind her desk. She shook her head. "I'll never understand why Mikayla would betray us like that."

Nobody had an answer.

"What do we do now?" Kim's question hung in the suddenly rancid air.

A little more bourbon was sipped. Nobody seemed to want to be the first to leap on top of that large pile of flaming dog poop.

"I guess that's for another day," said the mayor finally. "And with that, while I love you all, I'm throwing you out of my office and going home to my family."

Chuckles around the room. Final swallows were swallowed. Good-byes were said. The room cleared.

The suffocating odor of ugly unfinished business remained behind.

CHAPTER 47

THE DAY OF the neighborhood party for Elliott Webster and the Starwind construction crews dawned hot and bright.

The new footings for the first tower were being poured. The concrete for the second tower had been poured and steel beams were being erected. It was finally looking like a real construction site, Samantha thought as she crossed the lot at 4pm. It was exciting to see the progress after the disappointing setbacks from the two bombing incidents.

She could see several of the local residents starting to set out long tables and erect canopies and a couple of tents at the picnic site. It was obvious that the entire neighborhood had searched deep inside their garages and pantries to contribute to the party.

Mrs. Barkley and the ladies organizing the celebration had finally accepted that they just didn't have the physical space and equipment to do a proper open-air barbecue pit on the site. Only then had Samantha suggested they allow Elliott's long-time cook, Mama Jones, to send down some of her legendary smoked beef brisket. Mama Jones and Mrs. Barkley had bonded instantly over this community initiative.

Fifty pounds of brisket and fifty pounds of pulled pork would be arriving at 5:30pm. Samantha had no doubt that Mama Jones would deliver the fabulous meats precisely on time.

Small propane barbecues were being wheeled over and set up to do the burgers and dogs. Tables for the salads, buns, condiments and cold drinks were being covered with brightly colored vinyl tablecloths. One of the local teens had volunteered to be the DJ; he and a friend were busy testing the sound system.

It was an astonishing act of neighborhood kindness, thought Samantha as she began the rounds of hugging the ladies and their kids. "We are all so excited," she told Mrs. Barkley and some of the other mothers. "It is just wonderful of you to do this. The crews are really looking forward to tonight."

"You are changing our neighborhood. Finally, city hall doin' something for us!" Mrs. Barkley said, amazement in her voice. The other ladies nodded. "We're just grateful to that nice Mr. Webster for building this here."

More nods. More hugs. A couple of the men were dragging over coolers of soft drinks and beer. Recycling bins were set up for the empties.

Samantha realized again that this was costing the community money—and that the local residents didn't have a lot of that to spare. She choked up again as she understood the sacrifice that the neighborhood was making.

A couple of cases of boxed wine appeared from the back of an SUV. It was from Uncle Larry's Booze Barn. Samantha had secretly made a deal with Frankie to give them a big discount on the wine and beer, which Samantha would make up. No one would ever know.

Preparations continued throughout the late afternoon. The construction site closed an hour early to allow the crew to clean up and get ready. The sun was beginning its slow descent as Elliott Webster led his crews across the dusty ground to join the party.

At 5:28pm, a green van pulled up. A burly driver, lovely Starwind receptionist Jamaica Jones and her grandmother, the legendary barbecuer Mama Jones, emerged. Samantha quickly introduced everybody to everybody, and then scurried back to escort Elliott and the crew into the party area. There was a brief moment of awkwardness but everyone was determined to have a good time and within minutes the co-mingling and fun were under way.

The cold beer went down very nicely in the early evening sun. The kids happily gorged on pop and played their own games. Shouting and laughing was paramount. Some of the construction guys helped to organize a couple of games. The ladies finished laying out the salads and an entire table of home-baked goodies for dessert.

There weren't many formalities. Mrs. Barkley took a brief moment to welcome their guests and to thank Elliott for his project. Elliott took a brief moment to thank the neighborhood for doing this for the crew. Everybody cheered and headed for the food tables.

It was a fabulous, chaotic scene, thought Samantha. People were digging in. The construction guys were helping little kids to play games or devour hot dogs. Mama Jones and Mrs. Barkley shared the delightful task of serving the brisket and the pulled pork. They were laughing together as they piled the plates high with the succulent barbecue. The cold beer supply somehow kept even with the demand. It wasn't the miracle of the loaves and fishes, but it was close.

The local kid being DJ was playing a variety of music. Some of it Samantha recognized, much of it she didn't, but it all added to the magical atmosphere of the evening. At one point Jamaica Jones came over. "This is incredible! What a party!"

Elliott happened by at that moment, carrying a plate loaded with a pulled pork sandwich, three salads, two pieces of brisket and a large handful of French fries. A beer was cautiously balanced on the edge of the plate.

"Fabulous! I've never seen a community do anything like this for a local construction crew! Ever!" He stopped enthusing only long enough to hand Samantha his beer to hold so he could dive into the food.

Kim and Roy appeared, as did the mayor. The locals were surprised and delighted to have these VIPs join the party. Samantha finally got a bit of food before the brisket was all gone. It was delicious.

Then attention turned to the dessert table. It was all home-made by the neighborhood ladies. Sweet potato pies. Chocolate cakes. Brownies. Coconut cakes. Cherry pies. Peach Cobbler. Cookies.

There were groans of delight from everybody, then a rush to the table. It didn't take long for the crowd to happily plow through the baked goodies.

Samantha looked at her watch. The timing would be close, she thought to herself. She managed to nab a piece of cherry pie. So good.

Then Elliott hollered for a moment's quiet. He finally got it.

"This is not a time for speeches." The crowd chuckled. "And most certainly not any political speeches," he said as he looked at the mayor and the ward councillor.

"Hey!" Sonja Rodriguez said, laughing. The crowd applauded.

"What this evening really means is the linking of this neighborhood to the Delvecchio Bridge complex that we are building. Forever, I hope. But it also means the linking of our company and our men and women with your community. Anytime you need anything, you just let us know. Thank you. This has been just amazing."

As the crowd begin to applaud, Samantha heard the first faint tinkles. She looked at her watch again. Perfect. Right on time. The music grew louder. The kids were the first to hear it, as their ears were so highly attuned to recognize this particular sound. Then around the corner came two ice cream trucks, lights flashing and "It's a Small World" tinkling.

The kids all looked at each other. Nobody quite knew what this was all about.

Samantha smiled as she stepped forward. "This is just a small thank you from me to all of you. You have welcomed me into your community. The ice cream is all free tonight. I hope you enjoy it."

It was the perfect ending to the day. The kids whooped and sprinted to the trucks as the adults laughed. Mrs. Barkley and Mama Jones went over to her. "Aren't you the little devil," smiled Mrs. Barkley.

"She is a surprise, our Samantha," Mama Jones confirmed. "She almost gave Elliott a heart attack at their first meeting when she announced she didn't eat meat."

They all laughed. Elliott joined them and they laughed some more. He looked at Samantha. "What a great idea. Thank you." He hugged her.

The adults lined up for their ice cream treats after the kids were finished. The music soared into the evening sky. The laughter of kids and adults combined into a symphony of joy.

Chapter 48

THE SUN'S WARMTH was beaming on the Sapphire Blue pool when Kim and Samantha met late the next morning. They grabbed a couple of lounge chairs and a small table with an umbrella. They dumped their large bags of beach necessities and stretched out on the chaise loungers.

"It's been quite a week," Kim started. "I'm really glad you and Perk are back together. You were such an insufferable bitch for the past two weeks."

Samantha laughed. "Yeah. And you've been such a warm and happy person with the crap going on at city council."

Kim grinned. They relaxed in companionable silence. "Gosh, we haven't been down here much over the past couple of weeks, have we?"

Samantha reached over to pour a couple of plastic glasses full of rosé. "No. I've missed it. So much going on."

They watched a new family arrive at the pool. An older woman, two younger ones and a man in his twenties. Slavic features. They settled into a corner at the far side of the pool.

The Wives were in their usual regal location. Kids were bleating in the pool as they invented some game with barnyard animals. It called for a lot of oinks, moos and shouting.

"Great party last night," Kim observed.

"Wasn't it? The neighborhood did such a wonderful job. Such good people."

"Your ice cream truck surprise was really nice."

"I'm glad it worked out so well. They deserved a little treat. The kids loved it."

"I'm still surprised Perk doesn't have a better lead on the bomber. It scares me to think what might happen if another bomb blew up at Delvecchio and kids were in the area. Roy thinks Starwind's insurance company would cancel his policy if there was another bombing. The future of the entire project would be in jeopardy."

"Sheesh. Let's hope it never comes to that. It would be tragic for the community and the city."

"Yeah. You've got your problem with the construction. I've got mine with the mess with Mikayla at council."

"That is ugly. What are you going to do?"

"I don't know yet. My guess is we could suspend her, fine her her salary for a couple of months, suspend her, or try to force her out of office. The City Solicitor is reporting to us next week. It'll be nasty, however it ends up."

"Roy did good."

"He did, didn't he? And I never knew anything of what he was planning to do. Wasn't it amazing how The Observer turned on Mikayla? Their editorial was scathing, that whole 'betrayal of the public trust' thing. Somehow, they forgot to mention that she was leaking to them, but whatever."

"Do you think she'll resign?"

Kim was quiet. "I don't know," she said finally. "I would in that situation, but she is a real street fighter. I wouldn't count on it. If she doesn't resign, there isn't really all that much we can do formally as a Council to punish her or replace her."

Swim time. They both slid into the warm pool water and luxuriated there. As Samantha was floating quietly, she suddenly bumped into somebody. She spluttered a bit and opened her eyes as she stood up.

"Oh! Sorry! My fault."

"No problem. Hi. I'm Katherine. Ekaterina, actually."

"That's a beautiful name. I'm Samantha. What is it, Ukrainian?"

"Ukrainian and Russian. My family has ties to both nations. Our branch fled Russia a hundred years ago and ended up in Lviv in western Ukraine. The other branch somehow survives in St. Petersburg, despite the wars, Stalin, oppression and Putin. My sister is Juliya, my mother is Ludmilla Savchenko. They're over in that corner with my idiot brother Aleks."

"Nice. Oh, this is my friend Kim. She's a resident of the White building, I'm in Blue."

"Ah. We just bought a nice three bedroom in Red. Fitting, huh? My siblings think it is hilarious. My mother, not so much."

"How did you end up here?"

Ekaterina's eyes clouded. "My father died a couple of years ago. He fought the corruption in Ukraine most of his life. He was a lawyer. I think the strain and the pressure and the threats finally got to him. My mother decided to get out. We all have college degrees and speak English, so we were able to get Green cards. We wanted to be warm after the cold of Ukraine. Juliya got a job teaching at the University here, I joined a law firm, and Aleks is finishing his master's degree in computer science. So here we are."

"We'll have to get together for a drink," Samantha promised.

Kim nodded. "By the way, I'm the City Councillor for this area, so if you need anything just let me know."

Ekaterina's eyes widened. "You are an elected official? So young. So pretty."

Samantha splashed Kim. "Don't inflate her ego any more than it is. She's here to serve you. Take advantage."

"I'm always happy to help my constituents," Kim told Ekaterina as she pushed Samantha underwater. "Don't listen to this frustrated old hag. You call me anytime I can help."

They were all laughing as they separated and returned to their lounges.

"She seems really nice," Kim said.

"Doesn't she? And such a clever family." Samantha thought about it as she poured water for them both. "Their family must have seen a lot of history, living where they did and when they did. It would be interesting to hear their story."

Kim nodded amiably.

CHAPTER 49

DEVERON SNIVELY AND his sidekick were once again rushing out the side door of Whispering Palms when Samantha and Kim arrived for their next visit.

They sat in the car for a moment, watching the tall, skinny black man and the soft-bellied younger mixed-race man. "Boy, that's an odd couple. They always have that black satchel and always scurry out the side exit. They give me the creeps."

"Have you ever met Mrs. Snively?"

"Tamara, I think her name is. No I haven't. Mrs. Harris says she's a loner. She has her own one-bedroom apartment. I don't think she socializes much with the other residents."

They got out of the car and headed inside. As they walked through the reception area, they were saddened to see the black-bordered announcement of the passing of another resident of the home.

Kim put on her volunteer ID badge and went into the reading room to greet residents. Samantha put on her badge and went looking for Mrs. Harris.

"Well! I see you and the Sheriff are back together."

Samantha blushed. "How did you know?"

"Oh, honey, just look at yourself. You've got that glow back. It has to be a man. And the man for you is Sheriff Perkins."

Samantha smiled broadly. "You are so smart. Yes, we made up. I remembered what you told me. I made him lamb shanks. And wore a Little Black Dress. And poured some really good wine." She paused and winked. "The making-up was a lot of fun."

"I just bet it was. Yessiree, I bet it was. I'm glad for you."

They sat in companionable silence for a moment, both thinking their own thoughts about lovers and fights and making-up.

"I saw Mrs. Snively's nephew this morning as we arrived," Samantha said a few minutes later.

Mrs. Harris's face tightened just a bit. "Yes. We see them…a lot. There is something…I don't know, but my old teacher radar acts up whenever I see them here."

Samantha sipped coffee and looked around. No one was within ear shot. "How well do you know Mrs. Snively?"

"Ah. We speak. She doesn't come down much to socialize. I think she's lonely. Her memory is starting to go. I'm a bit concerned about her."

"Have you ever visited her suite?"

"Once. About a year ago. Nice apartment. She has a big armoire in one corner. Big padlock on it. I thought that was very odd. She said it was to keep the orderlies and cleaning people from taking her prized possessions. Then she scooted me out. I haven't been back again."

"Huh. Oh well, not my problem. Now, would you like to go for a stroll? It is lovely outside."

"That would be very nice, dear. Why not get Kim over here? Maybe Mr. Treadwell would like to join us."

Samantha's eyes sparkled as she thought about a little romance building. Mr. Treadwell was considered quite a catch at the retirement home. He had his own teeth and just one hip replacement.

Chapter 50

KIM WAS THOUGHTFUL as she and Samantha drove back to Sapphire Blue.

"What?" Samantha finally broke the silence.

"I…well, I don't know. But I just got the feeling from two of the residents this morning that they were hurting. Not just the usual aches and pains of getting old, which I have to tell you sucks and I don't even want to think about, but one of the ladies had bruises on her arm, and another had marks on her wrist. They looked odd to me. Neither one of them said anything, but they both sort of flinched when one of the staff walked through the room."

Samantha considered that for a couple of blocks. "I had a similar concern when we first started volunteering there. I mentioned it to Perk. He nearly bit my head off. He said elder abuse is a big problem in retirement homes and in society today, but that I can't go around accusing people without really good evidence. He was right, but I still think about it. I worry for the seniors. They are so vulnerable."

"Do you think we should talk to the GM? Mrs. Brighthouse seems like a pretty smart woman. She runs a good residence, I think."

"Gosh, that could—well, what if we are wrong? Older people do get bruises more easily. They accidentally bang into a piece of furniture or fall. The staff seems to be pretty decent, from the ones that I've met." She paused. "Well, there is this creepy nurse. Funny name. What is it? Cack—no, Krackle. He walked through the sitting room once and two of the women blanched and shut up on the spot. He struck me as creepy."

"Yeah, I know who you mean. Ethel told me once that she was scared of him."

"Who?"

"Ethel. She's a nurse's assistant. Gives medications to the residents. Helps out with their personal care. Really quiet."

"Yes, I've seen her a couple of time. Always doing the pills and injections and meds. Just sorta…mousy."

Kim nodded. "Yeah, that's her. Now. Krackle…Elmer, I think is his first name. He doesn't seem to have much rapport with the residents. Kind of dark and brooding. Maybe we should re-start our detective agency and help Perk out."

Samantha rolled her eyes. "Oh, yeah, that's what I'm going to do right after he and I just got back together. We broke up because I was trying to help him with the bombing case. Now you want us to investigate a non-crime at a nursing home where we are rookie volunteers? And don't even know if anything is truly wrong? I don't think so."

"Yeah, well, we'll see." Kim studied the streetscape. She noticed a heavy-set man wearing nothing but black shorts, black runners and sunglasses jogging slowly down the sidewalk, panting. Kim looked at him and muttered to Samantha, "Don't you just hate it when a guy's boobs are bigger than yours?"

Samantha rolled her eyes again.

Kim turned her head back to stare out the window. She looked hard at an older couple riding a big Harley that had just come up beside their car. "Man, that bitch pad looks comfortable."

"What? What did you just say?"

"The seat on the back of those big motorcycles where the women usually ride. They're called 'bitch pads.' Classy, huh?"

Samantha shook her head. "Sometimes I worry about you. Imagine my shame at having inflicted you upon the innocent citizens of Port Manatee."

CHAPTER 51

KIM'S COMMENT ABOUT resuming their detective work kept haunting Samantha. Because of a startling combination of dumb luck, creative thinking and bold action, she and Kim and Samira and even Rosie had helped to solve a couple of crimes in the past year and a half.

Despite that involvement, which always had the Sheriff tearing his hair out in frustration and fear for her safety, Perkins seemed to be back in some kind of like/lust with her. Which was a very good thing. And which she didn't want to screw up again.

Love? Oooh, let's not go down that steep and dangerous slope right now. After being betrayed by her husband, Samantha knew she had developed some very high fences around her innermost feelings. Being open to truly love again was hard. She knew she was nervous and conflicted about opening up too much. Maybe with more time. And Perk...he was so special. But still...

And who knew where his head space was about their relationship. Like most men, it seemed, they were pretty taciturn about sharing feelings about romance. A dozen roses from the grocery store on Valentine's Day was a pretty major expression of romance for most guys. It wasn't much to build on in relationships.

Damn. She shook her head in frustration as she acknowledged her own twisted inner self that she kept hidden from everyone else. She exhaled. What a screwed-up bitch she truly was. Especially about love, whatever that was. After her horrid experience with marriage the first time around, Samantha often felt she was scarred for life. Hopefully nobody would ever find out.

Anyway, enough gloom. But what was it with her and this Nancy Drew compulsion? Who was she to think she could solve society's ills and apprehend the guilty?

She sipped some lukewarm coffee and idly ran her finger around the plate where the crumbs of her croissant had flaked off. She licked her finger, put the mug and plate in the dishwasher and headed to her bedroom to get dressed for the day.

It was only a week before Kim's "Martinis and Manicures" fundraiser and she still had a lot of work left to do. Starting with Frankie over at Uncle Larry's Booze Barn. Or, as Samantha had nicknamed it, "The Second Happiest Place on Earth."

"We'll do the delivery by 1pm that day," promised Frankie. "I'll have two bartenders there by 3pm to do the set-up. It starts at what, 4:30?"

"Yes. I'm expecting the party to last about two hours."

"No problem. Whatever it takes. The bartenders will be there and will also do the bar clean-up. You prefer female bartenders since it is women-only?"

"Oh. Well, I hadn't thought about that. But yes, that's a good idea. I'd better make sure the two food people are female. Just to make it comfortable for everyone in attendance."

"Who's catering?"

"I talked a little boutique hotel called La Casa Adrianna into doing it."

Frankie's eyes widened. "You did? Holy Cow, that's huge. They don't usually do that sort of thing. Say, are you somebody?"

"No," Samantha said laughing. "But I know people. Sort of. Anyway, they agreed to do a Spanish tapas bar menu for the party. I think it'll be fun."

"Yeah. Golly. Uncle Larry's Booze Barn and La Casa Adrianna. You are the first person in history to link the two of us in the same sentence." Frankie shook her head. "Or event."

"OK, I think that's it. You'll give the bartenders the Kimtini recipe?"

"For sure. And I'll make them practice the night before so I can sample," she grinned.

"You've been great. Thank you. I've got to run," Samantha patted her booze concierge on the arm. She had already given them her credit card, and an impressive total had been rung through so far.

Samantha's errands for the party continued. She stopped by the florist to confirm the flower delivery, the chocolatier for the truffles and the party store for the gift bags. Then she drove into La Casa Adrianna to speak with Rosita.

"Ah, Senorita Samantha. How lovely to see you. And how beautiful you look."

"Thank you, Rosita. You are so kind. And you look great. I just wanted to touch base about the Martinis & Manicures party next week."

They quickly agreed on the tapas menu: Piquilla Peppers stuffed with shrimp salad; bacon-wrapped dates with goat cheese and pecans; olive tapenade; Spanish meatballs; croquettes with Manchego cheese and Serrano ham; and an imaginative pomegranate-pistachio crostini. There would be a Spanish cheese platter, and bowls of almonds and olives to complete the tasting feast.

Rosita thought having female servers was a smart idea. "We'll send a sous chef with the food to supervise the heating and serving," she said. "Our staff will get there by 3:15pm."

Samantha thanked her and rushed home. She called the Beauty College and confirmed two women to do her guests' nails. They would arrive at 4 to set up their tables and manicure supplies.

Military precision was the way Samantha liked to organize her events.

She then double-checked with the guard house at the front gate to confirm the arrangements for parking and security. Finally she sat down and mentally ran over the list. All good to go.

CHAPTER 52

"I THINK SHE SHOULD resign from this Council."

John Kelly was adamant as he kicked off the debate about how to deal with Mikayla Johnson following the leaking scandal that had dominated local headlines and talk shows for nearly two weeks. Public opinion on Boomer's radio program was deeply divided.

"I'm the longest-serving member of this Council, and I am disgusted by what went on. Her actions threatened the future of this Council at a time when we were just rebuilding trust with the public. The electors last year made it very clear that they wanted a clean, progressive city hall, council members with integrity, and wanted to leave the debacle of the last Council far behind. Quite simply, Councillor Johnson betrayed that public trust. She should step down. Now."

"Thank you, Councillor Kelly. Councillor March."

"As much as I would like to agree with my colleague, and as much as I despise what occurred, I don't think this is an action in which we should demand a resignation. If it is offered, fine. We'll deal with a by-election or make an appointment to fill that seat. But to force the councillor out I think goes beyond what would be reasonable in response to her actions."

"Thank you. Councillor Miller."

"I hate having to do this. It is not productive use of our time as an elected body. The public is not well-served by this entire process. We just seem to get some forward momentum going, and then something blows-up. Literally, in the case of the Delvecchio Bridge project over in Ward 3. Twice! That's a bigger concern to me. But we have to deal with this, so I propose that we take away her salary for two months. A financial penalty. That would be personally hurtful and perhaps make her think twice about any future...transgressions."

"Councillor Policy?"

"I abhor what has happened. Her actions have hurt the city and could have cost the taxpayers a lot of extra money if our City Manager hadn't been able to negotiate a marvelous deal with the landowner. I think it is clear that Councillor Johnson cannot be trusted with confidential information. I think she should be denied access to confidential material, being allowed to read it only while she is in the City Clerk's office. But it can't be delivered to her nor would she have her own private access to it for a one-year period."

"Councillor Sharpe?"

Kim slowly rose from her seat. It was well known that she and the Ward 5 Councillor had become antagonists in just the few short months since the new council had been sworn in. The bad blood had only gotten worse. With a split on how to punish the recalcitrant Ward 5 member, Kim's words would have a dramatic impact on the final outcome.

Mikayla Johnson continued to sit in her council chair. Her hands gripped the edge of the table. Her eyes remained downcast. Kim thought that she looked older and in pain.

She also remembered some of the mean and hurtful things that the Ward 5 Councillor had hurled at Kim during some of the debates.

"I agree with all of the sentiments that my colleagues have expressed," she began. "This has been a hurtful and unnecessary distraction from our doing the people's business. I fear that we have again lost the confidence of our public. We need to regain that trust. I ran, and I think got elected, because I couldn't stand what the last council, or more accurately three members of that council, did to this city. We became a national disgrace, a laughingstock of municipal corruption. My campaign promised a clean government, a city that would move forward with a stronger local economy, a more creative and fun city, a community that was socially progressive, financially conservative and environmentally sensitive. That is still my focus and I hope to work with all of you to see more progress on those things. That's why I'm concerned that if we are overly-punitive, the bad feelings will linger and fester and harm our ability to push forward. Our nation has seen too much polarization and fighting in politics. We don't need another elected body so filled with bile and distrust that nothing gets accomplished. What I am suggesting is a heart-felt public apology from Councillor Johnson. One that she would state in open council and put on the public record. Something that would acknowledge what she has done, what she intends to do about it, how she would change, and how she would like to go forward in the future. If that is honest and sincere, then I think the public would accept it and let us move on. If it is not done or is not sincere, or if promises are broken in the future, then I think we should demand her resignation."

Kim concluded and sat down. There was a breathless silence in the council chambers. Finally Mayor Rodriguez spoke.

"I think we have all been torn about what to do in this situation. It is unprecedented for us. I think all council members have made a responsible case for their position on how to proceed. To be honest with you, I had not made up my mind before the debate tonight. I wanted to hear from all of you, my colleagues, before deciding on my position. From the City Solicitor's report, we have the authority to take any of the actions that you have suggested. But, I find myself greatly persuaded by Councillor Sharpe's words. The deep schism we have in politics today is not good for our country. I think we have to consider how we are going to work together over the three remaining years of our term to keep moving our city forward. That to me is the most important part of this discussion. I think Councillor Sharpe's proposal gives us—no, gives Councillor Johnson—an honorable way out of this. And if it is done sincerely then it sets us up for working together in the future. I think that is really important. So that is my position."

The mayor paused. She looked around the chamber. Attention was riveted on her.

"I now wonder if the Councillor for Ward 5 would care to say something?"

Complete silence. For a long moment there was no response. The eyes of the other six council members were lasered on her. The audience was beginning to buzz over the tension. Finally Councillor Johnson lifted her head, took a deep breath and rose.

"I truly am sorry that we are here tonight. And because of something that I did. I admit that I did it and that I was wrong. I apologize. To this Council and to this City. There have been some bad things happening in my personal life in the last year or two. Maybe some of that seeped into my public life. Maybe I got too caught up in the politics and didn't care enough about public policy."

She took a heavy breath. She wiped her eyes quickly and then looked around the chambers. She swallowed a quick sip of water.

"I have been fighting depression for the last year or so. My father passed away, I have been battling some family disagreements over his estate. It has not been easy. And coming back to council after such a brutal election campaign, then the public pressures and the constant social media scrutiny and criticism once you're in office…well, that's something I hadn't experienced in my past terms on council. I haven't handled it very well. I have been really hurt by some comments that have been intensely personal and cruel. I'm going to go off social media. I have an appointment with a medical specialist to discuss my, ah, emotional state. And I am trying to get my meds sorted out."

She wiped a sweating brow. "This…this is really hard. To make my personal problems public. But I need you to try to understand the roller-coaster I've been on for the last year. I've just been, well, overwhelmed at times and rather than seek help I swallowed it all and it festered and then I lashed out. Too many people expect those of us in public life to be on call all the time, to be some version of perfect, to be pure or something. Well, I'm not. And I've been hurting for a while."

She stopped again and looked down. There was dead silence in the Council Chambers.

"I can understand why some of you said what you said tonight. I don't blame any of you. I also want to apologize to our City Manager for things that I've said about him. He is a good man and good for this city. I have no animosity towards him or our staff."

A shuddering breath. The room remained tense and hushed. Another nervous sip of water.

"I pledge to do better in the future. I promise to get my health problems addressed. I hope medical counselling will help with my emotional, well, you know. I really hope that will make me feel better and act more responsibly. I really do want to work with you and to make Port Manatee a better city. We might disagree on certain steps in the future, but I now know I won't experience them as personal attacks. You will never again have to worry that I will leak confidential information. I want to rebuild trust with you and the community. I will accept whatever decision this council makes. I really am sorry. I would like to do better in the remainder of our term. I hope I will have that opportunity."

With that she collapsed into her chair. The atmosphere had become subdued in the Council chambers. No one seemed to want to speak next. That was a tough performance to follow.

The Mayor finally cleared her throat and looked around at the council members. She stared at Kim, who finally pushed herself to her feet.

"I think we should acknowledge the apology from Councillor Johnson. I'm sure it was very difficult for her to say those things. Perhaps we all understand the demons that so often accompany being in public office, but too often we don't acknowledge them or seek help when they overwhelm us. It is clear this was an extraordinarily difficult thing for the Councillor to say in public. I think it was sincere and I am prepared to accept her apology and offer to reach out to help her if she wants it. I think it is now time to bring this episode to a conclusion, Madam Mayor. I would like to move that the Clerk publish the Councillor's words on the city website and record the apology in our minutes. I would also move that we note that the Council considers this to be a resolution to this unfortunate matter, but that any repeat offenses would result in a recommendation that the seat be vacated."

"Trust but verify, as President Reagan once noted." Kim sat down.

"I'll second that," said the Ward 4 Councillor. As the dean of the council, his change of position helped to sway the others. The mayor called for a quick vote and it was carried 6-0.

The mayor ended the meeting. The media rushed for Councillor Johnson who continued to sit in her chair. The rest of the council left the room as did the administration.

Roy grabbed Kim's arm when they were alone. "Great job, honey. You offered a reasonable way out for her. And we've got her on the straight and narrow for a while. I hope she will get the medical assistance she needs and get her family problems sorted out. She's right—there aren't many places that elected officials can hide or go for help if they have mental or emotional problems. Especially in confidence. You know that social media will find out and flay them. Well, I just hope that her admission and your motion will resolve the whole ugly mess."

Kim nodded. She was emotionally drained. They chatted for a moment and agreed to head back to his place for a drink—and whatever else might happen. Kim smiled to herself at those images.

She returned to her office, stowed her papers and locked her desk. She put on her coat and picked up her briefcase.

As she was turning off the light in her office, she was startled by Councillor Johnson who was coming out of her own office.

They stared at each other. Finally the Ward 5 Councillor nodded. "Thank you." She walked out of the room.

Kim sucked in her breath. Her eyebrows went up to her hairline. She shook her head, wishing she could accept the acknowledgement as a truce. Even after the emotional words tonight, her suspicious mind wondered if this was just a ploy in advance of some future battle.

Politics. She was still a newbie, but she could already feel herself being more careful with people. She was now trying not just to listen to the words, but to see behind their words and to understand their true motivations. She was more attuned to possible threats to her, politically and sadly but increasingly, physically. Violence against public servants was on the rise. The January 6 riot in Washington had terrified a generation of elected officials and horrified a nation. With the polarization of politics at all levels in America, and the incidents of physical attacks on politicians, it was a regrettable fact today that people in public office always had to be concerned about their safety and that of their family and co-workers.

It is a hard lesson for rookie politicians. The smart ones learn fast.

CHAPTER 53

"ONE OF MY undercover guys got a new lead on a drug supplier," reported Lt. Gomez at the weekly senior officer's meeting. "I've told you before that we've seen an increase in cocaine and fentanyl on the streets in the past few months. And other opioids." He ran his left hand through his thinning hair. Frustration was rampant in his voice. "We just clean up the Campanelli brothers and that sadistic lunatic El Jefe and somebody else pops up to fill the void with more street drugs."

Perkins tightened as he was reminded of the kidnapping of Samantha by the crazy Campanellis. He had shot one brother and the other had been killed by El Jefe's enforcer when the brothers got stupid and tried to rip off the drug lord. It was not a smart, life-enhancing career move to jerk off El Jefe. A string of dead bodies confirmed that. Several had not enjoyed a pleasant death. The former Central American drug lord was now doing hard time in a federal prison. The assassin who had wounded Perkins was dead, and Samantha was safe. But the stress of that time had never entirely faded.

Lt Gomez gulped coffee and continued. "My people took down a small-time seller the other night. We've been trying to roll somebody for a while, to get to the next rung up the ladder. This punk was finally, ah, persuaded to rat."

Knowing looks around the room. Nobody asked what form of persuasion had been used. It would have been legal, but there are always degrees of flexibility in gaining new street intelligence.

"The informant said the guy's been dealing drugs for a couple of years, but he's expanded in the last year. That would match the time frame after the Campanellis got taken out. Pills, but also heroin and coke. We've had eighteen street deaths related to this crap in the past six or seven months. The Medical Examiner thinks they've been from drugs that were made deadly. Either something added to them or they were cut badly in the meth lab." He shrugged. "Not that a drug dealer would care."

"Any idea where the source is?"

"No, not yet. Just the usual street transactions. Everybody buys from the next guy up the ladder, adds to the price, sells to his dealers, and it gets on the street. Kids are more vulnerable, but surprisingly these days so are some seniors. They've been experimenting with legal marijuana for pain suppression, but some of the older folks start needing a higher high. They get addicted to pills or Fentanyl or somethin'." He shook his head in dismay.

"Any leads on who's at the top of the chain? The supplier?"

"No. Nothing yet. We haven't discovered any new source locations. We don't know the home base. Our rat gave us a couple of names so we'll work on them in the next few days, see what's happening. We might go after a court-ordered wiretap if either looks promising. See what we can find out."

Perkins nodded and the meeting moved to the next agenda item.

"The Delvecchio Bridge bombings. What's the update? Any leads coming out of the Orlando bombing?"

"A few. They sent the dynamite remnants to the FBI in Atlanta. They're working on a match. FSU is currently doing an inventory of their supply of dynamite. Best of all, the Orlando cops found a security camera video of the area. It is night-time and the video is pretty grainy, but you can make out a single figure running from the scene. It appears to be a young male. He's wearing a jacket and jeans. They are trying to eliminate suspects but that's going to take time."

"OK, let's stay in close contact with them. That means sharing any intel or ideas. Do they have all of our on-scene photos and data?"

His officers nodded. There would be no hesitation in sharing evidence with the other departments investigating the bombings.

Perkins continued bluntly, "Stay on this thing, folks. We are not giving it up. I want action on this." Nods around the table. "Anything else?"

The head of this Intel unit spoke up. Lt Maria Salazar was a University of Georgia grad who had been with the department for seven years. She had recently been promoted to take over the Intel unit.

"This is nothing definitive, but we're starting to pick up noise and more on-line chatter about white supremacist groups in our region. We think there are three that have become more active since that raid on Congress in January, 2021. The BoogerBoyz, with a zee. Don't know what that name means. The Loco Locos. No idea where that name comes from. And third is The Red Guard. We assume it is named after the Chinese students that Chairman Mao unleashed to help start the Cultural Revolution. Those kids had contempt for the status quo. They quickly turned violent. Their actions set China back a generation in its development, and of course the country lost a lot of cultural treasures and intellectual prowess. Our preliminary intelligence suggests many of the same triggers here—the violence, the hatred, the public shaming. We are going to watch them much more carefully but I wanted to give you an early alert."

Perkins sat for a moment as his leadership team absorbed this disturbing news. He glanced around the table.

"Are they getting more active or more aggressive around our communities?" asked Captain Willie Williams.

"No, sir. Not yet. But our concern is if their on-line stuff starts to get more heated, or something triggers action and they erupt."

"Yeah." Williams was an old pro. He had a veteran's nose for problems. He and Perkins glanced at one another. "I don't like it," he muttered. He shared another look with Perkins.

"OK, Maria. Good early warning. Keep us informed. Anything else? OK, that's it. Stay safe, everybody."

Chapter 54

"WE'VE FINALLY DEVELOPED some intel on the bombings, but we are far from an arrest," Perkins confessed the next morning to FBI regional director James Robertson. "It appears to be somebody with a particular grudge or a statement to make or something, but there have been no public claims to the media, no calls for stopping anything. Your office is coordinating the data on the explosives. I thought the Orlando bombing might generate some fresh intel or a lead. We talked to Sherriff Ramos and our departments are sharing information. We're both in the dark right now, to be honest. None of the incidents make sense."

Robertson was silent. "I get it, Perk. If this is a lone wolf and nobody's talking, it is really difficult." He paused as he slurped coffee. "Listen, I have to tell you something. You won't like it." Perkins tensed. "I'm getting a lot of pressure to turn over the entire Florida bombing case to this Crunciman character at Homeland Security. Four different locations where bombs exploded. There seems to be increasing violence and damage to property. There is a growing sentiment in DC that this is domestic terrorism. That's why we've got the Homeland people, to handle these kinds of larger cases."

"Have you met that asshole?"

"Once, at a conference in Washington. I didn't like him. Rude, arrogant. His reputation is that nobody likes him except his immediate team, but he's produced some results in a couple of cases."

Perkins sucked his upper lip. "I didn't like him either. He showed no respect to local law enforcement or elected officials." He paused. "Listen, James, can you get me a few more days? I think we are getting closer."

Closer to what Perkins wasn't sure. He hoped Robertson wouldn't ask.

"Well, I can probably fight it off for a little while. I know the Under Secretary and she likes me. Their department is also trying to be more considerate of local conditions and personnel, but Crunciman probably didn't read that memo. Or care."

"OK, I understand. Let me crank up my people again. I'll be in touch."

Good-byes concluded the conversation. Perkins leaned back and stretched his aching neck. It cracked satisfactorily.

There was a sharp rap on his door. Perkins looked up and waved in Lt Salazar.

"We've just had a tip on that drug connection I was talking about," she told the Sheriff. "I want to apply for a wire-tap on some character named Granny. We don't know who he is, but his name has come up in a couple of conversations. It sounds as if he might be the banker."

"Great. Go for it. Make sure the legal beagles give you enough latitude to spread the surveillance as you need it. Let me know if you need more manpower."

Salazar nodded and rose.

"Before you go, anything new on the bombings, Maria? I'm getting heat from Washington to let them take over the investigation."

Salazar winced. She understood the tensions between feds and local cops, who resented the Washington mafia swooping in to take credit. She looked Perkins in the eye. "I am working on some new intel now. I'll keep you informed."

Perkins looked sharply at her. "OK, good. I'll try to keep the hounds away for a few more days."

She nodded and left. Outside his office in the hall, her knees weakened as she leaned against the wall. What had she just done?

Perkins began to tackle the ever-mountainous pile of paperwork and government forms. Mary peered in but didn't disturb him. She brought him a coffee as a reward for taking on the hated paper chase.

Another knock. Captain Willie Williams filled the doorway. Perkins waved him in, glad of the break.

Williams sat down gingerly. His solid bulk had been known to crack chairs of inferior design or workmanship.

"Didn't like that Intel yesterday about those far-right crazies."

Perkins nodded agreement. "Scary people. We knew they were around but they've never caused us any serious problems.

Sounds as if they may become a bigger danger. They can explode so quickly. Riots. Torch parades." He paused. "Do you think they are involved in these bombings?"

WIlliams pondered then shook his head. "Doesn't sound like their MO. And why?"

Perkins grimaced. "Just a thought. Back to these alt-righters. Thoughts?"

We need to do some rapid-response training."

"You're right. Can you take that?"

The Captain nodded, paused, and continued. "I did get thinkin' more about the bombing thing." Perkins tossed his pen on the desk. He respected the instincts of the veteran officer. "It makes no sense. The city wants this Delvecchio project. The community loves it. The contractor won the tender fairly and got unanimous approval from city council. Who would want the project to fail?"

Perkins studied the captain's face. "OK, who?"

"I figure one of three. First, a competitor of the winning contractor. Starwind? That right? Maybe somebody who's got a business grudge. Another construction company, they'd have access to dynamite." Perkins nodded agreement. "Except the tender's been signed, it's not like they're going to re-tender unless Starwind walks away. Mr. Webster has said that won't happen. So I don't see it as a business thing."

"Second, political. Somebody out to gain political advantage, or stop the current council from getting credit, or somethin' like that. Somebody trying to make a statement."

Perkins thought about that. They both swallowed some coffee. "Revenge included in that scenario?"

Williams face split in a wide grin. "Yessir, just might be." Perkins nodded back.

"Let's keep door number 2 open."

"Third," Williams continued as he nodded agreement, "we just flat-out got ourselves a nut case. Somebody who likes to see things go boom in the night. Or a fire bug. Or some kind of domestic terrorist. Or some nut with a cause. If that's the case, we've got a big problem. Unless the person makes a mistake or somebody talks, we're not likely to grab 'em. But usually if it's political, they want the publicity."

Perkins nodded again. "Yeah. I see that, Willie. I agree with you. So where are we?"

"Not real sure, Sheriff. Like I said, I don't see this as a business competitor. Not real sure I see a legit political angle yet. I sorta think it's a nut job, which is the worst case for us. But I thought maybe I'd mosey on up to the state penitentiary and talk to the former mayor and the two councillors who are enjoying the state's hospitality. See if they've got any interest in this thing. I'm not real sure they do, but we could at least rule one scenario out. We didn't look at Kowalski's wife, the mayor's sister, too close."

"It'd be a nice day for a drive," Perkins finally said. "Why don't you take Maria Salazar with you?"

Williams nodded agreement. He rose cautiously. The chair manufacturer earned a 5-star review on Yelp.

<h1 style="text-align:center">CHAPTER 55</h1>

"DYLAN CORCORAN IS a slimy little weasel," Williams reported back to Perkins the next morning. Lt Salazar sat quietly beside him. "Whiny. Lies to his mother, and she's been dead five years. Looks like shit on a shingle that's been left out overnight in the rain."

It was a pretty graphic description for 8am, thought Perkins as he gnawed on an apple cruller. But from what he remembered of the former City Councillor, Willie had him nailed.

"He wouldn't know anything about anything if the guards didn't tell him when to eat and when to take a dump and when to go to sleep. Now. Tom Brady. The other councillor convicted. Also a slimy little weasel, but smart in a slimy little weaselly way. I couldn't stand him. Smirks. Picks his nose and flicks off the snot. Made me ill. I could see him seeking some kind of revenge for ending up in jail. He's still angry but I don't think he's smart enough to pull this off."

Willie paused to inhale a sugar donut and a bear claw. It didn't take long. He gulped some coffee and glanced at his notes. Perkins sat patiently. It is always dangerous to interrupt a grizzly while it is chowing down. Salazar sipped lemon tea.

"Former Mayor Smithfield. The slimiest of the three slimy varmints. Still bitter about what happened. He has neither forgotten nor forgiven those who trespassed against him. He still thinks he was set up and blames Corcoran for squealing like a stuck pig to the DA. He is amazed that he got caught. He still thinks he should be mayor. And I think he thinks he will be again, even though the Judge banned all of them from ever again seeking public office. Jail is just an inconvenience for him, a temporary set-back, not a game-changer." He stopped and looked at Perkins very directly. "I think the guy is a wild-eyed nut-case."

He checked the box of donuts, his hand waving over the remaining selection. Perkins watched in silent horror. Not the double chocolate! Not the double choc—damn.

Williams brushed a chocolate crumb from his lower lip and finished his report. "I think Smithfield is a dangerous little man who shows neither remorse nor an understanding of what he did and why it was illegal. He thought he was above the law. Still believes that. I don't think his wife has much to do with him anymore. She's only visited a couple of times. His sister has been over from Jacksonville three or four times, and Greg Kowalski once. His niece has visited a few times, his nephew never."

He paused once again to consult his notes. He looked up at Perkins. "Frankly, Sheriff, I just don't get any kind of vibe that either former councillor is a criminal mastermind, plotting revenge and ordering bombings. I don't think they have the resources or the partners or the smarts. The ex-mayor is even weirder but he is the angriest. I'm just not sure about him." Salazar nodded agreement.

Perkins thought about it. "I think you're right, Willie. But it helps us eliminate some suspects. Besides, the Orlando bombing doesn't fit into any kind of local revenge plot here. I'll let Sheriff Ramos know what you got. Maybe he'll have some new ideas. Thanks, Willie. Good effort."

The huge captain nodded, tested gravity versus bulk versus strength once again, and won the battle as he rose from the office chair. He blocked out most of the hall lighting as he exited the doorway.

A few minutes later, Perkins connected with Sheriff Ramos.

"You were right," Ramos began. "Crunciman is a major asshole. Tried to take over. Threatened me. Tried to muscle his way in here. Wore his stupid sunglasses throughout our conversation even though we were in my office. He travels in a three-car regatta. He thinks he's a big timer. We bounced him."

"Yeah, I hear you. I couldn't stand him. But, FYI, I've been doing some back-channel work with James Robertson in Atlanta. He's under a lot of pressure to hand over the entire bombing investigation to Crunciman. I'm buying us a little time, but the pressure is growing. If all four of us work together, we might fight 'em off. James has been giving me some tech data on the explosives. Your people have sent the remnants to the Atlanta office. If we can match the dynamite fingerprint, if it was from the same batch, maybe there's a connection and we can work together with him on isolating the source and resolving this case."

"Our people are liaising with your and the other two Sheriffs' departments." He paused. Perkins could hear him sipping something that he assumed was coffee. After all, it was still early morning.

"I've had our Intel people spit-balling scenarios for this. Nobody can figure out a motive. Nobody is claiming credit. My people can't understand the whole damn thing. You got anything, Perk, anything at all?"

"I went through the same kind of role-playing with my people. One of our senior captains went up to the pen to talk to the three idiot former council members down here who got convicted of fraud and corruption. He just reported to me that he doesn't think any of them qualify as a criminal mastermind. Imagine my shock. Anyway, we keep coming back to some kind of lone-wolf domestic terrorist."

Ramos's frustration blew through the phone line. "Yeah, we're pretty much in the same place. We didn't have the civic corruption stuff, well, not that anybody got caught yet, but the whole explosion scenario at these early-stage construction projects just doesn't make sense to any of us."

Silence as the two experienced Sheriffs thought it through.

"Damn. Well, let's keep the Washington assholes away. Stay in touch."

"You too. Stay safe."

Chapter 56

JUDGE CYNTHIA GREEN was dubious but finally signed off on the wide-ranging wiretap for 'Granny' and associates.

"And you don't know who this person is? Or the other, what is it? A Mr. Snives??"

"No, Your Honor, we aren't sure of either identity. We suspect Snives is a nick-name. But we are confident that this tap will help us identify or lead us to a major drug kingpin, whoever he may be."

She studied the police officer in front of her for a long moment, and then scrawled her signature on the warrant request form and handed it to her clerk. The two detectives nodded their thanks.

Two hours later an electronic tap was on the home phone of one of the low-level street pushers they had identified in a previous raid. It was a break for them to actually get a wired phone—most of the drug dealers were now using burner cell phones which they threw away on a regular basis. This idiot lived with his aunt who didn't own a cell phone and claimed she never would.

"We're looking for somebody named 'Granny,'" Detective Greenblatt told the officers monitoring the tap. "Grantland? Grantholme? No idea of his real name. That's what we're after, to identify the top echelon." He checked his notes. "Oh, and we've also heard about somebody named "Snives." That's a crappy nickname. Anyway, do what you can. Call me when you get any hits."

The detectives hit the street again. They cruised through neighborhoods where urban renewal plans were non-existent. They updated the Sheriff on the successful wiretap warrant for "Granny" and for "Snives."

The streets were offering no clues. Or perps. Lots of users, some sprawled in back alleys and street corners. A couple of hookers on their corners early, desperate to earn enough for their own fix.

Barred windows on the few stores that remained on the block reflected the dying sun. Dull reddish-brown stains near a couple of gutters were all that remained of past gun battles.

It was a place of desolation. Of broken dreams. Of shattered lives.

Chapter 57

SAMANTHA WAS ONLY paying half-attention to Perkin's chatter. She was pacing through her condo. The "Martinis and Manicures" party was just two days away. Her cleaning service had been in today. Now she was inspecting every surface with gimlet-eyed intensity.

Rosie paced after her. She added her own critical exploration, although Rosie was more focused on possible treats to be found on the floor rather than admiring the high polish on the red oak hardwood.

Perkins was sitting on the couch swallowing his IPA. He cut a chunk of nice sharp Vermont cheddar. Rosie suddenly abandoned Mommy to spend some quality time with Daddy. She was rewarded appropriately.

"So anyway, the guys finally get a warrant for a wiretap on this low-level drug scum and we get a hit on a Snives. Odd name. Can't identify him. At least it's a lead. Not like the bombing stuff. We've still got almost nothing on that. We can't figure it out. Who would bomb a just-started construction site? And not claim the credit? It is just weird."

He finished his ale and set down the glass. He eyed the cheddar again. Rosie was guarding it. He risked a finger to carve a little piece for each of them.

Samantha continued to review the barracks. She flicked at a potential piece of dust and consigned the culprit to lint-heaven.

"What?" She twitched as Perkins touched her shoulder.

"I asked, would you like me to top up your wine?"

"Oh. Yes. Fine. Thanks." She looked around the penthouse. "Sorry, honey, I'm just focused on the final party prep."

He handed her the goblet. "The place looks spotless," he said as she ran a finger over the top of her elegant home entertainment center. She nodded with satisfaction at the result.

"This is such a big deal for Kim. Our first big fund-raiser. I want it all to go over so well. Oh, thanks," she said as he popped a pitted date stuffed with a bit of the sharp cheddar into her mouth. "The ladies have to be impressed. And they'll be checking out my home and my housekeeping," she added darkly.

"It will be a fabulous event," he reassured her. "One of the greatest social events in the history of Port Manatee," he said, loading up on brownie points that he could draw upon when future transgressions would require them. "And you are the hostess who will set the standard that lesser mortals will seek to match for the next thousand years."

Samantha broke into laughter at that and finally stopped her military-precision barracks inspection. She looked at Perkins.

"Sorry. My mind has been wandering. Where do you want to go for dinner?"

"We could order in," he suggested, kissing her left ear lobe. "And then see what else might transpire."

"Bring food into my nice clean house?" she demanded in horror. "Not a chance. The crumbs. What if something spilled?" She shuddered at the thought.

"Well, we've got Rosie the canine vacuum cleaner," Perkins reminded her.

"No. N. O. It's a warm night. How about we go for a nice seafood salad at The Drunken Monkey?"

"Whatever you desire. I think they'll let Rosie on the patio."

"Yes. Let's go."

They walked the two blocks to the beach-style restaurant where Carlos, the owner, welcomed them. He escorted them to a prime table and took drink orders. He got a bowl of water for Rosie.

"This was the place we first met," teased Perkins as they clinked glasses.

"Yes, when you tried to arrest me!" Samantha responded. She was still a little testy about that episode.

"Well, you and Kim and Samira against those drunken college boys who tried to hit on you," Perkins recalled with a laugh. "What a mismatch that was! The three of you standing together looking all valiant and indignant, the one guy on the ground puking after Kim, ah, disabled him with that kick."

"And you threatened to handcuff me!" Samantha reminded him.

"Yes. Good times."

The arrival of their seafood salads probably saved him from further damage. Then the waiter brought a small plate of cooked chicken for Rosie. He looked at the table and said, "Oops, no cutlery. Let me get you knives and forks." He turned away.

Samantha looked puzzled for a moment. "Knives. Weren't you mumbling about knives in the condo?"

Perkins also looked puzzled. Then it hit him. "Oh. No. Not knives. Snives. Whatever, whoever that is. Odd name, but it came up as part of a drug investigation. Along with somebody named Granny. We don't know who he is either."

The waiter returned with the cutlery. Samantha slowly un-wrapped it and began poking at the crab and shrimp in her salad. Perkins could see her mind spinning. He was hungry, so he dove into his salad. It was great. He dipped a quartered hard-boiled egg into the piquant citrus dressing.

Samantha finally ate a couple of bites. Perkins was half-way through his plate. Rosie had demolished the chicken and was lobbying for some seafood.

"Uh. Sweetie. This is going to sound sort of, well, odd." Samantha spoke slowly as she continued to poke around in her salad. She found a nice piece of lobster claw and popped it into her mouth. "You know that I never, uh, interfere in your police work…"

Perkins grimaced at that. There was significant evidence to the contrary. He put down his fork and knife. Somehow his salad had disappeared. He took a sip of his IPA and braced himself.

"…and this probably isn't really what you're after." She nibbled a piece of lettuce. He waited, trying not to show impatience. He'd learned that she would get there, but it was often a long and winding road. Where was Paul McCartney when you really needed him?

"Drugs, right?"

He nodded agreement.

"Well, here's the thing." She sampled another piece of the crab. "You know that I'm volunteering at Whispering Palms, the retirement home?" He nodded. "Well, I've seen a couple of guys there. They visit their grandmother. A lot." She picked another bite of shrimp and lettuce. "Like, every day."

Perkins was trying hard to follow the narrative, but the road signs were rather murky.

"Anyway, these two guys. One of them is named Snively. So, maybe his nickname is Snives. Rhymes with knives. That's what triggered my thinking here. And then there's their grand-mother. Mrs. Snively. Could she be 'Granny'? And the two guys always have this big black leather satchel with them. And they always sneak out the side exit. And besides, Mrs. Harris doesn't like them, and she's been a teacher for forty years and is really sharp," she finished in a rush.

Perkins was struggling to keep up, but the mists were be-ginning to clear.

"Wait. This young man is Snively. What kind of name is Snively? Anyway, nickname is Snives? The waiter said knives. That reminded you of this guy at the long-term care home. And you put together the grandmother and Mr. Snively and spun it to Granny and Snives and you think they might be dealing drugs?"

Samantha beamed at him. "Well, yes. Maybe. I don't know. But isn't that a pretty good, what do you guys call it, a deduction?"

She stabbed her fork into the last shrimp. She sipped her wine and eyed Perkins over the rim of her glass. He was deep in thought.

She quietly fed Rosie a bit of the cheese bread that had come with dinner. Sipped some more wine. She was feeling quite triumphant. Maybe being awarded her honorary detec-tive badge was a possibility again, even after she'd blown the last case about the bombings so badly.

Finally he looked across the table at her. "I believe you may have just cracked this case. Are you going to Whispering Palms tomorrow?"

"I could. It isn't a regular schedule for me, so sure, I can go whenever I want. Do you want to visit it?"

"I do. Not officially, but with you, just to see the place. Have a little look around. No uniform or anything. We'll take your car. When's a good time?"

"Uh, ten? I'll pick you up at headquarters? That'll get us there in time for morning coffee with the residents. I want you to meet Mrs. Harris. She's special."

Perkins nodded agreement. He looked around for their waiter. "Dinner's on the Sheriff's Department tonight," he smiled at her. "You're now practically a consultant on this case." The waiter presented the check. Perkins paid. He gathered Rosie's leash and looked at Samantha. "And as the Sheriff for this here town, I think you've earned a special reward tonight. Maybe you can think of something you'd like me to do for you?"

Samantha slowly ran her tongue across her lower lip. "Yes, yes I believe I can think of a suitable reward." He jumped up from the table. "Hang on, cowboy. Save your strength." She grinned lasciviously. "You're going to need it."

Chapter 58

SAMANTHA WHEELED HER convertible into the parking lot at Whispering Palms at 10:23 the next morning. Perkins sat in the passenger seat and looked as if he had just survived a disaster of monumental proportions.

"I've got to get you into a defensive driving course," he mumbled. Samantha ignored him as she hopped out of the car. Rosie followed her, happy to be back where all the nice old folks petted her. She was strutting across the lawn when an impudent squirrel raced across the grass. Rosie was outraged.

Perkins followed the two, limping just a tiny bit. Certain excesses the night before had left his right quad a little tight. Between the leg and the car-ride, it had so far been an alarming morning for the usually stalwart sheriff. The things I do in the line of duty, he thought to himself as he followed the two females who apparently now ran his life.

Rosie was greeted joyously by the residents. She immediately embarked on a victory lap of the common room. Samantha and the Sheriff stood just inside the doorway watching Rosie's parade.

"You brought her back! Wonderful!" They turned to see Connie Brighthouse standing beside them.

"Oh, hi, Connie. I want you to meet LeRoy Perkins. Mrs. Brighthouse is the General Manager here."

"A pleasure, ma'am."

"It is indeed, Sheriff. I hadn't realized you and Samantha were friends. She is turning out to be a treasure here at Whispering Palms."

"Yes, we are friends. She mentioned she and Rosie were visiting this morning. Since Rosie used to be my dog, I thought I'd see what was going on." Perkins grinned at the two ladies as Samantha blushed just a tad.

"Well, you are certainly welcome. And thank you for bringing Rosie again. Our residents love her. Forgive me now; I have a meeting with the nursing department." Her face clouded. "Our mortality rate has been increasing lately." She sighed and bustled down the hall.

"She seems very pleasant."

"Yes, she is. Runs a good home, from what I've seen. Oh, there's Mrs. Harris. You must meet her."

Samantha tugged on his arm and they walked over to the sturdy woman in her wheelchair. Samantha introduced them.

"So. You're the one who's got Samantha all aflutter," Mrs. Harris said with a twinkle in her eye.

Perkins laughed. Samantha blushed a little deeper.

"Well, ma'am, I'm not sure if she's aflutter or I'm just a flap-jack on her griddle, but yes, she is very special to me."

Mrs. Harris roared in laughter. "A flapjack on her...that's really funny. You're a southern boy, aren't you?"

"Yes, ma'am, I am. Proud of it."

"So am I. And I am very glad to meet you, Sheriff. I've been asking her to bring you in so I can size you up." She stared him up and down. "Fine figure of a man. Polite. Owns a dog. You have your own handcuffs. I suspect you can keep her in line most of the time. Yes, I think you'll do very nicely," she said, turning to Samantha who by now was beet red.

"You look after her," she warned Perkins as she started to roll away, "or you'll have me to deal with!"

Perkins flushed as well. There was nothing like a tough veteran teacher to bring back childhood fears and terrors.

They could hear her laughter as she rolled towards the coffee and cookies. Samantha just looked at Perkins and waved her hands helplessly. He nodded back, equally nonplussed.

Suddenly Samantha jabbed him with a sharp elbow. He flinched and looked at her. She was tilting her head at the lobby. Perkins turned slowly and saw two young men pass the registration desk and head to the elevators. One had a large black leather satchel that looked mostly empty.

Perkins watched them carefully as they shuffled in front of the elevator and then shouldered their way in when the doors opened. A couple exited the elevator, looking back at the two men. The door shut. The indicator hit 2 a moment later.

"That's young Mr. Snively," Samantha whispered to him. "Mrs. Snively's apartment is 209."

Perkins nodded, his eyes still locked on the elevator. "Where is the side exit you mentioned?"

"Down the hall about halfway. It is glass-walled, so you can see into it from the window in the north reading room."

"Why don't we just mosey over to the north reading room? Rosie looks fine for a few more minutes."

Samantha quietly led him out the door and down the hall. They moved into the reading room. There was no one else there.

Five minutes later two figures hopped down the stairs. The black satchel looked much heavier. Perkins silently followed their exit. He moved closer to the window and watched them jump into a late-model F150. Black. Big wheels. Tinted windows. He caught the first four numbers of the license plate. He scribbled them into his notebook.

"OK, good. Thank you. Let's get Rosie. I've got work to do."

It took some time to get Rosie extricated from the fawning seniors who were excited to see her again, but eventually they ended up back in Samantha's car. Rosie barked at the nasty little squirrel that had the audacity to reappear on the lawn.

"You did good," Perkins announced. Samantha flushed with pride at the compliment. Then she realized he was talking to Rosie as he offered a couple of treats.

She rolled her eyes, dashed through a yellow light, swerved around a senior driving a large gold Caddy as if he was practicing being a float in the Santa Claus parade, and pulled into the Sheriff's Department parking lot.

She thought Perkins fervently crossing himself was quite unnecessary.

He turned to her. "You did good too," he said with a grin. "I don't have any treats for you right here, but maybe tonight I will think of something special."

She melted as she stared at him. "Yes, I think you should figure out some treat for me tonight." Rosie alerted at the word 'treat' and peered anxiously into the front seat, her front paws scrabbling over the seat back. It just wouldn't do to miss any possible treats.

He gave her a quick peck and opened the door. He looked back at Rosie. "Come with me. We've got work to do. And Mommy has to get ready for her big party. To which neither one of us is invited," he said with a wink.

Rosie hopped out and he closed the door. "Thanks again. I think we're onto something. I'll call you later."

He and Rosie strode into HQ. Samantha looked at them as they disappeared into the building. She shook her head to refocus. She had to do the last fitting for her new dress, go over the final security and parking issues at Sapphire Blue, confirm the names of the manicurists, get the good china out and finish touching-up her penthouse for the party.

She fired up the convertible and tore out of the parking lot. A Deputy's SUV swerved desperately to get out of her way. Samantha just kept going. It certainly wasn't her fault if the Sheriff didn't hire very skilled drivers.

CHAPTER 59

"WELL, IT'S THE damnedest thing," Perkins reported to the Lieutenant who headed his Drug Task Force. "I think these two bangers are using their grandmother's apartment in this long-term care facility as their drug storage locker. And maybe as their bank. Whether Granny is running the thing or she is a dupe, I don't know. But I think you should set up surveillance for a couple of days and see what you can shake out."

"Running drugs out of a senior's home?" The LT was incredulous. "I've never heard of anything like that. Anywhere."

"I don't think anybody has. Who would ever think of that as the headquarters for a drug operation? Or a distribution location?" Perkins shook his head. "Oh, the plate is on a big black Ford truck. The usual pimped-out style. The plate's first four letters are TYGP."

The LT made a note. "We'll get right on it. I'll get a squad to look for these two and set up a loose tail. And we'll check out Granny. Snively, right? Hell of a name." He shook his head and went out the door. "Hell of a situation."

Perkins settled behind his desk to deal with the never-ending flow of paperwork.

Rosie decided to check on the snack status in the Detectives' bullpen.

CHAPTER 60

THE MORNING OF the 26th dawned as a beautiful Florida day. Martinis & Manicures Day.

Samantha spent the morning in final preparation. Placing the bouquets of flowers strategically throughout her penthouse. Ensuring enough serving platters were available. Brushing off the lanai one last time. Finalizing the eclectic playlist of interesting background music with Siri.

The caterers, liquor deliveries, bartenders, and sous chef began to arrive after lunch. The guard house re-confirmed the reserved parking spaces for guests. The two young manicurists arrived to set up their tables on the lanai.

"One's from Vietnam, one's from Louisiana," confided Samantha to Kim.

"So, neither one will speak much English."

Samira was next to arrive. The Sams Club members had agreed to come early to handle all the final details as Samantha got dressed. Kim was wearing a vibrant dark red pant suit. Samira was in a stunning forest green dress.

Samantha disappeared for a few minutes and got ready for her party. She reappeared in the living room to exclamations of approval.

"You clean up pretty good for a Yankee," Kim praised as she studied the midnight blue fabric that somehow shimmered and revealed varying hues of blue as Samantha moved. It was knee-length. Samantha wore a twisted gold necklace and two bracelets. Her burnished-gold hair was swept to one side. Her earrings were her mother's diamond studs. Her shoes were fabulous— matching dark blue stilettos that accented her long, beautifully sculpted legs.

"We all look great! I think we deserve a Kimtini!"

Samantha led the three to the bar, where one of the mixologists from Uncle Larry's Booze Barn was set up. "Three of them, please."

"My pleasure. I'm Sandy, by the way. And I love the Kimtini! Who thought that up?"

"We all did. It took some practice and some mistakes." The three friends giggled at their memories of the night they invented the cocktail. "But the end result is really good, I think."

Sandy expertly mixed the drinks, dropped in the five pomegranate seeds and presented the icy glasses to the ladies, who toasted one another.

"Ah, that's lovely," Samira announced after her first sip. The security buzzer went off. The first arrival. The party was officially off and running.

It seemed as if the 23 women leaders who had accepted the invitation were all anxious to arrive on time. 22 of the 23 entered within an eight-minute window. These were intelligent, successful women who respected time.

These were also the leading women of Port Manatee in business, the arts, law, the university, medicine, health care and banking. Samantha and Samira were busy greeting and welcoming them, and then introducing each to Kim who chatted with each woman individually.

The guests were smart, tough and creative. They knew how to dress and each had made a special effort for this party. Many of them already knew one another. Those who didn't quickly began to connect with others.

The Kimtini was a smash success. Sandy was kept busy mixing the special drink. The two waitresses from La Casa Adrianna began to circulate with the selection of special tapas. A few of the ladies wandered onto the patio and got their nails done.

The 23rd lady to arrive was 40 minutes late. Judge Cynthia Green explained she was late because she had been sentencing some scum-ball to 12 years in prison for elder abuse. She was applauded and a Kimtini was handed to her.

The volume picked up a decibel or two with each round of Kimtinis. The tapas were devoured as the guests exclaimed over the unique selection. There was soon a line-up at the manicure tables.

It became a magical evening of silk and luster and glowing women.

Talk ebbed and flowed amongst the guests as they sipped, nibbled and formed new groups only to break away moments later to create fledgling new packs and pacts. The dresses were as sparkling as the conversations. No matter their intellectual or professional achievements, none of the women wanted to be out-shone or out-shoed in such a gathering of esteemed peers.

Four potential business deals were ventured. Three charitable opportunities to improve the community were broached. Six recommendations for the latest hot restaurants were exchanged. One new romance was kindled.

When Samantha finally tapped her glass to get everyone's attention, it was obvious the party was a smash success.

"Thank you all for coming," she began as the room quieted. "Welcome to my home. This is the first time that we've done anything like this, and we are so grateful to each of you for making the time. And for contributing!"

The ladies laughed. They had all been at a hundred fundraisers in their careers. This one, however, would be memorable.

"You all know how important it is to have strong local government," Samantha continued. "That's why we got Kim Sharpe elected to City Council, and why we really appreciate your support for her political career. So, I'd like to ask Kim to say a few words."

There was the awkward light applause that always comes when one hand is holding a glass and the other hand is left to quietly tap the other wrist. It didn't matter. Kim looked around the room and smiled.

"When Samantha told me I was running for city council last year," she began as the guests chuckled, "I never dreamed that I would win. Or just months later be at a fabulous event like this evening." She turned to look directly at Samantha, who had stepped back to give Kim center stage. "I owe you a big "Thank You" for both events. You helped me to KICK ASS!"

A big cheer as everyone remembered Kim's devastating line against her opponent in the last election. Several smart questions about improving Port Manatee and the future direction of city council were asked by the audience. Kim handled them smoothly. She was turning into a more confident public speaker. Even the question about the bombings at the Delvecchio Bridge project she dealt with capably.

After allowing the Q&A to continue for several minutes, Samantha nodded to the servers and to the bartender. She then stepped back into the center of the room.

"I think that's enough formality for tonight. Kim wants to spend more time with each of you, of course. Let's get back to the party. I think we have some dessert items for you to sample, because there are no diets allowed here tonight! There is coffee and tea on the sideboard. And I know you're all busy and have to leave sometime, but there is a little thank you gift bag for each of you at the door. I hope you have enjoyed the party. We are really grateful that you came."

Applause. The servers circulated with trays of mini iced donuts, a decadent lemon tartlet and spoons of citrus sorbet. Two plates of hand-crafted dark chocolate truffles appeared.

Groups continued to form and then break apart in the natural ebb and flow as the party wound down. The first few to depart began to drift out of the condo. Samira was positioned at the door and made sure each of them got a gift bag and a big thank you. Air kisses were exchanged.

Kim was engaged in a deep discussion about future growth in Port Manatee with three of the ladies. The banker was particularly vocal. The manicurists began to wrap up their stations and were soon gone. The waitresses made a final sweep through the party with the dessert trays. Coffee was sipped. A few more guests departed, then the rest.

The clean-up of the kitchen was soon complete. The chef and servers left. Sandy wrapped up her bar and took her equipment with her. The people who had helped so much to make the party so successful were thanked profusely and received a gift bag. There would be big tips coming to all of them. Finally it was down to Kim, Samira and Samantha.

Samantha slipped off her fabulous heels and sank into the couch with a happy sigh.

"I think it was a smash success. Everybody seemed to get along. The food was great. The Kimtini a hit." She stretched in an exhausted way. "Kim spoke well. Good job, sweetie."

"I had several really interesting conversations," Kim contributed. "I'm going to follow up with three or four of them. There were some provocative ideas about city-building and what we at city hall can do to expedite some decisions. It was great, Samantha. Thank you so much."

"Yup. Great party, Samantha. This will be remembered in social circles here for a long time. I think we should keep this group together somehow. They are too smart and too caring for us to lose their support through lack of momentum. Not to mention that they are all well-off."

"I agree with you, Samira. Let's do that." Samantha yawned. "It will be interesting to see what donations might come in after this." She yawned again. "I'm beat. I'm going to bed. Thank you for helping me with this."

Her friends straggled out. Samantha undressed, got into comfortable pyjamas and was asleep within minutes.

CHAPTER 61

TWO MEMBERS OF the drug squad sat in an innocuous gray Honda sedan that needed a wash. They were parked in the strip mall parking lot across the street from Whispering Palms.

"Weirdest lead I've ever heard of," Detective Michael Brolio said to his partner.

"For sure. If the Sheriff hadn't been the one, I'da never given it a chance," agreed Detective Francesca Ortega. "Who ever heard of an old lady in a nursing home running a drug ring?"

The scraggly palm tree on the boulevard gave them a little shade as the morning sun continued its path upward. It was going to be another sweltering day.

The two detectives were used to waiting patiently on a stake-out. The LT's orders had been to do surveillance on the home, looking for a big black truck with two possible perps.

Almost an hour had drifted by when Ortega poked her partner. "Look. Big black truck all pimped out. Tinted windows. The whole shebang. Can you get the plate? OK, that's a match."

Brolio began to focus the long-distance lens on his camera as two men exited the truck. The tall lean one reached into the truck bed for a black satchel. It appeared to have something of substance in it because he hefted it up and then carried it towards the retirement home front entrance with his other arm extended a bit to help balance the load.

Brolio shot pictures as the two vanished into the seniors' home. He quickly checked the digital read-out. "Good. Got a couple of face shots." He downloaded the pictures to the on-board computer.

Ortega got out of the car. "I got this."

It was less than twenty minutes later when they saw the two men exit through the side emergency stairwell. The satchel looked even heavier than when they had entered.

"Snives is the tall, skinny guy with the satchel," confirmed Ortega. "Deveron Snively." She punched the computer in the car and waited a moment. "Huh," she grunted. "A couple of minor drug busts as a teen. Ran with a gang for a while. One charge of beating up some teenager. Got time served. Had a more serious charge of attempted manslaughter a year ago. Another gang thing. Nobody would testify against him, so the DA finally kicked it."

She hit more buttons. "Camero Gomez. Rap sheet is pretty light. One for holding marijuana, one for B&E when he was 17." She read his record carefully. "Another for theft under $5,000. Did a couple of months for that one. They've run together for a couple of years since they met in juvie."

"What about the old lady?"

Ortega summoned the computer wizard that connected her to the state police data center. She punched some buttons and waited. She grunted in frustration and hit some more keys.

"Well. She's not in the system under that name. Tamara Snively. I got a hit under Tamara Azikawe. I guess that was her first husband. Married three times, divorced a long time ago from her first two. She's had three kids with at least two different fathers. Her daughter died from cancer a couple of years ago. One son was in the army, now lives in San Diego. The other one is in and out of trouble in Miami-Dade. Deveron is Tamara's grandson."

"God bless our computer systems," Brolio confessed. "That just saved us a lot of shoe leather." He waited for the two suspects to get in their truck and drive away. Only then did he start the Honda and slowly pull out to follow the black truck.

Of course, the tracking device that Ortega had planted inside the back bumper of the truck made it a lot easier to follow.

CHAPTER 62

THE TWO DETECTIVES tracked the black truck for two days. It hadn't taken them long to confirm that they were chasing two drug dealers. Brolio continued to shoot pictures as they hit street corners where they gave baggies to their distributors for the street.

Money was passed. Drugs were distributed. Sales were made. It was a depressingly familiar scenario for the two veteran undercover cops.

When they reported to Perkins, their case was overwhelming.

"We figure it's time to bust Granny," Brolio told him. "We'll need a warrant and we'll need to figure out how not to scare the crap out of the other residents. We also need to decide if we do it when Snively and Camero are in her room, or do it separately and maybe arrest the two of them in the parking lot or somewhere to avoid any unpleasantness in the home."

"The GM there seems pretty grounded," Perkins told them. "Connie Brighthouse. Samantha knows her. I met her. Seems solid. Not sure she's ever had to deal with something like this, of course."

Both detectives smiled thinly. Yes, this case was one for the record books.

Perkins drummed his desk. "I'm thinking to do them separately. There is a big risk if we try to take them together in her apartment. If the bangers have guns, and that's a pretty safe bet, who knows what might happen. I'm thinking Granny won't be packing, but... Get her out of the place and then do the boys in the parking lot. It should just take a couple of squad cars and you guys."

The detectives nodded. "We'll need to get a search warrant for #209," Ortega said. "Judge Green should be fine. She gave us the wiretap."

"I really want to protect the residents," the Sheriff emphasized. "Let's avoid unnecessary noise, action, anything." He thought for a moment. "I wonder if we should get some inside help? There's this really sharp lady there, Mrs. Harris. I think we could get her to gather the other residents into the common room and keep them calm. Samantha and Rosie could help. And we need Mrs. Brighthouse to be aware. I don't know if Granny needs daily meds or whatever, so we'll have to check that out as well. I'm told she is a tough old broad who doesn't socialize much inside the residence." He snorted. "Maybe she'll make new friends in the slammer."

The detectives grinned and gathered their notes.

"Let me know when you want to do the raid," Perkins told them as they departed. "I need a little time to get Samantha and the gang ready."

Nods of agreement. The door closed. Perkins spun his pen on his desk. Raiding a seniors' home to take down a street drug operation! What was coming next in his city?

CHAPTER 63

THE FOLLOWING TUESDAY dawned sunny and hot. The logistics were in place for the take-down. Sheriff Perkins and Captain Williams had been briefed at 8am on the final action plan.

Detectives Ortega and Brolio would meet with Connie Brighthouse at 10am. Rosie and Samantha would arrive at 10:13. Rosie would entertain the residents from 10:17 until an estimated 10:58. Samantha would brief Mrs. Harris at 10:20. The two detectives would execute the search warrant and presumed arrest in 209 at 10:28. Mrs. Snively would be exited down the side staircase into a waiting police vehicle by 10:36. She would be taken directly to the Sheriff's department for processing and the formal arrest procedures. The two detectives would be joined by a forensics team in 209 at 10:49. It was expected they would be at their search for a couple of hours, finding and bagging evidence.

In the meantime, another plain-clothes team would be staking out the parking lot. Two squad cars would be waiting in the vicinity to help with the arrest of Snively and Gomez once they got out of their truck and began to move toward the entrance of Whispering Pines. Typically the two arrived between 11 and 11:30am. They would go upstairs to do their business, and the take-down would happen just before they started to enter the building. The theory was that the bag would be filled with drugs, money, and/or guns.

Perkins was emphatic that the safety of the residents was paramount.

By 11:30, the morning coffee klatch would be over inside the common room and the residents would be allowed to drift back to their own apartments, hopefully completely unaware of the drama that had gone on. Rosie and Samantha would safely exit the building at 11:45. Lunch at noon as usual in the home.

Easy. Simple. Neat. No hassle, no problems. That's what the raid team promised Perkins.

One little old lady in a long-term care facility. Two unsuspecting not-very-bright drug dealers in a parking lot. What could possibly go wrong?

ᑕHAPTER 64

"**W**ELL, THE FIRST thing was, Mrs. Brighthouse freaked," reported Detective Ortega late that afternoon. "She'd never experienced any police action inside a senior's residence, I guess. She panicked. We didn't expect that. She wanted to call their lawyers. We were kind of stuck. We couldn't deny her that right, but as soon as lawyers get involved, you know that it usually all goes screwy-bonkers. Anyway, she throws us out of her office while she calls the ambulance chaser."

Ortega swallowed some water. Perkins and Captain Williams listened in silence.

"Anyway, I guess her assistant was eavesdropping on her phone call and overheard something about Mrs. Snively. After we left the office she sneaks up to the second floor to squeal. We didn't know. Our timetable is starting to look a bit tight so we need to push this along. We don't want the old lady still around when the two punks show up and we take them down, right? We don't want any problems. We want it all nice and clean, just like you ordered. Meanwhile we check that Samantha and Rosie arrived, the rest of the residents in the common room start fawning all over the dog, great dog by the way, and we see Samantha briefing the old lady in the wheelchair. Mrs. Harris. That all seems to be going OK so we hustle back to Mrs. Brighthouse's office after the call to her lawyer is finished."

"We've got the warrant," continued Brolio, "so we're thinking that we're still good. Time's getting a little short so we drop a copy of the warrant on her desk and hustle up to find 209. Door's locked. We hear Mrs. Snively inside in her crapper flushing stuff. She won't let us in. We bang harder, she's hollering at us, the door is locked, and it's gettin' sorta messy. A couple of residents hear the commotion and they come outta their rooms. Last thing we want is an audience, right? We can hear the flushing still going on inside her room so we decide we need to go in by force. Well, not force, really. More of an enhanced entry protocol. Anyway, my size 13 gets the call. We bust into the room and here's this mean-faced woman screaming at us as she's flushing substances that we strongly suspect to be drugs. Most likely cocaine and fentanyl in little baggies. We dive for those to stop her. She is bellowing and clawing at us. The residents who aren't at the coffee party start to holler at us because they don't know what's happening. One guy shakes his cane, another one threatens us with his walker. They don't get that we're the good guys."

Perkins looked at Williams. Once that gigantic red screw-up ball starts rolling downhill, it's pretty hard to stop.

Brolio drew a deep breath and reviewed his notes. "There still aren't any residents from the party downstairs back on 2, so we figure Samantha and Rosie and Mrs. Harris have got things under control. Then Mrs. Brighthouse comes rushing up the stairs and looks at the broken door. Oh, did I mention when the door jumped out into the hallway and accidentally crashed into my foot, there was a bit of damage?"

Perkins made a note: call his lawyer.

"Anyway, we're inside the room trying to wrestle Mrs. Snively into submission. She's a tough old bat. She's hollering and squirming and I guess Mrs. Brighthouse had never seen a police take-down before so she's flapping her arms and shouting at us. We finally get the cuffs on her. The old lady, not the GM. We read her her rights, we drop the search warrant on her desk, the whole shebang. All nice and legal. Francesca pushes Mrs. Brighthouse into the hall. Well, not push so much as personally escorts out."

Williams side-eyed Perkins.

"It's a little hard to shut the door at this point because the door doesn't really exist except for a few shards of wood. You know, since it had attacked my foot. Some of the residents are now standing outside looking in and they see Mrs. Snively handcuffed and on her bed. They go crazy. Sort of mob mentality I guess, to protect your friends or somethin'. Anyhoo, they start to come into the room. We're trying to politely tell them no, stay out, this is a crime scene, and meanwhile the Snively b—uh, witch, is cursing a blue streak at us. I'm shocked she knew some of those words."

Ortega took a deep breath and picked up the narrative.

"Michael sees this huge chest of drawers in her room, an armoire I think they call it. There's a big lock on it. I mean, this is one big piece of furniture just to store grannie's panties, if you know what I mean. We want a little peek inside. We politely ask Mrs. Snively for the key. She says a couple of things about my mother that would not be appreciated at our family's Thanksgiving dinner table. Anyway, that's about when the shooting started."

Perkins' head slumped.

"Turns out that Tweedledee and Tweedledum have arrived early because Mrs. Snively gave them a panic phone call after the secretary squealed on us. They come charging into the parking lot about 80 miles an hour, slam on the brakes, jump out of their truck and our guys step out to arrest them. The bangers both pull out Glocks and start firing. Our guys dive for cover, get behind a couple cars, they're returning fire as these two are running for the front door to rescue Granny. From what we got told, Mrs. Harris and Samantha are in the reading room watching this go down. Mrs. Harris figures the situation out first and she tells Samantha to run and lock the front door. Samantha tears off, Rosie starts chasing her down the hall, the residents figure out there's a gun battle going on outside the big picture window in the common room, and a bunch of screaming starts. I heard it was sort of chaotic."

Perkins's hands had clenched at Samantha's involvement in the gun battle. The two detectives looked at him nervously. Involving the Sheriff's girlfriend in a gun fight probably wasn't going to lead to a quick promotion. And if you looked at their report on the raid in a certain mean-spirited kind of way, it was kind of a shit-show so far.

"Samantha gets to the front door and throws the lock. She's smart enough to turn around and get behind one of those big pillars in the lobby. Rosie is running around barking but finally comes over to her. I guess Mrs. Harris blocks the door to the hallway with her wheelchair and won't let anyone out, but the old folks inside are a bit, um, upset. We were told that a few comments might have been, ah, exchanged. A few coffee cups might have been accidentally broken. A few mini-muffins were maybe thrown. Apple spice, I heard."

Williams almost cracked a smile at that. He bent his head over his pad and made a couple more notes.

"Then the head nurse arrives to try to calm things down. We heard a couple of the old ladies used the opportunity to settle an old Bingo feud, something about mis-marking a card, by tossing a coupla muffins at each other. Some nasty words were exchanged. The nurse tried to break it up but I guess he really got it in the ear."

"The, ah, lovely ladies of a certain age said a few things to the nurse?"

"No, he actually caught a couple of muffins in the ear. Lemon-cranberry, we heard."

"What was his name?"

"Nurse."

"Yes, what was the nurse's name?"

"Head Nurse."

"I know he's the head nurse. Now, what is the nurse's name?"

"Nurse."

Williams slapped a big hand down on the desk. It sounded like a crack of thunder. Everybody in the room jerked.

The Captain carefully enunciated every word between clenched teeth as steam rose from his nostrils. "What. Was. The. Name. Of. The. Nurse?"

"I. Told. You. Nurse."

"For the last damn time, tell me the name of the head nurse who was in this incident!"

"Oh! Gosh. This is really funny, Captain, you're just going to split a gut laughing." Ortega eyed William's ample torso and regretted that last phrase. "Anyway," she hurried on, "now I've got you. This is so funny. The Head Nurse is named Nurse. Nick Nurse. Isn't that a riot?"

This time it was Williams who bowed his head. Perkins was stone-faced. Ortega waited a moment. Looking back on that last line, maybe 'riot' wasn't the best choice of words. However, no thunderbolts struck her so she continued the narrative.

"Anyway, upstairs, we've both got our guns out because we don't know if the fight is coming inside or not. The Snively ogre still won't give up the key to the armoire. We remind her of the warrant. She reminds us to go and get—well, that suggestion may not be pertinent right now. She's writhing around on the bed, her hands cuffed behind her back, she's hollering about police brutality—as if!—the other residents are getting a little restless, Mrs. Brighthouse is dashing around between looking out at the parking lot and inside 209 and trying to calm the angry residents and keep an eye on Mrs. Snively. We're still trying to figure out the gun battle and we keep hearing shots fired, we can hear more sirens on the way, and then one of the residents comes out of her room into the hallway and says we're all on TV."

Perkins groaned. He couldn't help it.

Detective Brolio bravely picked up the next phase.

"Anyway, the old folks all want to see themselves on TV so they disappear into their rooms. Turns out the local cable channel has a helicopter covering the scene. Great, right? Nothing like a little free publicity for our Sheriff's department."

Williams grabbed Perkins' arm to stop him reaching for his service revolver.

"Ah. Well. So, about that moment Francesca spots a necklace on Mrs. Snively and it looks as if there's a key attached to the chain. She asks very politely if she could remove the necklace to admire it. Mrs. Snively said some more things about Detective Ortega's mother and somehow the chain got a little broken when Mrs. Snively needed a bit of help to take it off."

Perkins interrupted. "But if her hands were behind—. Oh. Never mind."

Brolio nodded. "So Francesca somehow finds the necklace in her hands and gosh, there's this key attached, and so she deduces that it just might open the lock on the armoire and she tries it and wow, it does. Mrs. Snively is really hollering at that point, saying some really mean things about my mom and dad and suggesting that I was in the church scratching myself when they got married, nasty stuff like that. Kind of hurt me, to be honest. Maybe I have a case for slander. Anyway, Francesca opens the lock and pulls open the doors and holy crap, there's these stacks of cash on the shelves. Never seen anything like it. I mean, it was piled up. And a bunch of little baggies of pills and white powder we believe to be cocaine. Mrs. Brighthouse has just come back and she sees that and stops dead and says, 'Oh my' and sinks into a chair. Mrs. Snively is screaming her head off that she's never seen that money and didn't know anything about drugs being in there."

Perkins made another note: see my therapist. He thought for a moment, scratched that out and made a new note: get a therapist.

"The shooting has stopped," Detective Ortega continued, "and we're not hearing anything inside, so we figure the cops outside have made the arrests. We've had our radios turned down but we fire 'em back up and suddenly hear one of the guys shouting that they've got one perp down but the other is entering the building. Well, that changes things. We make sure the residents are in their rooms watching themselves on TV, so they're all real happy. We can't shut Mrs. Snively's door because of course that door doesn't really exist anymore. So we shove her in the bathroom and shut that door. Mrs. Brighthouse decides to sit in a chair in the far corner of the room. I have to say that she's looking a little pale. Not really sure why."

Perkins was looking a little pale himself as he stared daggers at the two detectives. They both swallowed hard but courageously continued. The phrase "career-limiting" crossed Brolio's mind.

"Looking back on it, I guess it may not have been the typical day of a quiet seniors' home administrator," Ortega admitted. "Oh well. Things are pretty calm now, and we're crouched inside 209 when we see the emergency exit stairwell door open. This tall skinny dude holding a gun comes through, looks around, sees the door on the hallway floor outside his grandmother's room and for some reason he goes ballistic. Starts waving his gun around and cursing and threatening things. Well, we didn't think that was good for the residents, you know, for their health and well-being. You were real emphatic that the residents be safe, Sheriff, we remembered that. We lean out and he takes a few shots at us so we duck back inside and then lean out again and we both fire and somebody hits him and he drops to the floor. His gun falls so we sprint down the corridor and Michael kicks the gun away and I get the cuffs on him and we figure out he's only been hit in the right arm, barely a scratch, hardly even worth mentioning."

She drained the last of her cold coffee.

"Then we check for casualties. Sadly, the grandfather clock at the end of the hallway didn't make it. Unfortunate. We're pretty sure it was one of Snively's bullets. Right through the 6." She paused in thought. "That would hurt. But it would have been quick."

Perkins sighed and made another notation. "And was that when the SWAT arrived?"

"Oh yeah. Didn't we mention them? The officers in the parking lot called for them after their little gun battle out front. Seemed a bit unnecessary to us, as we had everything pretty much under control, but whatever. Anyway they come bursting in, you know how those guys act, the black helmets and the armor and the big guns and the testosterone and everything. Kind of over the top, but... Anyway, they crash through the front door that Samantha had bravely locked, oops, I guess that door's sort of a mess too—you know, it being glass and so on. So they come plunging up the stairs, Rosie sees 'em and decides they're a bunch of new playmates so she's chasing them, Samantha is chasing after Rosie, Mrs. Harris is rolling after Samantha, the residents in the coffee room are now free and they spill out still having their muffin battle and I guess it's all a bit of a circus."

"A bit of a circus," Perkins ground out, teeth clenched. Williams patted his arm.

"The SWAT guys scared the hell out of the residents on the second floor, by the way. We didn't think that was very good for police relations with the seniors," she sniffed. "Not like how Mike and I treated them."

Perkins head slumped lower.

"Well, really, Sheriff, when you add it all up, we executed the search warrant, we discovered large amounts of money and drugs, we arrested the three primary suspects, and the only real damage was a couple of doors that can be easily replaced. Oh, and a couple of drug dealers with flesh wounds, but really, just between us, who cares? Oh yeah, maybe we need to add the SWAT guy who fell down the stairs and broke his leg because he is one of ours, but that's not our fault. I'd say all in all, this was a pretty successful day for the drug squad." Ortega paused and looked at her partner. "Oh yeah. And some mini-muffins that got sorta trampled to death," she concluded brightly.

Detectives Brolio and Ortega beamed across the table.

Suddenly a frown crossed Ortega's face. "I guess the bird's the one casualty."

"The...bird?"

"Some innocent bird caught a bullet. It was only a sea gull, so nobody'll care. Besides, we think we can talk forensics into saying it was one of the druggies' guns that shot it."

Perkins massaged the back of his neck. For some reason he had a bad headache. He could feel the tension throughout his upper body. His left arm throbbed with shooting pains.

"What about the broken elbow?"

"On the SWAT guy? Well, yeah, but that's not on us either. It happened when the EMT guys were rolling the gurney to the ambulance. I guess one wheel got caught in a loose brick in the sidewalk or something and the gurney sorta tilted and the poor guy hit the deck hard. So really just an arm and a leg. And the bird. That's it."

Perkins swallowed hard.

"Oh, and the clock."

Brolio looked at his partner. "Did the fire alarm go off before or after that?"

Perkins felt a twitch starting in his right eye.

"Oh. Yeah. Kinda forgot about that too. But that wasn't our doing either. Some staff member in the home, for some obscure reason that I don't understand, sorta got all shook up by the morning's activities and I guess she yanked the fire alarm. Can't imagine what she was thinking. The FD just comes in and confuses things at a crime scene, you both know that. They're sorta pushy, with their red trucks and flashing lights. And we all know they just wanna play with their big hoses alla time."

Perkins was, for one of the very few times in his career, absolutely speechless.

Brolio thought for a moment and then added, "Actually it was kinda lucky that somebody called them, you know, because of that fire in the kitchen."

Perkins' hand shook a bit as he added that to his list.

"We heard the cooks forgot about the latest trays of muffins baking in the oven when they hid in the walk-in fridge after the shooting started. Wimps. I guess the baking got a little scorched and started the kitchen fire. Pumpkin spice, I think they were."

Perkins' shoulders slumped. His right eye looked as if it was sending out a Morse code message.

"Boy, those sprinklers in the kitchen really soak the place," Brolio continued. There was a bit of awe in his voice. "Some foam or somethin' really came down. The kitchen appliances and counters got soaked. I guess it'll take a clean-up crew a day or two to get rid of all that. But again, not our fault."

Perkins slid a little lower in his chair. He was looking a lot older than the day before.

"Besides," Brolio concluded, "they can order in for a day or two. Prob'ly be a nice change for the residents. Chinese, maybe? You'll prob'ly get a nice note thanking us."

Perkins just stared at them with weary, vacant eyes.

Williams was a very smart officer. He stepped in quickly. "OK. That's enough. Thanks for your report. We'll have some follow-up tomorrow. Leave now." His tone left no question that this was an order.

The two detectives scurried out gratefully. They were both somewhat surprised they still had their butts attached to their bodies.

Perkins rested his forehead on the desk.

Well, it had been a nice career as Sheriff.

Chapter 65

THE LOCAL MEDIA went berserk. Several regional media outlets picked up the story. Three national TV networks, one of them legit, and one newspaper chain glommed onto the story with considerable glee.

Social media was brutal. And almost always incorrect, not that that mattered.

Phrases and headlines such as "Wild shooting spree terrifies retirees" and "Screaming not Whispering at the Palms" and "Terrified Seniors ducking bullets and tossing muffins" shot through the World Wide Web. A food blogger commented on the variety of muffins being offered at the long-term care facility. She added muffin recipes of her own, including one with flax seed and mashed turnips. No one downloaded it.

A pro-gun web site analyzed the weapons fired and called for armed vigilantes in long-term care homes to protect innocent retirees. It also suggested that residents in these homes should be armed.

A late, late, late night comedian did a skit about the raid, focusing on arresting the grandmother. If you weren't connected with the Sheriff's department, it was sort of funny.

The Public Information Officer had never fielded so many media requests in her three years in that job.

Perkins refused all interview requests. He let the word seep out internally that any officer commenting on camera would be—well, the exact repercussions were not exactly spelled out, but the implication was very clear to all. No one spoke.

The PIO issued a terse statement on the incident:

PORT MANATEE SHERIFF'S DRUG UNIT ARRESTS DEALERS

A major source of drugs sold on the streets of Port Manatee has been shut down after a successful raid by the Drug Squad.

More than $634,000 in cash was confiscated during the raid. Drugs with an estimated street value of $218,000, primarily cocaine and fentanyl, were also confiscated. Three handguns were safely taken off the streets.

Arrested and charged with a variety of offenses including trafficking in narcotics and weapons-related charges were: Tamara Snively, 78; Deveron Snively, 24; and Camero Gomes, 23.

There was some slight property damage and a few minor injuries incurred during the arrest. Further charges are pending. The investigation is continuing.

Chapter 66

"I WAS SITTING WITH my husband on our balcony last night, having a glass of wine. I said, 'I love you so much, I don't know how I could ever live without you.' He said, 'Is that you or the wine talking?' I said, 'That's me talking to the wine.'"

Samantha, Samira and Kim laughed at the overheard comment from The Wives throne room by the pool. Perkins offered a tired smile. Roy Crawford was busy reading his city hall emails on his iPhone.

The Sunday following the Whispering Palms debacle. Everybody had needed a day off. Perkins was exhausted. He'd been leading the clean-up of the fallout from the raid. Media had been unrelenting for two days, until their attention was diverted by a Hollywood starlet who had been caught in a Beverly Hills faux castle complete with a working S&M dungeon.

The owners of the long-term care home had not been amused by the events at Whispering Palms. Their lawyers had been muttering about various lawsuits and payment for trauma and damages.

The Sheriff's department's insurers and legal advisors had been flummoxed by the raid and were scurrying like cockroaches in a dirty kitchen when the light snaps on. Perkins was sticking by the long-established precedent that if the police had a valid search warrant, they weren't responsible for any damage caused.

Samantha and Rosie were both fine. In fact, both seemed rather exhilarated by the experience. Mrs. Harris was still laughing at the muffin battle. Nurse Nurse had eventually extricated the muffin debris from his ear. Repairs to the doors, the kitchen, some mussed flower beds and the hallways were all compete. Mourning for the grandfather clock continued.

The residents couldn't stop buzzing about the adventure; their own heroics grew with each telling. It had gotten their blood flowing like nothing in recent memory. Their horrified adult children were ignored.

Mrs. Brighthouse had become a victim, unfortunately. She had decided to transfer to another facility.

The sea gull had been buried in a quiet ceremony. Attendance was sparse.

"The stupid thing is, in a certain sense, the raid was quite successful," Perkins said as he sipped a cold beer. "We got the three arrests, we broke up a drug ring, and we recovered a bunch of money, drugs and guns. I think we'll convict all of them. But Lordy, what a wild day."

"Roger just had a colonoscopy," reported Wife #4. "The doctor told me that despite what I thought, his head wasn't up there."

Kim, Samira and Samantha went into hysterics. Roy and LeRoy looked at each other.

"Why don't we offer the home a lump sum settlement and get out of it?" suggested the City Manager. He was a veteran of frequent nuisance lawsuits that are routinely filed against municipalities. "The city is going to get sued since your department has immunity. It isn't worth the lawyer's fees and the hassle. We'll pay whatever the clean-up crew charged and give 'em a flat fee for the clock and everything else. Heck, for 25 grand we're probably out of it."

Perkins pondered that advice. It sounded pretty good to him.

"I'm trying to get my husband to take up curling," reported Wife #8 as the last of the rosé got poured for the coven of Wives.

"Why?"

"Well, just once, I'd like to see him with a broom in his hand."

CHAPTER 67

THE EXPLOSION WAS the biggest and loudest of the mysterious bombings. It ripped through the early construction of an office tower in suburban Gainesville. No one was injured but the damage to the budding project was extensive.

"We've got nothing, Perk," reported Gainesville Police Chief Erica Courtenay. "The site was fenced but unguarded. No cameras in the area. No reports from eyewitnesses. The developer is pretty clean. It's a good project. Nobody can figure out a motive."

"Huh. Much the same scenario as the bombings we had here, and the one in Orlando," said Perkins. "It really is odd."

"Our people figure six sticks of dynamite," she continued.

"The explosions seem to be getting bigger each time."

"Really? Then the perps are getting cockier. Maybe they need the bigger bang each time."

"Yeah. Listen, Erica, I've been working with James Robertson, the FBI honcho. We're trying to coordinate information. The dynamite's fingerprint seems to be consistent. If your ballistics people can feed anything like that to his office, it might help."

"Sure. I'll tell them immediately."

"One final question. This one will seem odd. But did anybody report hearing any banjo music anytime around the explosion?"

Sheriff Courtenay didn't laugh the way Perkins expected. "You know, it's funny you would ask that. One of the cops first on the scene interviewed a couple of kids on bicycles. They both swore they heard a banjo playing from a car that sped away. Our guys never connected it to anything."

"Our media is playing up this stupid 'Banjo Bomber' thing. We have no idea what that all means."

"Well, you never know what little thing will crack open a whole field of investigation."

"You're right. Oh, one more thing: watch out for some Homeland Security ass name Crunciman. He likes to swoop in with his entourage and try to take over. You may wish to resist that. But James tells me he's applying enormous pressure in Washington to take over the entire investigation. Unless we get some leads on this damn case, our local investigators will probably get kicked out. I hear it is getting harder to resist, especially when we don't have much." He paused. "I just don't like Crunciman," he admitted. "He was rude to my Mayor and my department. His ego is almost as big as his head."

"Well, yeah," she chuckled. "I can't stand those blowhard feds either. Thanks for the tip."

They hung up. Perkins swivelled in his office chair. He thought hard. The clues were vague at best. What possible connection could there be between banjo music, dynamite, and blowing up emerging construction projects? And then the big question—why?

There had to be a thread connecting the dots. He couldn't imagine what it might be. But he knew the pressure to solve the bombings was going to explode any day now. He could feel Crunciman's cold, stinking breath on his neck.

CHAPTER 68

THE EXPLOSION WAS the biggest and loudest of the ones that had occurred recently at Port Manatee City Council.

The surprise was, it didn't come from Mikayla Johnson.

"It is reckless and unprofessional for the Sheriff's Department to raid a long-term care facility like it did," steamed Councillor Fred March. "Especially when it is near my ward. I understand from people who were there that there were seniors held against their will in one room! Others were nearly caught in the crossfire of deputies shooting it out with a couple of druggies! The terror these poor seniors must have gone through! The property damage! The risk to human life! What on earth was the Sheriff thinking? Since when do we endanger the lives of our most vulnerable citizens—while they are in their own home! Maybe it's time for a new Sheriff in town!" He concluded his rant, glared around the council table, and sat down heavily.

Kim shot out of her chair. "Quite frankly, Madam Mayor, we should be applauding the Sheriff and his officers. They arrested three people deeply involved in the drug trade in this city…al-legedly, I guess we still have to say…and those drugs were going to harm kids and teens and people all over our city. The damage to human lives that fentanyl causes is horrific. And I understand the raid resulted in the confiscation of over $800,000 in street drugs and cash from this illicit operation. And they took away three guns."

She took a deep breath and a small grin appeared. "Besides, to be quite honest with you, and I am a volunteer at that home and visit the residents regularly, the incident seemed to thrill more of them than traumatize them. They are still buzzing about it." The smile faded. "The key point is that we need to support our Sheriff and his department when they are working so hard to get drugs and guns off our streets and keep our city safe."

Councillor March glowered at her and was about to rise again when the mayor called on the Ward 5 Councillor.

"I want to support my colleague from Ward 3," Mikayla Johnson began. Kim nearly fell off her chair. "I agree with her that the Sheriff's department has done great work in breaking up a drug ring in our city. I'm not sure that all members of this council fully understand the damage that drugs are doing to our children. If we can stop another conduit for street drugs, then I am all for it. And if there was some minor damage, well, perhaps the City Manager can tell us our exposure?"

"Councillor Johnson asks a very good question," Roy Crawford began. "I have met with Sheriff Perkins about this situation." He neglected to mention it was over a few beers by the pool, but that wasn't important. "There was a valid search warrant for the premises. The Sheriff's department has immunity in such a case. Most of the time the property owner sues the city. Our insurance will take care of the costs, and I have instructed them to settle quickly so the exposure to the municipality will be quite negligible."

"That is good news," continued Councillor Johnson. "I think that we should congratulate the Sheriff's department for this action."

"Well. That's going to make it harder to string up those two idiot detectives," Perkins muttered to Samantha as they nestled on her couch watching the cable TV broadcast.

Rosie didn't seem that interested in the political debate. She snored quietly at their feet. Her two front paws twitched as she dreamed of squirrels on the lawn at Whispering Palms. One of these days...

"Gosh, Kim spoke really well," Samantha said. "And I'm stunned at the transformation of Mikayla."

"Yeah. For months she's been madder than a grizzly with a toothache. She made it sound as if we really knew what we were doing at the take-down." He paused. "Let's just hope she never finds out the true story."

"I guess that incident a few weeks ago when Roy trapped her on the leak really did change her."

"Yeah. Guess so." Now that the political debate was over and his job was apparently safe for a few more days, Perkins was getting a lot more interested in Samantha's hidden assets. She kissed him deeply and then lay back and enjoyed the sensations as his hands roamed.

"Isn't it interesting how on a council, so many different elements can come together," she murmured. "All these people of different backgrounds, focused on so many different and unique parts of a city. The diverse issues that councillors have to deal with...public music concerts one minute and then some hot political issue, and then new techniques for blowing up old policies and—hey!"

Perkins had sat up abruptly. He left her sprawled inelegantly on the couch. Her clothes were somewhat askew. If her mother had arrived at that precise moment when Samantha was a teenager, she would have flung Perkins out the back door of their house and locked Samantha in her room. For about ten years.

"What you said. All these different elements coming together. Music and science and politics and everything. Where does that happen all the time?"

Samantha was busy straightening her blouse and re-hooking her bra. She looked at him with narrowed eyes. "Do you really want to be asking dumb questions when, if you play your cards right, you could be carrying me into the bedroom?"

Perkins sat up, eyes focused on a distant vista. "It happens at a university. A college. That's where they offer all these different programs. Music. Engineering. Political science. Philosophy. And lots of young people are radical; they are passionate about some cause. Geez, Samantha, that might be the thread I've been searching for!"

"What are you talking about?"

"The bombings! A university offers all—wait! Isn't the daughter of the, who is it, the, the—oh, the Kowalski family. Isn't she in poli sci at FSU? The ex-mayor's niece? Oh man, this feels right."

He jumped up from the couch. Rosie woke up. The squirrels were still winning.

Samantha sprawled on the couch as she finished rearranging her clothing. "I'm lying here and you're thinking about some other girl?" she asked peevishly.

"What time is it? Oh, good, not even nine o'clock. Make some coffee for me, will you, honey?"

He bent over to pick up his phone. Samantha just couldn't resist. One firm kick into his right buttock sent him slumping to the floor.

"Oh, sorry," she said insincerely. "I had a sudden leg spasm. How do you want your coffee?"

Chapter 69

"Chief Greene? Sheriff Perkins here, from down in Port Manatee. Sorry to bother you at home this late, but we are working on the bombings that've been going on across Florida. Your office said you wouldn't mind."

"No problem, Sheriff. The bombings recently? The one in Orlando? And didn't you have a couple?"

"Yes, those." Perkins sipped a bit of coffee. "Well, I'm not sure they do tie into FSU, but I got a lead tonight that I need to check out. It's a bit of a long shot, but we don't have much else. What I'm wondering is if you have a radical group on campus? Maybe involving political science, engineering, environmental studies, the music department?"

"That's a crazy mix of subjects. But sure, we have a bunch of radical groups on campus. It is a university. There are always radical groups. Our intelligence people keep a casual eye on them, but frankly it's almost always talk. A lot of talk, mind you. A few students get hot for a cause, form a group, sit around, drink coffee or beer, sometimes puff a few joints, and figure out how to make the world a better place. They're almost always harmless. After they graduate the group breaks up. New ones form. It's a cycle. Sometimes they do some good." Perkins could almost hear the shrug.

"Would you ask your Intel team about any groups that have been formed in the past year or so? Somebody who would have experience with explosives. And maybe some interest in local politics. Not state or federal. And if anyone named Katherine or Kate Kowalski might be involved."

"Sure, I'll get on it right away. Lemme make a note of the spelling. With a K, right? OK. We'll get back to you tomorrow morning."

"Thanks, Chief."

Perkins hung up the phone and sat back thoughtfully. Samantha looked at him with a small pout. She was still rather cranky. He had never abandoned her at such a moment before. There would be retribution.

Chapter 70

"Her nickname is Killer Kowalski. There was some big-time wrestler in the 1950s and 60s named Killer Kowalski. He was famous for the Claw Grip. He won some championships, for whatever that's worth in that scripted sport," Captain Ming Tranh laughed.

"Why is she nick-named 'Killer'?"

"Apparently in her political science class debates she's an absolute destroyer. So with that last name, it was a natural."

Perkins sipped his morning coffee and thought about that. "What about her link with somebody in engineering or some field where explosives might be involved?"

"That was a little harder but we found a connection with a guy in Environmental Sciences named Billy Broadhurst. They get taught to use dynamite in case of blockages in a swamp or something. Word is that he's got the hots for Kate. She's a pretty cute little thing. From what my people tell me, she's got him by the short and curlies. He is very committed to saving the planet."

Perkins thought some more. "And the music department connection?"

"Nothing."

"Anybody else in their little group?"

"Yeah, actually. A woman named Eloise N'domo. She's in the Urban Architecture program. We don't know much about her but apparently the three of them are tight."

Perkins thought some more. "This has been very helpful. Thank you. Uh, how would you and the Chief feel about my sauntering up there to have a little chat with the three of them? Not together, of course."

Tranh paused as he thought through the implications of letting an outside law man interview students on campus. "I'll check with the Chief, but she's usually pretty good about helping other cops. I'm not sure you want to do the interviews on campus though."

"I understand. That's no problem. Would you or somebody want to be there?"

"I would assume so. Again, I'll check."

"Great. I could come up tomorrow."

"I'll talk to the Chief now and email you directions if it's going to be alright."

"Perfect. Thanks for the help."

Chapter 71

ROSIE LED SAMANTHA into the Whispering Palms Retirement Home. Rosie carefully checked out the squirrel situation. None of the audacious little buggers appeared on the lawn.

Mrs. Harris was a little down. "We had another death last night. It was unexpected. I thought she was in pretty decent health, but she just...died. That's the fifth one in the last couple of months. It is upsetting," she concluded as she absently stroked Rosie's fur.

Samantha looked around the reading room. She saw Elmer Krackle staring at her. She didn't like the nurse; he seemed creepy to her. They both shifted their eyes. The quiet nurse, Ethel something, moved silently down the hallway. Her eyes were cast down. Her mousy brown hair needed urgent professional attention. Nothing that perhaps two days of shampooing, coloring, trimming, moisturizing, curling, retrimming, volumizing and a covey of stylists couldn't improve.

Rosie wandered off to share her unique blend of comfort and pleasure with the other residents.

"Is everybody OK after the, uh, the..."

"Shootout?" Mrs. Harris finished for her. "It's OK, honey, we're all big kids here. Most of us have been through harder situations. Yeah, we're fine. Some of our kids are freaked, but we're fine," she concluded with a chortle.

Nurse Krackle walked through the room to the hallway. He glared at two of the residents. Samantha could almost see them shrink away.

"I don't like him," she muttered quietly to Mrs. Harris. "I don't know why."

"Nobody likes him. I think he's put some of the residents here in restraints at night so they can't get up. Nobody will talk about it. One of the ladies had an accident one night when she couldn't get up to go to the bathroom. She had to lie in her own urine all night." Mrs. Harris shuddered at the idea. "She complained. Nothing happened. I guess they are so short-staffed that management is scared to discipline the staff."

"I've seen a few bruises, on arms or wrists," Samantha agreed. "Nobody wants to talk about them?"

"Everybody is scared. If the nursing and personal support people don't like you, they might fiddle with your meds, or restrain you at night or not come when you call. Many people living here need help to get up or to eat or take their medications or go to the toilet. It can be really hard."

It was unusual for Mrs. Harris to complain, Samantha knew. This was a startling revelation.

"Have you talked to Nick Nurse?"

"I did. Once. He was sympathetic. Said he'd talk to his staff. There was some short-term relief. But without a General Manager right now, it is slipping again."

Samantha shook her head in dismay. Long-term care facilities apparently could be dangerous and treacherous places, socially and physically.

CHAPTER 72

"HELLO, MR. BROADHURST. THANK you for chatting with us. My name is LeRoy Perkins. I'm the Sheriff down in Port Manatee. You've met Captain Tranh."

The young student shifted uncomfortably in his chair. The meeting was in a small board room in a building, owned by a friend of Tranh's, near the campus. Nobody wanted these interviews done on university property. The deniability factor hovered.

"How do you enjoy your Environmental Sciences courses?"

"I believe we have to develop a better understanding of earth sciences and how our population relates to nature. We're destroying so much of our natural environment. Shame on your generation!"

Perkins looked at Tranh who gave a tiny shrug.

"Does that include erecting buildings in cities?"

"Of course! That's one of the worst things you've done. The urban sprawl, the concrete and steel structures. Not using wood or natural products. Not building roof gardens and vertical green walls and bicycle parking and..." The student shook his head in disgust.

"Do you think it's your duty, your obligation, to save the planet?"

"That is such a stupid phrase! Typical of you old, out-of-touch bureaucrats and boomers. You don't get it! We need to take action now to stop the waste and the hypocrisy and the plundering of the earth's riches. You make me sick."

"Do you learn how to use dynamite in your classes?"

"Sure."

"Do you like banjo music?"

"Who doesn't?"

"Do you know a Katherine Kowalski? Kate?"

His face changed in an instant. "Yes. She's sort of my girl-friend. She just doesn't know that...well, we're...we're..." He shrugged in confusion and irritation.

"And have you gone on any little road trips with her?"

"Why? What do you mean? Why am I here? "

With that he crossed his arms and sat back.

***

"THANK YOU FOR meeting with us, Ms. N'domo. We just have a few questions to help us on an investigation. How do you like your urban design courses?"

"My generation has to fix your generation's screw-ups. It'll take decades to turn around what's been destroyed. For shame! The waste. The pollution. The bad urban design, wrecking our cities. The past thirty years will go down in the history of city-building as a monument to your generation's arrogance, laziness and stupidity."

Her dark eyes flashed. Both Tranh and Perkins couldn't help but flinch a little at her vituperative comments.

"And do you feel you have to help fix that?"

"In any way that I can! The time for talking is over. The time for action has come. Your pathetic societal norms and your economic failures mean my generation has to take over." Her tone was low, angry and biting.

"Would that include blowing up buildings under construction?"

She snorted derisively and refused to answer.

"Oh. Do you like banjo music?"

This time she snorted like an angry rhino, shook her head, got up and stomped out.

***

"IT IS MY generation's obligation to change our society: Our cities. Our sense of community. Our political leadership. All because your generation has failed us in so many ways."

Perkins wasn't going to take that bait. Neither was Tranh. A lot of politicians and political decisions over the past couple of decades simply couldn't be defended.

"Do you include your uncle in that last group?"

"You leave him out of this! He got railroaded in court. You were part of that despicable attack on him. I remember you. He'll be back, you just wait and see. And I'll be there to help him reclaim his seat as mayor! He will transition my generation to take over the power. And I will!" Her eyes were bright and shining. "We're going to start with the cities and then reform the states and then we will reclaim Washington!"

Perkins paused to let the rhetoric hang in the air. Tranh looked at her with interest.

"Tell me, Ms. Kowalski, what size of shoe do you wear?"

"7 ½. The same as my mother. The same as ten million other Americans. Why?"

"Have you visited your uncle while he's been in prison?"

"No."

"You realize that they keep records there of all visitors?"

"Oh. Well. Maybe. Once or twice."

"Or maybe five times?"

"Why do you care? What is this all about?"

"Do you care for banjo music, Ms. Kowalski?"

"Oh, pluck you!" She stormed out of the room.

CHAPTER 73

"IT MIGHT BE them," Perkins reported back to his senior management team the next morning. "Three fervent kids. They're angry about the environment and politics and the state of our cities and a bunch of other stuff. Hard to disagree with some of their beliefs and complaints, mind you. But they might also be guilty of these bombings," he repeated as he blew out his cheeks in frustration. "But I can't prove it."

Silence around the conference table. They'd all been in a similar situation at some point in their crime-fighting careers. A lot of criminals had walked away, laughing at the cops because even though the police knew they were guilty they couldn't come up with evidence that would stand up in court.

Later that morning Perkins phoned Elliott Webster. "How's the Delvecchio Bridge project coming along?"

"Really good. We've almost made up the time we lost due to the bombings. We should be back on schedule by the fall. The foundations are all completed and we're starting to raise more steel next week. We agreed to add two more floors to each building. All good."

"That's great. Congratulations. Uh, Elliott. A question. Have you ever had anything to do with the Kowalski family in St. Augustine?"

"Never heard of them."

"Billy Broadhurst?"

"No."

"Eloise N'domo?"

A pause. "Yeah. She's known to a lot of contractors in Florida. She's a really radical urbanist. Hates steel and concrete towers. Wants to build with wood and natural fibers. Hates hi-rises. Wants medium density only. Hates big business. Wants little co-ops and community builders. She's a fierce social media blogger and she's picketed a couple of projects. Why?"

"Her name came up in our investigation of the bombings."

"Huh. Yeah, I could see that. She's pretty angry with our industry. And architects. And urban designers. And—well, everybody."

"Yeah, I felt that. We've got a really good sense of three students who might be doing the bombings. We just can't prove anything."

Webster absorbed that. "Well, damn." He paused. "Let me know if I can do anything to help. I'd really like to get it solved. My insurance people are still being rather…uncooperative. If we got a conviction, that would help. It's a lot of money for a mid-sized contractor like us to be out."

"I hear you. I'll keep in touch."

An hour later his phone rang. He happily stopped doing paperwork and looked at the caller ID.

"Ah, the pride of the FBI. How's Atlanta doing? Can the city survive your ego?"

"Always a pleasure talking to the Sheriff who is back with that gorgeous redhead. What did you have to do, grovel?"

"Nah. That's a purely FBI tactic. I just stood up in my manly way and she collapsed into my arms."

James Robertson roared with laughter. "Oh boy. I can't wait to tell her that when we meet."

"Yeah. Maybe not."

Robertson was still stifling his laughter when he turned to the reason for his call.

"My lab guys traced the dynamite you sent with the explosive fingerprints left on the debris from the bombings. They have a 94% certainty of it being the same batch as one that was sold to Florida State University a year ago. The Environmental Sciences Department."

Perkins slowly exhaled. "Good. Really good. Thanks, James."

Robertson's voice turned more serious. "Look, Perk, your time on the bombings is pretty much over. I've been fighting Washington but with the lack of progress or arrests in the bombings and the on-going media attention, I think Crunciman is about to win the bureaucratic battle and take over the entire investigation."

Perkins paused before replying. "All I can tell you is that I think we finally have a solid lead and we're pursuing it right now. Just buy me a couple of more days."

The FBI Regional Director waited a long minute. Perkins could imagine the various bureaucratic pluses and minuses that were going through his mind. This had become a major unsolved crime in his territory. "OK. I'll see what I can do. But your time is about done."

"Thanks. I owe you one."

"Oh yes you do. And I'll be around to collect one of these days. I can't wait to meet Samantha. With any luck I can have your relationship ruined before dessert!"

He hung up as his laughter echoed down the line.

Perkins stared at the phone. Why was his hand suddenly sweating?

CHAPTER 74

LATE THE NEXT morning Perkins was still fighting the paper wars when the receptionist buzzed him.

"There's a Ms. Kowalski to see you. She doesn't have an appointment."

Perkins blinked in surprise. "Ah, I'll be happy to see her. I'll be right out."

He immediately called for Deputy Chad to join him. He wanted a witness for this interview with the angry college girl. Maybe she would admit to something.

He strode into the lobby area and looked for the pretty FSU student who had shredded him a couple of days previously. Nobody. There was a middle-aged woman sitting primly in one corner, and two young lawyers with their briefcases in tow on a bench under the windows.

Perkins turned to look at the receptionist. She pointed to the woman in the corner. When he began to walk towards her, she rose and also advanced.

"Sheriff Perkins? I'm Shirley Kowalski. Kate's mother. We, well, we need to talk. Please."

Quickly covering his surprise, Perkins shook hands and guided her into his office. "This is Deputy Chad. I've asked him to join us." She nodded noncommittally and wearily sat down in one of the office chairs that faced his desk.

"Would you care for a coffee? Water?"

"Coffee would be nice. A bit of half-and-half please."

Mary must have been in a benevolent mood that morning. She quickly produced a cup for the woman and put down a bottle of water as well. She closed the door on her way out. Mrs. Kowalski sipped. Perkins studied her. She was in her fifties, some gray in her brown hair, still slender and attractive. Her eyes were sad.

After another sip she looked directly at Perkins and drew a deep breath. "You must be wondering what I am doing here. It's simple. I'm here to confess to the bombings." She held out her hands as if waiting for the handcuffs to be slapped on.

Deputy Chad looked at Perkins who was studying the woman. "That is quite a confession, Mrs. Kowalski. Would you like to tell us why you did them?"

"I believe we have to change how we build cities. This is my form of protest. Just take me away. You can close your investigation now. I'll confess to everything."

Perkins scratched his left ear. "OK. But isn't setting off a bomb a pretty, uh, radical way of protesting? What if some kid was in the vicinity?"

"Oh. No. That would never happen. I was always very careful."

"And how did you learn about using C-4?"

"Oh, my husband is in construction. And I studied it on-line."

"And where did you buy the explosives?"

"I can't tell you."

"Uh huh. Your husband, perhaps? Isn't he in construction?"

"No! He, he would never do that." Her face was flushed. "He wasn't involved."

"So who helped you?"

"Nobody. I swear. Nobody else."

"What size of shoe do you wear, Mrs. Kowalski?"

"Seven and a half. Why?"

"And why did you choose these particular buildings as targets?"

"Uh, well, I, I just did."

"You understand that the Delvecchio Bridge complex includes a children's playground, social housing, space for artists and will help to rejuvenate a neighborhood in this city that needs a lot of help? The damage to the community would have been immense, not to mention causing the likely bankruptcy of a family construction business and causing hundreds of job losses to local families? Frankly, Mrs. Kowalski, you don't strike me as someone who could be that cruel."

At this, her face crumpled into tears. She sobbed into a lace handkerchief that was clasped in her left hand. Deputy Chad looked across the desk at Perkins. The Sheriff looked back at the woman and waited until she was under control.

"Look, Mrs. Kowalski, let me be honest with you. I think you are a very nice woman. I also think you are lying through your teeth and had nothing whatever to do with any of these bombings. I think you're covering up for your daughter and trying to shift the blame away from her."

"I am not covering up! I am not lying! It happened just as I said! I did it myself, all on my own! Nobody helped me!" She stared at him defiantly, gasping for breath.

Perkins let her emotions settle. "Why would you do something like this? I mean, your story just doesn't make sense. They didn't use C-4; they used dynamite. And frankly, Mrs. Kowalski, I just don't think you are capable of using explosives. You know we'll check everything you tell us, and it won't add up."

Her face crumpled again. More tears began to stream out of the corners of her eyes. "Kate is so young. Her whole life is ahead of her," she sobbed.

"Sure. I know you want to protect her, but you can't help her this way."

"She is my only daughter." Mrs. Kowalski was weeping openly. Her voice cracked between the sobs. "She's a bright, beautiful girl with a great future. I love her so much." She took some deep breaths and tried to compose herself. The officers waited.

"But she got tainted by my idiot brother in jail. He convinced her that he had been wrongly convicted. I'm terrified that she might have thought that by vandalizing that Delvecchio project she would give him a platform for re-election."

She nervously swallowed more water. Her handkerchief was soaked with tears. It was obvious that her stamina was reaching its breaking point. She looked gray and exhausted.

"Then she got hooked up with some really radical woman in urban something, and this boy who is chasing her around like a love-sick puppy. Kate is such a beautiful girl. Her father and I have been chasing off guys since she was about 14. And a couple of dirty old men," she added darkly.

She was struggling now, her strength ebbing as her emotions poured out. "This young man apparently has been bragging about doing something big to impress Kate. When she told me about your interview I knew the police had suspicions. I have been terrified for her. I had to do something to save her so I decided to sacrifice myself." She dabbed her eyes again. "That's just what mothers do."

CHAPTER 75

"WE'D LIKE TO charge all three," said Perkins firmly, "but I'm not sure we're ready yet."

"I agree. And on what charges?" Doug Saunders had been re-elected recently for his second term as District Attorney. He was a no-nonsense type.

"My inclination is to go after public endangerment. I guess you could look at terrorism. Public mischief? Vandalism?"

Saunders grunted. "What about the mother?"

"Ah, let's let her walk. I know you could charge her with obstruction of justice or lying to a police officer, but I just don't see the benefit."

"OK. I'm easy. Mothers. Gotta love 'em."

"Captain Tranh is picking up the three kids. I think they're going to do them simultaneously. Then they'll bring 'em down here in separate vehicles. They will be kept in separate cells. We will interrogate them and then you can determine if and how you want to charge then."

Saunders nodded. "Dumb kids. I hate to see their lives ruined over something this idiotic, but we can't ignore the explosions and the endangerment of public life and safety."

Perkins nodded. Justice had to be done. Public safety had to be protected. Three smart young people were about to learn a hard lesson: there were consequences to actions.

<h1 style="text-align:center">CHAPTER 76</h1>

THEY THOUGHT THAT Billy Broadhurst would be the first to crack, probably in the first two minutes of his interrogation. He blubbered a lot but admitted nothing. He whimpered something about true love. He then refused to answer any more questions. His tears and sobbing made it difficult for his questioners to hear him. Finally his parents were called and they hired a lawyer. Nobody was very optimistic.

Eloise N'domo continued to icily stare down the questioners. The tattoos that covered her left arm and shoulder included a dragon and a vengeful god of some denomination. She fiddled absently with the multiple piercings in her ears, nose, right eyelid and bottom lip as she listened to the questions. She denied everything. She said she'd never participated in any bombing. She had a few choice insults for the police. She demanded legal representation and refused to answer any further questions. She threatened lawsuits and made accusations of police harassment.

Kate Kowalski was the puzzle. She was a very pretty girl. Long brown hair. Neatly dressed in a short skirt. She denied any involvement in any bombings. The officers listed the bombings and the evidence against her. They told of her mother's 'confession.' At that she burst into tears, broke down a bit more, but never admitted to being part of any bombings. In fact she denied it strongly.

She did confess that she and her dad loved banjo music. Then she asked for a lawyer.

It was a stalemate for the interrogators. Nobody was happy.

The police interviewers and the DA's office were left in a quandary. They had lots of circumstantial evidence but in court it would be iffy. With no confessions, there remained doubt. Was it worth taking a chance and charging them?

DA Doug Saunders said no. Not at this time. Insufficient evidence. He ordered them released.

Perkins and his team were frustrated.

"Keep hunting," he finally told his investigators. "Keep searching. Chase other leads but keep digging into those three. Something stinks. We must be missing some link. We've got to go deeper."

<h1 style="text-align:center">CHAPTER 77</h1>

PERKINS SAT ALONE at his desk. This entire case was blowing up on him. And the clock had finally run out. The FBI Director had called him an hour ago to tell him that Crunciman and his pack of feral federal wolves would arrive tomorrow at 7am to take over the bombing investigation.

N'domo's lawyer was threatening a lawsuit for false arrest or confinement or some other legal intricacy. She was also threatening a few other nasty little surprises to throw at the Sheriff's department. Harassment. Disrespect by police. Black Lives Matter. Some other things.

Kate Kowalski's lawyer was demanding the unredacted police reports that led to the students being picked up and interviewed. He was getting very provocative. Kate continued to deny anything to do with the bombings. She and her mother had become very close again.

Billy Broadhurst, his lawyer and his family did nothing.

Perkins pondered that as he sat in his office. It was after 6:30pm. He was exhausted. He was hangry. The case was driving his entire force to the brink. It was the talk of the detective's bullpen. They were coordinating with Orlando and the other bombed sites. There was little progress from any of the other jurisdictions.

The DA was going after a court order to get access to computer and cell phone records for all three suspects. That was going to be a battle they might not win.

Tranh and his team at FSU were digging deeper into the university experiences of the three desperadoes, as one detective had nicknamed them. They were also looking for connections to other radical groups. So far it was a dry well.

The ADA was working with his Tallahassee counterparts on deeper background information about the trio. Nothing of substance so far.

On an impulse, Perkins called Samantha. "Any chance you're free for a late dinner? I'm still at the office."

Samantha stopped nibbling on her dinner salad. "Sure. I haven't even thought about dinner so that would be nice. You sound tired," she added.

"Yeah. I suppose so. This bombing case is driving us nuts. Everybody's putting in really long hours but we can't seem to get a break." He sighed loudly. "Why don't I pick you up in an hour or so? I'll get home to clean up and see how Rosie is doing."

"Great. Casual?"

"For sure. Maybe a burger or something. You decide. I'll see you soon."

"Bye."

She hung up. She put away her dinner dishes, stuck the salad in the fridge and cleaned up the kitchen. It would be a light second dinner for her tonight. She changed into a short white summer skirt, sandals and a multi-colored blouse.

She was waiting at her condo's front door when Perkins' car pulled up. Rosie and Perk both kissed her hello. She got a little more tongue from the puppy. Perkins really is exhausted, she thought.

"I thought going to Chico's Burgers might be fun," Samantha told him after buckling up. She had discovered the funky little joint near the Delvecchio Bridge project.

"Great. Good choice."

He headed the SUV towards Chico's. As Sheriff, he had to be on call all the time, so even his personal truck had a police scanner and a roof-top flashing light that could be activated when necessary.

The wooden shack had six mismatched tables on its cracked concrete patio. There were five more under a thatched roof that provided some relief from sun but not from rain. There were seven rickety wooden bar stools of mixed heritage. They were nestled around a plywood plank sitting on two old wooden saw-horses that hosted a tub of ice water to chill the beer and sodas. That was the bar. Mixed drinks were not encouraged, unless you wanted some cola in your beer. There was a rumor of a dusty box of wine somewhere on the premises, but nobody had ever confirmed it.

Experienced patrons served themselves from the ice bath and replaced what they had taken so the beer supply was always cold. It was sort of an honor bar. If you got caught not honoring the bar or your bar tab, you were kicked out. Forever. No appeal. If you were lucky, Chico's mother wouldn't grab the machete hanging in the back room and severe a finger or two. But you would never be allowed to return.

And as the burgers were fabulous, that was a serious penalty. Samantha ordered a single patty blue cheese burger. Perkins was more ambitious—double patty, bacon, American cheese and caramelized onions. Extra crispy fries on the side.

"The fries aren't very good for you," Samantha commented as they both popped an icy cerveza. Rosie was intoxicated with the aromas coming from the barbecue pit that served as a kitchen. She strained at the leash that tethered her to the table.

"Yeah." Perkins took a huge slug of cold beer. He rolled his neck, trying to work out the kinks. Another big swallow helped to lubricate his tired muscles. It was pretty obvious to him that a few more quaffs would provide important additional muscular relief. Clearly an astute medical diagnosis.

He finished the first can in record time. He got up, went to the tub and grabbed two more lite beers. He threw a few more cans into the ice water and returned to the table.

"Oh, thanks," Samantha said.

"What? Oh, did you want another as well?"

Their platters arrived. The big bowl of crispy fries sat in the middle of the table as they each prepped their burgers. Rosie was very attentive as Samantha and Perkins took their first big bites. There was quiet at the table as they savored the juicy burgers and the toasted sourdough buns.

A moment later Perkins came up for air. "Man, that's good." He took another big draft of beer and then a handful of the fries. He dipped the ends in ketchup and then chomped down cheerily. "Oh. So. Good." He finished his second beer and popped the third.

Samantha held out for a moment but then dipped into the fries. A throaty sound of approval had Perkins grinning at her. Rosie pushed into Samantha's leg and was rewarded with a bit of burger.

It didn't take them long to finish. The sun had set and lights glowed around the little shack. The tables were all full and there were a dozen people at the bar sharing the seven stools.

Chico's mother stomped by. There was gossip that she had smiled once in the spring of 2013, but nobody could swear to that.

Chico was sweating at the barbecue, the grease flare-ups highlighting his swarthy face as he slapped more of his secretly flavored burger patties on the grill. Rosie got Samantha's last bite of burger. Perkins finished the bucket of fries and his final beer.

"Well, I might live," he said wearily. She patted his hand comfortingly.

Chico's mother leaned over without a word and cleared the table. Turning-over tables was the key to success in the restaurant industry. Her business model was brilliantly simple: drink beer, eat burger, pay cash, tip big, get out. 54 minutes to churn seats was about right in her view.

It would have taken a CEO, two MBAs and a highly paid consultant six months to design such a business strategy and publish their corporate mission statement.

Samantha's cell phone buzzed discreetly. She sighed but picked it up as Perkins dropped fifty bucks on the table. You didn't want to short-change Chico's mother. You also learned not to expect change at Chico's. But the burgers were worth it.

He was patting Rosie and getting her leash sorted out from where she'd stepped all over it when Samantha leaned over and grabbed his arm in a fierce clutch.

"We've got to go!" she hissed at him. "Now!"

She jumped up from the table and hustled toward the SUV. Perkins followed, confused. He got Rosie in the back seat and then jumped in the driver's seat.

"What's going on?"

"That was Mrs. Barkley! Their Neighborhood Watch group at Delvecchio Bridge just spotted a guy sneaking into the construction project. He must have used something to snip the lock on the fence!"

Perkins didn't hesitate. He shoved the truck in gear and swiftly swung around and headed for the development site. He grabbed the radio and called in the situation. He ordered units not to use sirens. He told the dispatcher that he was 90 seconds out. She confirmed the orders and three patrol cars responded. They were all racing to the condo project that had already been bombed twice.

"I thought they had a security guard on the premises?"

"They do. I guess he's on a bathroom break," Samantha told him.

"He's never heard of a pee jar?" Samantha stared at him.

They were approaching the site. Perkins killed his head-lights. They rolled quietly onto the bare dirt. It took a moment for their eyes to adjust to the darkness.

"There! See him?"

Samantha still didn't see anything and—wait. She spotted a tiny movement on the ramp that led into the pit where the foundation was anchored.

"Stay here. Monitor the radio. Tell the dispatcher the situation."

He quietly exited the car. Samantha hesitantly picked up the microphone. "Hello?"

"Who is this?"

"Uh, I'm Samantha Summers." She spoke in a near whisper. "I'm with the Sheriff. He just left the car to go into the construc-tion site at Delvecchio Bridge. He told me to call you."

A puzzled silence. "OK. I guess. What's happening there?"

Samantha reported on the situation. She explained it was dark on the site. And she was firm that Perkins was wearing dark clothes and other officers should be careful.

"Got it. Stand by. Stay in the car."

Samantha clicked off. Rosie was whining in the back seat.

Perkins moved quietly through the construction site, duck-ing behind a big yellow Caterpillar bulldozer to stay hidden. He could hear other vehicles approaching but he was obviously the first responder.

Man, he hated bombs. They were just nasty things. But this might be their best chance to catch this mysterious Banjo Bomber. And even as he thought that, he suddenly heard the distinctive banjo plucking from the "Deliverance" theme.

That must mean something, it occurred to him. And it couldn't be good. Like an impending explosion?

This was a situation officers were trained to avoid. A dark night. An unfamiliar physical location. A dangerous unknown suspect. And no back-up. High risk situation. Grave jeopardy of injury or death to the officer.

He also knew there was a possibility the person was arming another bomb that was an enormous and imminent threat to the neighborhood. He didn't know when it could explode, but it was probably soon. It was another big risk for an officer—to be exposed like that. The book said wait.

Perkins didn't hesitate.

He crept forward until he was at the top of the construction ramp that led down to the foundation. He looked carefully.

There! He saw a figure moving stealthily in a dark corner. The three-quarter moon provided some illumination. Perkins carefully and silently started down the slope, trying to avoid kicking rocks. He was nearing the bottom when his foot caught some loose gravel. The noise seemed like a hundred cannons to his ear. Stealth was over.

He extended his gun arm, moved his left arm away from his body and turned on the powerful flashlight. In a second he had spotlighted a figure crouched beside some steel and concrete pillars. Hands seemed to be wiring something together.

"POLICE! Freeze! Do not move! Now, stand up slowly and hold up your hands!"

The figure didn't move for a long moment. Then it slowly rose. Man? Woman? Perkins wasn't sure. Suddenly the figure ducked and ran for the far corner of the pit and tried to scramble up the dirt wall. Perkins advanced quickly. "Stop! This is the sheriff!"

The figure slid down the wall and tried to duck away from the light. A rock bounced in front of Perkins' leg. He could feel the sting of a sharp edge on his left shin. He moved three steps closer.

"Deputies Moore and Cortez right behind you, Sheriff. OK to turn on lights?"

"Come on down. We've got him cornered."

The three officers now spread out at the bottom of the pit, their guns drawn and pointed at the suspect. Flashlights from the two new officers swept around the huge pit. Nobody else was found. The suspect was turning his head left and right looking for an escape route. There was none.

"Lie down! Arms extended! Do it now!" The two deputies were shouting and moving quickly towards the body that finally dropped to the ground. Cortez moved in with the cuffs.

"We've got a lot of dynamite here, Sheriff," reported Deputy Moore a moment later. Perkins continued to stand, gun drawn, as his officers secured the suspect and the pit. Two other patrol cars had arrived and established a safe perimeter. "He was getting ready to blow them. There's detonation cord all over. And a timer right here. He's got six, no eight, wait, ten sticks of dynamite down here. Man that would make a big bang."

Moore checked out the wiring. "He was just about ready to connect, set the countdown to detonate. We got him just in time. Two or three more minutes and this place would have been one hot mess."

Perkins breathed deeply. He holstered his weapon and came down to confront the suspect. Cortez jerked the suspect upright. Perkins shone his flashlight on the person. It was a man. Well, that was a bit of a surprise.

"Who are you? What's your name?"

A pause. Then a groan. "Bobby."

Perkins waited. "Yeah?"

Another sigh. Another pause. "Broadhurst."

Just then the security guard appeared at the top of the pit, coffee in hand. "Hey, guys, what's happening?"

CHAPTER 78

BOBBY BROADHURST LOOKED around the interview room at HQ with interest. Perkins and his team studied him through the one-way mirror. He was early 20s, shaggy-haired, stubbled, dirty and he gave off a stench of three-day sweat and something even more unpleasant from his clothing. Or his armpits.

He was drinking from a bottle of water that was almost empty. Perkins' initial impression was that Bobby was not going to be heading up the quantum mathematics team at MIT any time soon.

Detective Rhonda Sanchez looked at Perkins with a raised eyebrow. He nodded. She was one of his top interrogators. He'd called her in to conduct this session.

He watched through the mirror as she opened the door and sat down across from Bobby and went through all the legal preliminaries. Then she plunged right in.

"Why are you blowing up buildings, Bobby?"

"To help my cuz. Billy. He's tryin' to impress this girl at FSU."

Perkins blew air out of his cheeks. A whole bunch of things just clicked together with that one simple sentence.

"Where did you get the dynamite?"

"Oh, from Billy. He's got lots of it at the University."

"Did anybody else help you?"

"Nah. I've been usin' dyn-o-mite since my pappy taught me years ago. We used tuh blow up beaver dams 'n stuff in the swamps."

"Do you know Eloise N'domo?"

"Nope."

"Kate Kowalski?"

"Sure. She's Billy's girlfriend. Except she don't know that. She's real purty." He gave a brown-toothed smile. "She smells real good."

"So, Billy asked you to do this?"

"Well, yeah. I was happy tuh do it. I like seein' things blowed up. And I made real sure not to hurt nobody."

"Uh huh. And why did Billy think your blowing up these buildings would help him get together with Kate?"

"Um, guess Billy thought if this-here Delvechy thing went boom, it wouldn't get built an' that'd make Kate's uncle the mayor. Agin." He paused to finish the bottle of water. "He's in the state pen, stoopid sumbitch."

More connectivity in this puzzling, frustrating case snapped into place. What were once obscure, separate facts were suddenly weaving a coherent narrative for Perkins.

"You know what you did was wrong, don't you?"

"Well shoot. Nah. Jus' helpin' out muh kinfolk."

Perkins had heard enough. Detective Sanchez would clean up the details. He left the room and returned to his office. He called Samantha. He'd sent her home with Rosie. It was 2:30am but she answered on the first ring.

"It was Billy Broadhurst's cousin doing the bombing. They had some twisted idea that it would get the former mayor re-instated, and that would make Kate grateful to Billy and they'd sail off happily into the sunset. Unbelievable. Dumb kids."

Samantha could hear the anger and frustration in his voice. "Well, at least it's over. You got them."

"Yeah. I guess Elliott Webster will be happy."

"I'm sure he will. And he'll want to thank you, and Mrs. Barkley and the Neighborhood Watch group at Delvecchio Bridge."

"So will we. The neighborhood did a great job. I'll call Mrs. Barkley tomorrow to thank her personally."

"That will be nice. She'll really appreciate it."

"I'm beat. Can you keep Rosie tonight? I'm just going to crash in the office for a couple of hours."

"Sure. You must be exhausted. Try to get some sleep. I'll talk to you in the morning." She looked at the clock. "Well, later this morning."

CHAPTER 79

AT 5:48AM, PERKINS rose from the battered couch in his office. He shaved and showered in the officers' locker room. He felt like crap. His shin had a big purple lump. His eyes were scratchy. He had been in better moods in his life.

At 6:59am, a four-SUV convoy swept into the Sheriff's headquarters. Crunciman and his cronies were dressed in black, wore mirror sunglasses, and strutted like peacocks that had just gotten lucky with the cutest peahen in the flock.

Perkins, Captain Williams and several other senior officers met them outside the front door.

Perkins enjoyed slowly and precisely informing Crunciman of the brilliant detective work of his department that had solved the Delvecchio Bridge bombing case. He was forceful in his comments. Crunciman bristled at several of them. Wiser heads and the very large bulk of Captain Williams ensured a peaceful if not happy discussion of the case between the two law enforcement leaders.

At 7:07am, the convoy had swept out of the parking lot, disappearing into the hot Florida morning.

At 7:08:30am, Perkins and his senior team were sprawled in his office chortling over the entire episode. The donut devastation was awful. The laughter was robust around the room.

An hour later, Perkins phoned FBI Regional Director James Robertson in Atlanta. They laughed together at the scenario. It was not yet possible with today's technology to hi-five over the cell phone towers, but Perkins and Robertson came very close.

Perkins phoned the other Police Chiefs and Sheriffs from the other cities where bombings had occurred and shared the information on the arrest of the Banjo Bomber. There was considerable relief among them all.

Perkins then ordered the PIO to send out a press release.

The resolution to the bombings drew much less media coverage than the explosions themselves.

CHAPTER 80

"WE NEVER EVEN considered relatives doing the dirty work," Perkins admitted to Samantha before dinner that evening. He had spent the day cleaning up the Banjo Bomber mess. "Everybody was so focused on the three kids after we finally discovered them. We did pretty well to figure that out, but we ignored the possibility of outsiders assisting them because we thought it would be one tight little secret cell. We sort of figured out the connection between Kate and her uncle and returning him to the mayor's office, but we underestimated Billy's infatuation. Eloise, as it turned out, was the only one with pure motives—to improve urban design and living, at least as she defined it. But she had no part of the violence."

He swallowed some ale. "It was a hard conversation with her lawyers. I told them she is no longer a person of interest and that we have no suspicion that she was involved. They seemed to accept that. Whether she will, in this environment of mistrust towards law enforcement, I don't know. Hopefully no lawsuit from her."

He nibbled some cheese. Rosie got a nice little dividend. "Billy was arrested as an accessory. He's now in custody. I expect he'll plead guilty. He'll spend some time in jail. So will his cuz."

Samantha poured him another IPA. "I'm going to bring Mrs. Barkley and her group of women down to headquarters and present them with a plaque for community service. They seem kind of excited about that. What they don't know is that Elliott Webster is going to present them with a $50,000 scholarship fund to help their kids pay for college."

"Oh, that's wonderful!" Samantha didn't mention that it had been her idea to set up the fund. Elliott had loved the idea.

"He told me that if ten sticks of dynamite had blown up the foundation and the steel again, it would have terminated the project. They probably wouldn't be able to get insurance, and the workers might have rebelled. Construction likely would have stopped. That would have been tragic for the community."

"It would have been awful. And it probably would have bankrupted his company," Samantha said heatedly. Perkins nodded. "Imagine that wonderful family business and all those jobs that would have been lost. And my park for the kids!" She bit off a swallow of Sauvignon Blanc.

Perkins patted her hand gently and continued his summary.

"Kate Kowalski is the last piece out there. She is the hardest one to clean up. Technically we don't think she had anything to do with the actual bombings, but I remember what her mother said in my office. I just find it hard to believe that she didn't either provoke Billy into this crazy plan, or that she didn't at least know about it. I suspect she was controlling him with sex, or the promise of it. He's a weak little puppy. The DA is looking at an accessory charge against her, but I'm not sure he can make it stick. I think she's a pretty tough girl who's not going to crack. I suppose Billy might squeal on her, but he's really infatuated. So, she may well walk away scot free." He grimaced at the idea. "She'll make a heck of a politician some day with that Teflon skin and lack of morals."

Samantha thought about that as she sipped her wine. Rosie didn't seem to care as much about the fate of the students; she was much more concerned about the fate of the cheese plate and the equitable distribution of its contents.

"Oh," Perkins concluded. "The banjo music. Bobby just liked that song. He played it just before he set off each explosion. Some sort of theme song or something." He shook his head. "Some psychiatrist at the prison will have a field day exploring that."

CHAPTER 81

THE DINNER TO celebrate the home's survival of the drug dealer shoot-out at Whispering Palms and the help from Rosie and Samantha during the drama was an occasion. The residents had decided to dress up. Samantha was glad she had worn an attractive dress of cream silk with black accents on the neck and shoulder cut-outs, black heels and a black bead necklace.

She had overcome Perk's grumblings enough to get him into a jacket and crisp open-necked blue shirt. Rosie was her usual cute self. She seemed to know that, as she went preening through the crowd of seniors in the large sitting room.

The cocktail half-hour ended at 5:30 and the ensemble moved into the dining room. Samantha and the Sheriff were seated at the table of honor in front of the big picture window that looked onto the garden. They were welcomed by the head of the Resident's council, Ruth Goldblatt; the interim GM, Roger Storey; Head Nurse Nick Nurse; and Mrs. Harris.

Rosie was seated between Samantha and Mrs. Harris. She sat proudly, her coat shining in the evening light. Samantha had spent much of the afternoon giving her a bath and a good brushing. Her coat glistened, Samantha observed somewhat enviously.

Perkins broke the ice by telling the table about some of the strange and amusing laws still on the books in various states:

* It is illegal to sing in public while wearing a bathing suit—in Florida.
* In Idaho, it is illegal to fish while you are on the back of a camel.
* In Kentucky, you can't hold ice cream in your back pocket.
* In Gainesville, Georgia, it is illegal to eat chicken with a fork. Interestingly, Gainesville is titled, "The Chicken Capital of the World.

The laughter soon generated other stories as the salad course was served. Rosie was not very enthusiastic about salad, so she settled to the floor with her head between her paws.

The room buzzed with talk and laughter. A little wine had been poured for many of those in attendance. A slight flush appeared on a few weathered, powdered cheeks.

The main course was poached chicken with grilled asparagus and scalloped potatoes. It had been a while since Samantha had eaten scalloped potatoes. They were really good. Not a creamy, buttery calorie in the serving.

Rosie received a nice plate of chicken. No asparagus. No potatoes. She scarfed it down in record time and began to negotiate for a little extra from the plates on the table.

Samantha looked down at her and said, "Be a good girl. No begging at the table."

What Rosie heard was, "You are such a lovely girl. Would you like some more chicken? Well, just ask politely."

So she did.

Mrs. Harris rewarded her. So did Nick Nurse. Perkins sighed.

Dessert was cherry or apple pie. With ice cream, upon request. Perkins requested with some enthusiasm. Samantha fought a battle with her thighs and her conscience and won a partial victory with the cherry pie but no à la mode.

The speeches after dinner were not lengthy. GM Storey welcomed everyone, said how happy he was to be their new manager, got a little laugh by saying he hoped the excitement of recent weeks was in the past, and introduced Mrs. Goldblatt.

"We have wanted to do a little something for our two special new friends here at Whispering Palms," she began. "First, for the beautiful lady with the gorgeous burnished-gold hair." Samantha bowed her head in modesty. "She has added so much to our lives and brought us all such joy and enchantment." Samantha's cheeks turned a bit pink at the praise. "So our Crafts Committee wanted to make something very special for her." Samantha cleared her throat. What a lovely gesture. She was sure she would enjoy it. "Rosie, would you join me?"

Samantha sagged back in her chair. Perkins looked at her with a big grin on his stupid face. She glared at him. He covered his mouth with his napkin to keep from laughing out loud.

Rosie bounded to the front of the table. There Mrs. Goldblatt unbuckled her old, store-bought collar and replaced it with a beautiful hand-made leather collar with a shiny gold star stamped with her name hanging from the front. Rosie gave the nice lady a little kiss.

Warm applause from the crowd. Rosie had become a celebrity at the home.

"Now," continued Mrs. Goldblatt, "we also wanted to honor one other lovely lady. Also with such beautiful reddish hair. Samantha has not only enriched us with her visits, but she showed enormous bravery during that nasty episode a little while ago when she rushed to lock the front doors. That kept out the shooter for a precious bit of time and let the police take action. We think she certainly saved some of us from injury or maybe even worse. She has become a very special friend of Whispering Palms. Samantha, would you come up?"

Big applause. The people who could rise rose. Perkins escorted her out of her chair and gently pushed her to the front.

Mrs. Goldblatt hugged her and then stepped back. "Samantha, we so enjoy your visits. Thank you for adopting us. And for bringing Rosie. On behalf of all of us at Whispering Palms, we want you to have this gift from us."

With those gracious words, she picked up a beautifully decorated package and presented it to Samantha, who promptly hugged her again and tried to fight back tears.

She stood there, holding her gift. "I just want to say that this is so very special. I thank you. And you all mean so much to Rosie and Kim and me. We love coming here. As long as you'll have us, we'll keep on visiting."

Another nice round of applause. The guests began to disperse. After all, it was almost 7:30. *Jeopardy* was on soon.

At the head table, Samantha was urged to open her gift. She carefully unwrapped the bow and paper and lifted the lid. And gasped. It was a beautifully hand-tooled leather necklace with a small gold star at the front.

"This is exquisite," she announced to the table. "Thank you so much." She looked at it some more, then at Rosie. "Oh! Now Rosie and I can dress up together!"

Rosie wandered over to see what the fuss was all about. Wait, why was Mommy holding Rosie's new collar? She scratched at her neck. No, she had hers on. Well. Copycat. At least Rosie could be a fashion icon for Mommy, leading the way with her cutting-edge fashion choices.

She wandered off in case a random piece of chicken had suddenly dropped to the floor.

Several of the residents retired to the little bar adjacent to the dining room for a nightcap. Samantha, the sheriff, Rosie and Mrs. Harris joined them.

"What a lovely evening," breathed Samantha happily as she lifted her glass of Drambuie on ice to salute the table. "Thank you again."

Heads nodded and smiles were offered. Talk was light. Drinks were finished and the crowd began to scatter.

"I'd better take Rosie for her walk," Perkins said. Samantha nodded as she got up and turned to Mrs. Harris.

"May I see you to your door, Madam?"

Mrs. Harris laughed. "You may."

They began the journey down the hall to the elevators. Perkins put a leash on Rosie and headed for the exit. He was surprised to find a pair of malevolent eyes following him. Elmer Krackle stared at the pair before ducking behind a door.

As Rosie wandered around the lawn looking for nocturnal squirrels and the perfect place to do her business, Perkins thought more about the angry nurse. What's with the bitterness?

He remembered Samantha had said something about indications of abuse in the home. Could there be any truth to them?

Samantha rolled Mrs. Harris's wheelchair up to her apartment. She unlocked the door and they went in.

"Oh drat. Samantha, would you mind doing me a little favor? I forgot my meds. Ethel at the Nursing Station will have them."

"Of course. I'll get them now."

Samantha walked down the long hallway to the desk and its back room where the on-duty nurse was located. No one was at the counter. She looked into the room behind. The light was on and there seemed to be somebody inside.

"Hello?" No reply.

Samantha quietly went around the desk and opened the door to the office. Nurse Ethel was standing at a counter preparing medications. She was startled when Samantha appeared.

"Oh! Gosh, you scared me." She nearly dropped a vial of clear liquid. There were several syringes standing ready. Samantha could tell she was flustered.

"Sorry. I called from the desk, but nobody answered. Mrs. Harris needs her medications for tonight."

"Oh. OK. I'll get them. Just let me finish preparing the insulin for my patients."

Samantha nodded. She looked around the little office. There were racks of pill bottles and jars of medications to be given to the residents.

Ethel was usually so quiet but tonight she seemed very nervous. She began chattering to cover it up. "There are so many medications I have to give out every day. So much work. And some of the patients don't take care of themselves. They don't deserve to..." She stopped abruptly. "I try to tell them, I try to warn them. But they don't listen. They don't do what I want them to do."

Samantha was listening with half an ear. The racks of medications were startling to her. So many of them. Each resident had his or her own drawer. Charts and schedules of when the meds were to be taken filled a tack board.

"Pills for everyone. Opioids for some for their pain. Insulin for the diabetic patients. So many of those. Mr. Chan. Mrs. Thessalin. Mr. Cummings. Mrs. Squire." She abruptly shut up. She kept her head down. Samantha kept looking around.

Ethel was quiet again. Samantha looked at her discreetly. The nurse was in her 40s. Her hair was a tangled mess of brown and gray. She was very thin. Her uniform had a couple of stains on it. Her once white shoes were no longer pristine. She seemed nervous for some reason—preoccupied perhaps.

"Uh, the pills for Mrs. Harris? I can take them down to her. That will save you a bit of time."

"I guess that will be alright. Here." She grabbed four pill bottles from Mrs. Harris' slot and put one pill from each in a small plastic cup. She passed it to Samantha. She then began pushing the rolling cart of medications out of the nursing station. She wouldn't look at Samantha as she left.

Samantha shrugged, thanked Ethel as she maneuvered the cart and carefully left with the pills.

She returned to Mrs. Harris's room and gave her the prescriptions.

"Boy, the nurse seemed awfully weird. Kind of mousy, isn't she?"

"Ah. Ethel. Yes, she is. You practically don't even notice her. Then she is just there. Odd woman. And not a happy person. I've always thought she was hiding something. An old love lost, maybe? I know she's not married and doesn't seem to have a family." Mrs. Harris sniffed. "She could certainly make herself a little more presentable."

Samantha got a glass of water and handed it to the older woman. She began to swallow the four pills she had to take at bedtime.

"She was complaining about all the medications that the residents have to take," Samantha continued. "And she said something odd about some of them not looking after them-selves. I thought it was a peculiar statement for a nurse to make."

"That is peculiar. Ethel seems to have some inner demons. I've never quite figured her out. She doesn't have that, what is the word, precision? that most nurses have. I think that nasty Elmer Krackle really dominates her." She paused as she took her final pill. "I don't like that man."

Samantha nodded agreement. "He is a creepy guy. And I still think some of the residents are afraid of him." She took the empty pill cup from Mrs. Harris and tossed it in the garbage. "I can't put him together with the bruises I've seen on a few of the resident's arms and wrists, but I certainly have suspicions."

Mrs. Harris was obviously tiring. Samantha looked around the apartment to see if she needed anything else before going to bed. "I guess Ethel will be doing her rounds now. She shouldn't bother you. I told her I would make sure you took your pills." She paused again for a final check. "I guess she'll be giving the insulin shots to Mr. Chan and Mrs. Squire and the others."

"Forgive me, dear, I'm getting a bit sleepy. Would you just help me to—wait, what?"

"Uh..."

"Did you say she's giving an insulin shot to Mrs. Squire?"

"Yes, I think she said that."

"Mrs. Squire isn't diabetic!"

"But...but...why would she be...oh my God! You don't think..."

"We have to stop her! Mrs. Squire is a friend of mine. Her apartment is 278, way down a corridor at the far end of—oh I don't have time to explain it to you! Take me there!"

Samantha didn't hesitate. She opened the apartment door, wheeled Mrs. Harris out into the hallway and started pushing.

"Down this hallway! All the way to the end! Hurry!"

Samantha pushed harder. Her heels were not made for sprinting. She kicked them off. The faux marble tile felt cool on her bare feet but she got a better grip and moved faster.

One of the gentlemen from the bar appeared out of an elevator. "Get the Sheriff! Now!" commanded Samantha. "Tell him to go to 278 immediately! 278!"

The man gaped as the wheelchair whizzed by him. Then he collected himself and pushed the down button to return to the lobby level and find the Sheriff. The door dinged.

Samantha and Mrs. Harris continued their desperate sprint down the corridor. Samantha had to swerve suddenly as another door opened and a resident strolled into the hallway. Everyone yelped in surprise.

Another door opened. It was becoming an obstacle course. Mrs. Harris clung desperately to the armrests of her wheelchair as Samantha tried to accelerate. She swerved again to avoid an elderly man.

Samantha was beginning to gasp for air. Pushing a wheelchair at high speed was a taxing endeavor. She made a note to add it to her cardio workouts.

The end of the hallway loomed. "Turn left here," Mrs. Harris ordered. Samantha slowed and managed an elegant wheelie around the corner. She didn't use her turn signal but figured she could be excused this once.

"There's a right turn just down here," Mrs. Harris told her. "We're getting close! I just hope we're not too late! Come on!"

Samantha did a wide right turn and barrelled into the dimly lit hallway. She could see the nurse's medication cart at the end of the corridor, half into a room. She grunted and took a deep breath as she tried to add a couple of MPHs to her speed. Mrs. Harris leaned forward to assist aerodynamically.

She could hear a few more doors opening behind her as they flew down the corridor. There were shouts of "What's going on?" and "Hey!" and "Be careful!" Samantha had to swerve again as a door ahead of them opened suddenly. Mrs. Harris hung on grimly, waving her cane at the woman in the doorway.

A moment later they arrived at 278. Samantha skidded to a stop. Mrs. Harris reached out to push the med cart inside and jabbed her cane into the door to open it fully. It swung open and Samantha took the two crucial steps that wheeled Mrs. Harris into the dimly lit room.

A lady in her 80s was lying in her bed. Samantha assumed it was Mrs. Squire. Nurse Ethel was holding a syringe and was about to inject her with a clear fluid.

"STOP!" Mrs. Harris hadn't been a successful teacher for 40 years by being timid or soft-voiced. Her tone froze the nurse. Mrs. Squire didn't seem to be conscious. Samantha was still trying to take in the situation.

"Ethel! Back away from the bed!" Mrs. Harris commanded. Ethel paused. She looked around. "Now!" She dropped her hand with the syringe in it. She looked down at Mrs. Squire. Then she looked at Mrs. Harris. Then at Samantha.

She gripped the syringe as if she was going to slash at them. "Drop it, Ethel! Now!"

Tears began to appear in the nurse's eyes. She waved the lethal needle at them but then sagged and the syringe suddenly fell to the floor. Her face crumpled as she choked out, "Why did you stop me? Her time had come. The Voices told me so."

A cold shiver went down Samantha's spine. The nurse's tone was faint, almost disembodied. It was eerie. And frightening.

Mrs. Harris was made of sterner stuff. "Ethel! Listen to me! Step away from the bed. Come over here. Now!"

A pause. Samantha stood there, frozen, as the scene slowly played out. She was scared to move in case it startled Ethel or she grabbed another syringe and tried to use it as a weapon against the two of them.

Mrs. Harris seemed to understand that as well. She subtly rolled her wheelchair a foot or two forward, but it was enough to block Ethel's direct access to the medication cart. Samantha breathed a sigh of relief.

Ethel seemed to be in some sort of suspended animation. She moved very slowly. Her gaze was far away.

Samantha could hear footsteps pounding down the hall-way. A man's boot. Good.

The Sheriff burst into 278 a moment later. He skidded to a stop as he did a quick assessment of the situation. It made no sense at all to him. Rosie bounded in and looked around the room.

"You OK?"

"Yes," Samantha whispered.

"Mrs. Harris?"

"Yes."

"Who's the...why am I...what's going on?"

Samantha could sympathize with his confusion. She wasn't completely sure what was going on.

Mrs. Harris had no such compunction.

"I think we've just broken up a series of murders of innocent residents here, Sheriff. I think you should put the cuffs on Nurse Ethel." She paused as that sunk in. "Then I think you and your people should have a long, long talk with her about the recent unexplained deaths here at Whispering Palms."

That galvanized Ethel. She cried out and lunged forward, hands extended, clawing for the medicine cart and its sharp needles. Perkins move swiftly to block her. He grabbed her with one hand and spun her around the wheelchair. Mrs. Harris thrust her cane between the nurse's legs. Ethel and Perkins tumbled to the hard tile floor. Samantha could hear the air go out of the nurse. She lay wailing on the floor as Perkins sat on her.

"Give me the adhesive tape on the cart." Samantha grabbed it and ripped off two long strips. Perkins used them to bind the nurse's wrists behind her back before hauling her onto the chair beside the bed. Ethel slumped there, tears streaming down her cheeks. Her head was bowed and she was exhaling loud, tortured sobs.

Mrs. Squire still hadn't moved.

CHAPTER 82

"THE WHOLE STORY is unbelievable," Perkins announced two days later to Mrs. Harris and Samantha. They were in a small conference room at Whispering Palms. GM Roger Storey and Head Nurse Nick Nurse sat at the table. They were both bewildered by the narrative and stunned at the outcome.

"After we took her down to headquarters, she was sort of frozen. She said something about E-somebody or something told her to. It took us two days to figure out that information from her. Who is Elmer?"

"Elmer Krackle, likely. A nurse who worked here. He disappeared the night of the arrest. Nobody's seen him since."

"Dark hair, dark eyes, mean expression on his pock-marked face?"

"That would be him."

"I saw him glaring at me the night of the dinner. Creepy looking dude."

Deputy Chad made a note.

"Anyway, we didn't get anything out of her that first night. The next day it was if some switch flipped on. She started talking." Perkins paused and looked down at the table. He shook his head. "None of my interrogators had ever heard anything like it before."

He swallowed some coffee and went on. "She said she was on a mission to cleanse society. The Voices told her what to do." He drank again and shook his head. "To be honest, it was scary to listen to her."

He looked at Mrs. Harris. "You were right. You were the first one to figure it out. She's responsible for at least five, and we think maybe six, murders here at Whispering Palms. We also think she's responsible for two, and probably more, murders at another long-term care home where she also works. She would inject a very high dose of insulin into her victim. They would go unconscious and then die. I guess it was painless for them. It certainly was effective. And nobody suspected anything. There are rarely autopsies done on a nursing home death. They happen so frequently. Most medical professionals assume the death is natural or from underlying health causes. Family members are sort of prepared for the inevitable. They never question the passing. So these deaths are almost never reported to law enforcement. And therefore not investigated."

He looked down at the table. "I guess the insulin dissipates in the body. What evidence would there have been left to prove murder? And who would have suspected anything was amiss? In some ways it is almost a perfect crime scenario."

Silence in the room as the full horror of the situation seeped into every crevice of their minds.

"The reality is, if she hadn't blabbed to Samantha, and Mrs. Harris hadn't made the connection to Mrs. Squire, and if Ethel hadn't confessed eventually, I'm not sure the authorities would have ever discovered these crimes."

No one spoke as that sombre reality settled in the room.

Finally Perkins shook his head. "What you can do is help me find this Elmer Krackle character." He rubbed his hands together. "We would very much like to have a little chat with him."

CHAPTER 83

THE MANHUNT FOR Elmer Krackle accelerated rapidly.

FBI Regional Director James Robertson authorized electronic surveillance on Krackle's credit cards, cell phone and bank accounts. Michael Crunciman of Homeland Security stunned Perkins and his department by agreeing to check international travel and do a bulletin to police forces and border security agencies in Canada and Mexico.

A third interview with Ethel had produced little of use. She had frozen again. She occasionally spouted incoherent phrases. She sat in a slumped pose. She often shook. It was the interviewer's opinion that she had serious mental health issues. Perkins authorized a referral to a state hospital for a psych evaluation.

Chats with other staff members and several residents at Whispering Palms had been fruitless. One man said he remembered that Krackle once mentioned he liked his spurs; no one recalled him riding horses, and spurs and nursing shoes didn't go together. The officer interviewing the resident shrugged. Perhaps the elderly gentleman was having a bit of a memory issue.

It became apparent quickly that Krackle was not well liked by any of his patients. Quiet talks with several residents did in fact reveal that he would sometimes forcibly restrain patients in their beds. They had been scared to tell anyone in authority because Krackle had threatened them with worse treatment. He had even withheld food and water, and had not let some of them go to the bathroom when needed.

Perkins was sickened by the stories. His determination to get the perpetrator drove his entire department. The reports of elder abuse and murder shocked even the most hardened police officer.

"We have no evidence of Krackle leaving by ship or by plane," reported Crunciman's assistant. "His passport hasn't been used. He doesn't have a NEXUS card or another form of approved travel documentation. Or at least not under that name."

"His credit cards haven't been used in the last two days," reported Robertson. "He did use his bank card to withdraw the daily maximum of $600 from his account. We assume he is now running somewhere in the US using that cash. That will run out soon if he has to pay for food, gas and motels from his stash. He may have more cash but his checking account has only $1,377.69 in it and doesn't show any other sizeable cash withdrawals recently. He could be traveling by bus or train, but we suspect car because his is missing. A 2016 Camry. Gray."

The Sheriff's department had no trouble getting a search warrant for his apartment. It revealed little but dirty clothes, a messy bedroom, a bedside table with a lot of porn, food spoiling in the kitchen and a half-starved cat which the deputies turned over to the Animal Shelter. There were a few trinkets from past vacations—the St. Louis Arch, the Alamo, Bourbon Street. There were many pamphlets from an obscure religious sect that was predicting the imminent end of the world. Their previous predictions of Armageddon had proven to be misguided, but their literature seemed more enthusiastic about their next date for the extinction of the Earth.

Talks with the superintendent at the apartment building were uninformative. The manager spoke better Spanish than English. He seemed nervous about talking to law enforcement officers. The two deputies suspected a stash of weed somewhere on his premises, and maybe a couple of illegal immigrants as well.

Perkins didn't care about that.

"If he drove north at first, which is probable, he could be anywhere in the United States." His crisis team all studied the large map of the continental US. "Once he got to the Florida panhandle, he could have gone west, north or east."

Frustration flooded the conference room. Krackle had no living relatives as far as the federal agencies could determine. He had been born in Galveston in 1974. Both parents were deceased. No siblings. He had lived in Florida since 2008. If he had any friends, the investigators hadn't found them. He filed his taxes on time. He had a modest annual income of $41,000. He had no police record other than a DUI when he was 22.

Whispering Palms had done a rather cursory background check on him. "The reality is that nursing staff are in such demand that long-term care facilities will take anybody with a nursing certificate—and be grateful to hire them," confessed Roger Storey. Krackle's credentials had come from a little-known religious college in Central Texas. He had earned mediocre Cs and a couple of Ds. But he had passed.

"He doesn't seem to have a home base to return to that we have identified," advised the psychologist that the department occasionally hired to bring insight into the personality of suspects in difficult cases. "Almost everybody has a base, somewhere familiar that they consider to be safe. That's the tendency for people in times of strife or danger—get to a secure place where they feel comfortable and protected. Their family. Their hometown. Whatever."

"Re-check your notes," Perkins ordered the officers who had done the interviews at Whispering Palms. "There's got to be some clue, some obscure fact that we're missing."

Officers sorted through their note pads again. "He might like Tex-Mex food," offered one after analyzing the take-out menus at his apartment. "Maybe he hikes. One of the residents said something about walking by a river—she was a little vague," reported another. "He sometimes wore glasses." "He had dirty fingernails." "He usually wore black and silver shirts under his nurse's jacket," contributed another.

Perkins pursed his lips in frustration. Wayne Cooper continued to stare at the notes he'd been making steadily during the discussion.

"OK, thanks. Anything else right now?"

Shakes of heads around the table. Papers were shuffled into stacks. It had been an unprofitable meeting. Nobody was happy. How could this guy be defeating the combined police muscle that Perkins had assembled?

"Let's keep watch on his banking and credit cards. And travel." Perkins nodded at Crunciman's representative, who nodded back. "Go over your notes one more time. There has to be some link, some hint that..."

"Sheriff. Hang on. I might have something," Cooper said as he slowly raised his head. The room froze. Cooper's insights were usually incisive, sometimes stunning in their leap forward. "I'm not positive, but I think he is hiding in San Antonio."

CHAPTER 84

THE PURSUIT QUICKENED. Perkins called San Antonio Police Chief Laura Delgado. "He did that to seniors living in a home?" She was outraged. "My father is in a long-term care facility. I'm going to check them out tonight!"

Perkins gave her the details they had on Krackle. "We don't have an address in San Antonio and we are not positive he is there, but one of our smartest analysts figured he was running to San Antonio. I've learned to trust Coop's instincts."

"You don't mean Wayne Cooper?"

"Yeah."

"Wow. I've heard of him. Anytime you big uglies in Florida get tired of him, just send him to me in San Antonio."

"Yeah. No. But I'd be happy to send you a few pounds of alligator meat."

"Ugh. Double ugh. This is beef country. When you get smart enough, you should try some. How did Cooper figure it out?"

Perkins laughed hoarsely. "He put together some widely separated and, to the rest of us, unrelated small clues. 'Walking by the river' became your Riverwalk. 'Likes spurs' became your NBA team. Other stuff. Scary how his mind works."

"Yeah. Still think he'd be better here than in that humid climate of yours. It's prob'ly killing brain cells every day."

"Oh. You've met our Senator." Delgado chuckled. "Listen, Chief, I want this guy. It is one big, ugly mess that we are uncovering here. I'm worried he's running for the Mexican border and will disappear down there."

"I understand. I'll brief my people immediately. You'll liaise with Captain Lopez. You'll hear from him later today."

"Thanks, Chief. I appreciate the help."

"Killing innocent seniors in their beds. Unbelievable. If you need anything else, just holler."

Less than two hours later, Perkins took a call from Texas. A gravelly voice marinated by years of unfiltered cigarettes spoke.

"Captain Eduardo Lopez, Sheriff. Chief Delgado gave me this case. What an ugly crime. I've never heard of anything like it."

"Nobody here has either. What do you have for me, Captain? We want this guy."

"We happen to be testing a new Artificial Intelligence vehicle license scanning system through our traffic cameras. This will be a great test. My people are feeding the data in right now. If he's driving in our city, we'll get him. If he's heading for the airport, we'll get him. If he's running for the border, we'll get him."

"That's the best news I've had today. Thank you. You've got my cell number as well? Good. Don't hesitate to call me at any hour."

CHAPTER 85

IT WAS 6:57AM when Perkins' cell phone buzzed. He was already in his car heading for HQ. He hit the hands-free audio.

"Perkins."

"Sheriff. Good morning. It's Eduardo Lopez, SAPD."

"Captain. Good morning. I'm hoping this is good news."

A pause. "Yes. I guess. We spotted Krackle's car at 11:36 last night, heading south. Our A. I. system alerted us. We got the Staties involved once he hit the highway south towards the border. They stopped him on I-37. We figure he was running for the crossing at McAllen or Brownsville."

"What happened?"

"The Texas Highway Patrol stopped him in the middle of nowhere about 2am. Three patrol cars. The plates matched your information, so did the make of car. The driver was not, ah, cooperative initially. He sort of waved a pistol out the window. Maybe took a couple of wild shots. The officers were not amused. Some gunfire was returned. Krackle was wounded. Our guys are OK."

"How badly?"

"Oh, nothing serious. Hand. A nick in the forearm from a ricochet. They took him to a local hospital to clean him up. He's in the jail at McAllen right now. Your guys are welcome to pick him up and take him back. He said a few things about Texas, so he's not real popular down here."

Perkins grinned into the phone. If there was one thing he knew about Texas, it was that you don't mess with the state, its history, its barbecue, The Alamo or football.

"No extradition problems?"

"Nah. Your warrant will be good. And frankly we'd just as soon get rid of this scumbag. I can't believe he doesn't like Texas brisket." Perkins could hear the exasperation in the Captain's voice. "He's just a perverted little bastard. He fits better into Florida society than our pristine lifestyle here."

Perkins couldn't help laughing. "OK, thank you. I'll send a couple of guys to drag his sorry ass back here. They'll coordinate with you. Your guys did a great job. I'll be telling your Chief that."

CHAPTER 86

"I THINK HE'S SCAMMING us. He's just trying to avoid a needle on Death Row," claimed Detective Rhonda Sanchez. Perkins had assigned her to be the lead interrogator upon Krackle's return to their jurisdiction.

"I'm not so sure," returned ADA Frank McWhirter. He was a tough-minded senior lawyer in the DA's office. He handled many high-profile capital crimes. "We've already got back a preliminary report from the psychiatrist on Nurse Ethel. She says that quiet little gray-haired Ethel is one seething mass of twisted morals and is not capable of separating the Voice she claims to be hearing from stuff that Krackle was supposedly telling her. She just keeps claiming that the Voice told her to inject patients to kill them. She says it was to help cleanse the universe." He shook his head. "We figure she's nuttier than a tin of Planters and that she'll never go on trial for these murders. Without her testimony, it makes the case against this Krackle filth pretty iffy."

"Just what are you saying? He's going to walk on this whole mess?"

McWhirter looked down at his hands. He twisted them for a moment. "The reality is, what have we got against him? He frowned at some people at Whispering Pines. Maybe he used tie-downs on some of them, but no formal complaints were ever filed. His lawyer would argue that was to protect seniors from harming themselves. As far as we know he never injected a lethal dose into any resident. He hasn't admitted anything to Detective Sanchez in her interrogations. I don't think we have a case."

The frustration level in the Sheriff's meeting room was edging into the volcanic.

"He's as dirty as a manure spreader at the end of a dusty day!" Sanchez was clear about her feelings. There were supportive nods from around the table.

"Then bring me the evidence. Look, I don't like this any better than you do, but so far I've got nothing to work with that will stand up in a jury trial."

A lengthy pause. It got uncomfortable. Perkins finally stood up. "OK, we're not going to settle this today. Rhonda, have another run at him tomorrow. Frank, we'll try to find you something on the scum ball."

The meeting adjourned. Frustrated staff filed out. McWhirter finished stuffing his briefcase. This was the really lousy part of the job, he thought as he closed the bag.

Perkins wrapped up his long day and headed for Samantha's.

Chapter 87

"So that's a big part of the problem," Samantha told Mrs. Harris the next morning as they sipped mid-morning coffee and watched Rosie romp through the meeting room. Her new collar shone in the morning sun. "The police have no formal complaints, no record of abuse to residents, no evidence that Krackle actually wrongly injected anyone here, and no testimony from anyone as to his influencing Ethel. It is all circumstantial. And he seems to be a very cunning man without scruples. He's admitting to nothing."

Mrs. Harris set down her cup on a side table. She glared out at the world at Samantha's news. The world blinked back in dismay. Mrs. Harris was one tough customer.

"Would it make a difference if there was a series of complaints about cruelty and abuse from residents here?"

"I'm not a lawyer, but yes, I would think so."

"OK. Have a couple of deputies here at 2pm. Maybe a lawyer or two. I'll take care of the rest."

Samantha immediately got on the phone to Perkins. He was cautious and curious, but agreed to have two deputies visit the home, along with somebody from the DA's office.

New GM Roger Storey appeared in the doorway. He watched in awe as Rosie performed her therapeutic magic. "Amazing," he muttered to Samantha as she went to get Rosie and take her home. Samantha smiled and nodded.

At 2pm Samantha returned to the home. Mrs. Harris was acting as Sergeant-Major. She had the deputies seated at two tables in separate corners of the meeting room. The ADA and an assistant were at another. Then the parade began.

One by one, more than a dozen residents came forward to file formal complaints against Elmer Krackle. The stories they told were horrifying. Three of them had pictures of bruises on arms and wrists from restraints. The stories were all consistent: Krackle often tied his patients down at night despite their resistance; if they threatened to complain or report him, he said he would withhold food and medicine.

It was a reign of terror. If they misbehaved, he would deny them water or refuse to help them to go to the bathroom. If they said they would tell their relatives who visited, Krackle threatened to adjust their meds or deny them pain killers or other medications.

It had all been whispered about in recent weeks amongst the residents, but no one had had the courage to come forward.

"I just started to find out about all of this recently," reported Mrs. Harris to the detectives. "Friends here were starting to tell me. Then it all kind of blew up with the gun fight and the fall-out from that, and the deaths of my friends." She sighed loudly. "It has been a very traumatic time. But when I heard you need complaints to be made against that horrid little man, then I knew we all needed to step forward. Will this give you enough evidence against him?"

"Yes, ma'am. We'll be reporting this to the Sheriff immediately. I think the DA will file a raft of new charges of elder abuse against this human slime ball, regardless of the murder charges. This will keep him locked away for a very long time. Thank you for stepping forward and for organizing this... confessional."

Samantha was tight-lipped with anger as the reports of mistreatment of these lovely older people mounted up.

"I fear this sort of thing is more prevalent in some long-term care facilities than we realize," said GM Storey. "Residents are so vulnerable, particularly if they need a lot of assistance in getting out of bed, dressing, eating, and so on. And if they don't have any relatives to advocate for them, they are often alone and scared. Some have dementia. Most have health problems of some kind. They all take medications. We're understaffed a bit, but this facility is better than most."

It was hardly a ringing endorsement of the industry.

Samantha clenched her teeth to avoid saying anything angry and bitter. Storey was new; maybe he'd improve things.

Mrs. Harris was slumped in her chair as the final interviews concluded and the room cleared. Samantha realized how physically and emotionally draining this entire episode had been for her. She shook her head and went behind the wheelchair.

"Let's get you to your room for a little nap," she said firmly. There were no protests.

"Oh, thank you, dear. Hang on. Could we swing by the desk to check my mail?"

"Of course." Samantha pushed her down the hall to the main reception area.

"Any mail?"

"Yes, Mrs. Harris, a big envelope just arrived for you." The receptionist put the envelope on her lap and Samantha continued the journey to her room. A moment later she had Mrs. Harris beside her bed.

"Huh. That's a bit odd," Mrs. Harris said as she wearily studied the return address. "It is from one of Lillian Goldschmidt's daughters. Remember her? She passed away a few weeks ago. We were good friends."

She slit open the large envelope and withdrew a letter and another envelope. She read the letter and the passed it to Samantha.

Dear Mrs. Harris:

I know that you and my mother were wonderful friends at Whispering Palms. My sister and I, and our families, are still absorbing her passing. It was unexpected. That's why it has taken me quite a while to go through her belongings.

I found this letter, which was addressed to you. I have not opened it.

I hope you are well, and perhaps this note from my mother will comfort you.

Sincerely yours,

Rhonda Blumenthal

Mrs. Harris carefully opened the sealed envelope. She read it intently. She flinched a couple of times as she absorbed the letter from the grave. She re-read it and then put it on her lap and wiped away a tear. Then she looked up at Samantha and, for the first time in her 86 years, swore. "I think we just nailed the bastard."

Samantha took the letter with a shaking fist. It was handwritten in a small, tight, elegant script:

My dear Latoya:

I am writing you in case something happens to me. I am getting weaker and am not feeling that well because of my heart condition. You will have noticed that.

Last night, Nurse Ethel and that mean Mr. Krackle were in my room. They thought I was asleep. He kept telling her that my time had come, that the Voices were speaking, and that she had to cleanse the world.

She was moaning. He insisted that she was doing a good thing. It was very scary.

We have talked about our suspicions of something going on here at the home. I don't trust either one of them. I think he is evil. I think she is weak. I am afraid. I am going to tell my daughter on her next visit.

Be very careful, my dear friend.

Warmly,

Lillian

"Her daughter's next visit never happened, of course. Lillian was killed the next night. I always thought it was a suspicious death."

"This is stunning. I'm certainly no lawyer, but I think this might be something like a death-bed confession. I think it will stand up in court. May I take this to Perk?"

"Yes. Immediately. This is a voice from the grave, but I want it to be heard loud and clear. And I want justice for my friend."

With that she passed Samantha both envelopes and both letters. She slumped in her chair, clearly exhausted. Samantha helped her onto the bed, smoothed a comforter over her, and left her to rest.

She took the envelopes and headed for the Sheriff's department.

Chapter 88

"THE COURT MIGHT treat it as a dying declaration," said DA Doug Saunders. Perkins had phoned him as soon as he had read the letters to Mrs. Harris and asked him to come over. Sanders re-read the second letter carefully. "It is rather unusual in a trial for a judge to allow this type of evidence, but I know of at least two cases in other states where a letter like this has been allowed. One was a wife who was scared of her husband; I think the other was also a wife who got tangled up in some religious stuff and allegedly committed suicide. It can be difficult to handle from a legal point of view," he concluded, "but this is the first real break in our investigation of murder with this Krackle piece of..."

"As a minimum it should give our interrogators a lot more leverage."

"Yes. And it might scare him enough to crack. His lawyers will have a hard time dealing with a kind of death-bed statement from a respected older person."

Samantha sat quietly, watching the professionals in the police and court systems try to work out the strategy that would put away a man she knew in her heart was a murderer. She had explained the way the letters had come into her possession. Saunders and Perkins were both satisfied with the process and the chain of custody.

She admired what they were doing. She was, of course, already highly attracted to Perkins but seeing him in his professional capacity was very stimulating. She crossed her legs. Maybe it was time to play the naughty Sheriff and the stern librarian.

"Samantha and Mrs. Harris will have to testify as part of the chain of evidence of these letters, but that's no problem. The letter from Mrs. Goldschmidt is hand-written and will stand up to cross-examination. The timing all fits."

Perkins nodded at the assessment. "What if we used this new information to have another run at Ethel?"

"Sure. Good idea. If she is totally kookoo-batty, then she doesn't matter to the case. But if we dangled her evidence and this letter in front of Krackle, his lawyers might start to believe she might testify. That could push a plea deal, which would save everybody a lot of time and trouble."

"OK. I'll instruct Rhonda Sanchez to use it."

The meeting broke up. After dinner that night at her condo, Samantha went into her room and changed into a severe mid-calf length skirt and starched blouse. She walked back into the living room and stood in front of Perkins.

"I'm afraid you are in very big trouble," she told him. "You have several long over-due library books. Come with me. Now."

His eyes lit up.

CHAPTER 89

THE FIRST ROUND of Kimtinis was served. Perkins helped Samantha pass the icy-cold drinks to Samira, Kim, Roy Crawford and Mrs. Harris.

"This is to you," the Sheriff said, looking at the very smart woman in the wheelchair who was obviously delighted to be invited to Samantha's home. "Your efforts in gathering the residents to file complaints, and then handling the letter from Mrs. Goldschmidt the way you did, well, they cracked the case wide open."

"Hear-hear!" echoed round the living room. Rosie sat quietly by the wheelchair. She was optimistic about the bacon-wrapped mini-sausages.

"So, he finally confessed?" asked Kim.

"Yes. It took a long interrogation, but even his lawyers finally realized the preponderance of evidence. They advised him to confess and plead guilty if the DA took capital punishment off the table. He'll be going away for the rest of his life."

Samantha listened quietly as the conversation buzzed around her living room. She was tired but pleased with the outcome of the investigation. She was also shocked at what she had discovered about the evils of some long-term care homes and how residents were treated. She vowed to herself to continue to fight that. Kim was drafting a motion at City Council that would urge the State government to develop better oversight of seniors' care.

Samira said she would bring up the problem at the VA Hospital. They had to better protect patients being sent to these homes after their medical treatment in the hospital was complete.

Mrs. Harris had some valuable contributions about improving life in seniors' residences. Roy Crawford talked about new zoning bylaws that could be implemented to encourage more 'grannie-flats' in residential districts that would allow seniors to stay in their own homes, or independently but with another family.

Perkins caught Samantha's eye and smiled. Samantha smiled back. Tonight everything was all good, but it had taken a terrible toll getting here.

Samantha sipped her Kimtini and glanced down at her hand. Oops, a chipped nail. Time to visit the spa.

She smiled to herself as she looked around at her friends and her lover, took another sip of her drink, glanced back at her hand, and thought, what a great combination for any woman— Martinis. And Manicures.

THE END

About the Author

GORD HUME IS the creator of the popular "Samantha and the Sheriff" adventures. This is the fourth book in the series, which has generated an enthusiastic readership in North America and beyond.

Gord is also the author of seven non-fiction books on building better cities and improving communities. The books have been highly popular amongst municipal leaders in more than 22 countries around the world. Gord has been a sought-after keynote speaker at major conferences in the United States, Canada, Europe, Asia and New Zealand. He was elected to London City Council four times.

He has enjoyed an award-winning career in broadcasting; founded a newspaper; and been a leader in many civic, charitable and community foundations and organizations.

Gord loves exploring the culture, cuisine and history of people and nations around the world. He has visited nearly forty countries during his life-long passion for new adventures and experiences.

Gord now shares his time between London, Ontario and St. Pete Beach, Florida, where he continues a busy schedule of writing and doing media commentary on current affairs.

Enjoy all the "Samantha and the Sheriff" adventures:

Sapphire Blue

Alligator Alley

Singapore Bling

Martinis & Manicures

Torches & Trouble

Cossacks & Caviar

www.ingramcontent.com/pod-product-compliance
Lightning Source LLC
Chambersburg PA
CBHW070623170726
48291CB00003B/848